"Kill her now, Adam." The grouchy one.

"I give the orders." The leader. "We could have fun with her first." A belt being unbuckled, followed by the sound of a zipper sent a cold shock of fear through Coral. They wouldn't risk being caught by the police, would they?

"Wait. I'll take her out." The third, steady voice. It still reminded her of—no. It was the head injury playing tricks with her. She tried to see past the flashlight in her eyes, held up her arm to protect her vision. Only when the man held his flashlight to his face and his features came into view did Coral know she wasn't hallucinating. She had recognized a familiar voice. The only man she'd ever loved, the man who'd broken her heart, the man who'd promised to always be there for her but then left their marriage in favor of his career, time and again.

"Trevor?"

Dear Reader,

Welcome back to Silver Valley!

Incognito Ex, Silver Valley P.D. number eight, is my favorite SVPD book to date. Coral and Trevor once had it all, including a marriage that both allowed to fail for myriad reasons. When they come face-to-face again, during a night of Russian organized crime madness, it's not a forgone conclusion that they'd made a mistake by divorcing. But as the stakes rise and both of their lives are at risk, all of the resentments and sorrow of the past melt away to reveal the truth: Trevor is the only one for Coral, and she for him. But there are some big issues to solve first, like how to stay alive while being stalked by a former FSB/KGB agent!

While the situations and characters in my stories are fictional, emotions are universal. We've all wondered about our choices, past and present. Perhaps, like Coral and Trevor, we've felt the pangs of regret over ending a relationship too soon. I hope you enjoy the suspenseful ride with Coral and Trevor, but more than anything, I hope their love brings you healing in your life, too.

I love to connect with readers! Please find me at my website, www.gerikrotow.com, and on Facebook, www.Facebook.com/gerikrotow, and Instagram, www.Instagram.com/geri_krotow.

Peace,

Geri

INCOGNITO EX

Geri Krotow

HARLEQUIN
ROMANTIC SUSPENSE

Recycling programs
for this product may
not exist in your area.

ISBN-13: 978-1-335-62666-0

Incognito Ex

Copyright © 2020 by Geri Krotow

This edition published by arrangement with Harlequin Books S.A.

For questions and comments about the quality of this book,
please contact us at CustomerService@Harlequin.com.

Harlequin Enterprises ULC
22 Adelaide St. West, 40th Floor
Toronto, Ontario M5H 4E3, Canada
www.Harlequin.com

Printed in U.S.A.

Former naval intelligence officer and US Naval Academy graduate **Geri Krotow** draws inspiration from the global situations she's experienced. Geri loves to hear from her readers. You can email her via her website and blog, gerikrotow.com.

Books by Geri Krotow

Harlequin Romantic Suspense

Silver Valley P.D.
Her Christmas Protector
Wedding Takedown
Her Secret Christmas Agent
Secret Agent Under Fire
The Fugitive's Secret Child
Reunion Under Fire
Snowbound with the Secret Agent
Incognito Ex

The Coltons of Mustang Valley
Colton's Deadly Disguise

The Coltons of Roaring Springs
Colton's Mistaken Identity

The Coltons of Red Ridge
The Pregnant Colton Witness

The Coltons of Shadow Creek
The Billionaire's Colton Threat

Visit the Author Profile page at Harlequin.com for more titles.

To Hope Stephan

Your strength and courage inspire us all

Chapter 1

"Mom, please calm down. Nobody's going to kill me, for heaven's sake!" Coral Staufer pinched the bridge of her nose, warding off the headache that her mother's repetitive concerns inevitably triggered. It wasn't that she disagreed with her mom, either. Silver Valley wasn't the quiet, safe place it had been when she'd come back three years ago. She'd learned that firsthand this past winter, when she'd lost everything she'd worked so hard for in one catastrophic explosion.

The mere mention of Russian Organized Crime, or ROC, still made her stomach heave. And hadn't she had her share of tense nights out here since she'd made the choice to camp on her property in her trailer instead of the hotel provided by insurance, or at her parents' place?

Still, her safety wasn't something she wanted to continually revisit with her parents. Why hadn't she kept her phone ringer turned off?

Because you don't want to worry Mom or Dad.

"You're our daughter. Of course we're going to be concerned about you, living out on Brenda's property after what happened." Her mother paused after mentioning Coral's aunt, her mother's younger sister. Three years out, the loss of Aunt Brenda still hurt her mom deeply. "Today the papers reported that they still haven't gotten all of those Russian gang members out of Silver Valley. There's always more than what we know, Coral."

Yes, indeed. Living with a Marine intelligence officer turned undercover agent had taught her that the hard way, hadn't it?

"There are always bad guys, Mom, no matter where I live. You were more worried when I lived in California, weren't you?" Her time in the greater Los Angeles area had begun with college and ended with…a divorce.

Her mother's pause told her that she was trying to say the right thing in the least annoying way, which meant Coral wasn't going to like what came next. "Honestly, honey, no, I wasn't as worried then. Your dad and I knew you had—"

"Stop." She didn't want to hear the rest of it, hear how in her parents' eyes she'd made the most colossal mistake of her life when she'd left her five-year marriage.

Reminding herself that this had nothing to do with her failed relationship, that her parents were simply disappointed that she hadn't come out for the family dinner as planned, she began again.

"I am so sorry I missed our time together this week, Mom. As my event schedule fills up I need more time here at my place, is all."

She'd had to cancel with her family only an hour before the big sit-down due to an off-site event that had had last-minute changes. And to be fair, she'd been in no mood to sit with her parents and three older brothers and get treated like she always did—like the little sister who made poor decisions.

"I'm sorry, too, Coral. I'm happy for you, really. It's about time that your business expanded again. And I know it's been a nightmare for you since the gala. Please remember, honey, like we've said many times, you always have a place here at home." Home for Mary Staufer was on a quiet suburban cul-de-sac in Silver Valley, outside of Harrisburg, Pennsylvania.

"And like I've said, Mom, your place is a forty-five-minute drive each way from where I need to be right now—on my own property." She had Coral's Catering and Events to run, no matter that her main venue was in the midst of being rebuilt from the ground up, or that she had no idea how long she'd have to deal with her temporary living accommodations since her house had been severely damaged, too.

"I understand, really I do. I'm not trying to take your independence away, honey. You're a grown woman. Just pay attention and stay safe. Here's your dad." Ah, the classic method of hanging up without hanging up—getting her father on the phone.

Her dad was far more understanding in tone but still

encouraged her to think about getting a guard dog, protection that would stay by her side while she was on her property. She ended the weekly call to her parents with a mixture of gratitude for their love and exasperation for their refusal to accept that she was almost thirty years old, no matter what they said.

Only after she'd disconnected the call and shoved her phone in her back pocket did she remember what she'd wanted to ask her parents. The lockbox she'd found in a pile of rubble earlier today sat on her kitchen table, dusty but otherwise not the least bit dinged up. Anticipation curled in her belly at the thought of Aunt Brenda burying some kind of treasure or, more likely, cash. Aunt Brenda had been known to stash bills in the oddest places. Coral had found money all over the farmhouse when she'd moved in three years ago, almost a thousand dollars' worth. Bills were stuffed into nooks and crannies, including the back of the linen closet and a chipped ceramic flour bin.

She didn't know where the box's key was and wondered if her mother had a clue. Aunt Brenda's health had declined so quickly there was no telling where her mind had been in her last days.

She'd ask her parents about it the next time they spoke. Chances were she'd find the key in the meantime.

Pulling a chilled bottle of pinot grigio from the camper trailer's tiny refrigerator, she forced her shoulders to relax. With a quick twist of her corkscrew and a smooth pour into a stemless acrylic wineglass, she decided to make the most of what was left of the evening before she grabbed much-needed sleep.

The summer twilight underscored for Coral why she'd come back home to Silver Valley, Pennsylvania, to start over three years ago. The sunset, so late after a delightful day of event planning, streaked crimson to the east, promising another warm day tomorrow. Cicadas hummed, but it was nothing like the full-on symphony August would bring. Toads, unseen but ever present in the former farm fields, croaked with warbled jubilation. It was still only mid-June, but an early heat wave had plunged her south-central Pennsylvania hometown into summer in a few short days. After the horrid Arctic winter they'd had, followed by a long, wet spring, Coral relished the heat. Her skin felt like a sponge soaking up every bit of the warmth and humidity. She held the cold glass of wine in her hands and sipped, allowed the full, crisp flavor of the grapes to smooth over her tongue before she swallowed.

She'd come back here after her divorce with a broken heart and a sense of disillusionment only a failed, married-too-young marriage can bring. Her parents had been tremendously supportive of her while still trying to convince her that she'd made a mistake. As if her ex would have changed his mind and agreed to stay at the snap of her fingers.

It had been more complicated than that.

Not one to wallow, she acknowledged that her disastrous marriage had taught her how to appreciate the little things. Being married to a Marine who was constantly deployed made the dependable routine of her life in Silver Valley all the more comforting. She'd also learned that total self-reliance was her best path in life if she wanted to avoid getting her heart broken again. Which was why she'd taken on the monumental work needed to get Aunt Brenda's historical property and buildings back up to code and launched her catering and event-planning business. Coral had put her stamp on the inherited barn when she redid it to be an event venue.

As much as she prided herself on her ability to handle anything thrown her way, she'd been sorely tested this past spring. Even the lessons from her broken heart, now mended, seemed minuscule in comparison. Her gut-souring ball of nerves had finally eased after a solid month of despair last February, after the January explosion that had leveled her main money-making venue. The historical barn that she'd converted into a top local wedding and event destination had been destroyed in a blink.

It no longer mattered that her schedule had been booked through the next two fiscal years as word had spread about the authentic location, superb catering and accommodating service. It didn't hurt that she'd gone to high school with two of central Pennsylvania's best wedding planners, either. Silver Valley already had the Weddings and More Barn, owned by Rob Owens and located on the other side of town. She'd launched Coral's Catering only after consulting with her main competitor. Instead of competing, though, they'd helped one another's businesses take off, recommending each other's venues when their dates were full. And now Rob had generously allowed her to use his barn for some of her events, especially until she was able to schedule warm-weather tent festivities.

It could be much worse, but she wanted her venue back, her home rebuilt.

Her business had started off as a premier spot for Silver Valley events but quickly rose to compete neck and neck with the top spots in the larger Harrisburg and Susquehanna regions. She'd even started to have nibbles from New York City and Philadelphia as the popularity of country-set weddings grew.

The wine's sharp taste did nothing to soothe her heartache as she looked at the remains of the barn that had served as a permanent fixture in her life's backdrop. The historically significant and beautiful building had been reduced to piles of rubble. The newly built framework offered little solace, as it was still months from completion.

She'd lost it all. The hardest part for her to accept initially was that there was nothing she could have done to prevent the total destruction that occurred last January. There had been an altercation between law enforcement and Russian Organized Crime. Her high school friend and gala organizer Portia DiNapoli had narrowly survived an assassination attempt and, along with some SVPD officers, had saved the lives of over two hundred attendees at a local charity gala. Whenever she got really low about having to start all over again, Coral reminded herself that no one had been harmed in the criminal explosion and fire. Nothing else was of higher importance.

The gala had been to benefit the library and homeless shelter, the latter a good gratitude check whenever her self-pity swelled. In the fifteen-foot trailer that had become her home, she had far more shelter than many of the local homeless. Living single wasn't always easy, but she had so much to be grateful for, including good friends and her family, no matter how intrusive they felt at times.

The loss of the barn was the absolute pits, for sure, but what really irked her was that its destruction underscored what she had and had not accomplished over these past three years. The structure's empty shell was a harsh reminder that other than her thriving company, she'd not moved forward in her personal life since leaving Southern California.

Since she'd left Trevor.

You left him?

She allowed herself a quiet chuckle in the summer night. He'd left her first, if she was being honest. Not intentionally to break up their marriage, but to meet the demands of his career. First his military obligations and then continued service to his country as a civilian. He'd been gone more than he'd been home, and she knew they'd both expected too much from their marriage. You couldn't work on something that had barely gotten off the ground when both people weren't in the same geographical place for more than a month or two every year. The expensive trips to exotic ports to meet up with him couldn't make up for the long nights alone in their apartment.

Darkness completely engulfed her on the tiny canvas chair, a folding hammock style that had become part of her outdoor living room. She sat in the small clearing where she'd parked the camping trailer, which had turned into a great little home since May, when the weather had become more temperate.

Right after the explosion, she'd had to stay elsewhere. The blast had destroyed a good half of the farmhouse, also historical and her home. Her parents had convinced her to stay with them, which seemed a viable alternative until the wear and tear of driving to and from the slowly progressing construction site each day wore her down. After a few short weeks, she'd begun to count the days to warmer weather, or at least, warm enough, when she could be on her property while the renovations continued. Even without her permanent venue, the property was where she felt the most creative and productive. Besides, she needed to be nearby for any construction concerns that arose.

The fancy camping trailer had its own generator, which she only ran as needed on the hottest of days. It was noisy, and she preferred to fall asleep to the sounds of the farm fields and woods that surrounded her property.

Thank goodness her never married aunt Brenda had gifted her the farm upon her unexpected death, right as Coral's marriage was falling apart. As much as Coral had wanted to continue her event-planning business in California after the divorce, she'd needed the comforts of Silver Valley more than she'd realized. For as beautiful as she'd found California, where her ex had been stationed at the US Marine Corps base Twenty-Nine Palms, there was nothing like the endless greens and blues that melted together to form the Appalachian Mountains that surrounded her hometown.

Stars sprang out across the dark sky, and she tilted her head to watch them, searching for a meteor. Her kind of camping was definitely "glamping" compared to the wilderness treks she and Trevor had taken. Thoughts of her ex had been popping up more lately, as annoying as the ubiquitous gnats and mosquitoes that she worked hard to keep away, as bug bites in the event tent weren't anything she wanted her clients and their guests to experience.

Her memories of Trevor seemed different lately, not the usual rehashing of the failed relationship she'd initially done in her first months back in Silver Valley. Back then she'd gone over every freaking inch of her marriage, wondering where she'd gone wrong. It was like sifting through the rocky barn rubble for a diamond. When she'd figured out that it hadn't been solely her burden, that Trevor had had his part to play, she'd finally let it go. Lots of people had a failed first serious relationship. She and Trevor had made the added mistake of making it legal, was all. They'd been kids when they met and never really outgrew seeing themselves as that young, carefree college couple.

But the burned-down barn mocked her day after day, stabbed at the most tender spots left over from her broken heart. Not that it hadn't healed. It had. She just had a few sores left that clearly needed to be patched up, judging from how often Trevor had crossed her mind these past couple of weeks.

She took another sip of wine. Maybe it was time to do whatever it took to start dating again. Until now she'd only spent every possible date night here, on her property, in the barn. Helping others with their happily-ever-afters.

Moving back into the trailer to grab her bug spray, she didn't turn on any lights to encourage the flying demons. It wasn't as if she needed extra illumination—the space was small enough that she knew every inch of it. Her fingers felt the cool aluminum can on the tiny kitchen counter and grasped it. As she stepped back outside, Coral heard the unmistakable sound of men's voices floating across the field.

She froze.

It's just teenagers passing through.

Her logical mind wanted to brush it off, reassure her that her parents were overwrought in their concern. But the cold reality of ROC's insidious infiltration into Silver Valley and her ratcheting heart rate disagreed. She drew in a deep breath, forced herself to focus. *Think.*

The construction workers had left for the day almost five hours ago, so it wasn't the familiar sound of voices interspersed with pounding hammers or whining drills that she'd heard. Her event tent, located on the other side of the property, was set up and ready to go for next week's wedding reception. It'd been important to do a trial run with the behemoth structure, as this was her first event back on-site.

She'd arranged to begin the other event tasks earlier than usual, too, but her small staff wouldn't arrive to prep the decorations or cook what could be frozen ahead of time until noon tomorrow.

Whoever was out in her fields didn't work for her. It didn't mean they were criminals, though, did it?

Call the police.

She would, but only after she made certain they were on her property and that it wasn't just a group of bored teens. SVPD had bigger fish to fry—like ROC bad guys.

The rumbling voices stopped, and she waited. Maybe it *had* been a couple of teens walking down the main road, or biking, shouting as they rode the undulating highway. She stood a full quarter mile from the road, but a good breeze could carry voices that far, especially at night.

Except there wasn't a hint of wind tonight. The still air was why the mosquitoes were so omnipresent.

As the silence lengthened, she thought maybe she'd imagined the sounds. Until a sharp epithet carried across the field to her ears. Fear shot down her core, and she immediately regretted not going to the family dinner. Fear and regret weren't going to keep her safe, though. Trespassers were on her property, and Coral didn't entertain uninvited guests.

She acted on instinct, using the checklist her ex had drilled into her head to help her survive the long months he'd deployed, leaving her alone and at times vulnerable in Southern California. Using caution to be as quiet as possible, she stepped backward until her butt hit the trailer and reached inside the door, her hand closing on the hunting rifle she kept propped against the doorjamb, just in case. "In case" usually meant the errant black bear or a deer so injured by a car strike she had to put it out of its misery. Fending off attackers wasn't high on her list in the hometown she knew so well. Until January, when outside forces had invaded the serenity bubble she'd lived in since moving back, the hunting rifle had stayed locked in a case in the old den of the farmhouse.

She only had birdshot on her at the moment, having left buckshot locked in a basement safe in the part of the farmhouse that had remained intact after the explosion. Birdshot would give enough of a kick, though, to at least scare off the intruders. At a minimum it would buy her time to get away. All of this depended on them not having their own firearms, of course.

Coral wanted to crawl into her camper, lock the door and pretend she'd heard nothing. It'd be easier. But it might be a deadly choice. Why had she allowed her mother's fear to seep through her peace of mind?

Another loud verbal exchange ricocheted across the field. Whoever was here didn't realize she was on the property, or they'd be a lot quieter. She made her way toward the voices, and within twenty yards or so she saw flashlight beams swinging across the field on the far side of the barn's foundation. Where the barn had once stood, the framework for the new building had begun to take shape. She looked through the skeletal structure to where at least two men methodically ran their lights over the ground. Using the darkness and her knowledge of the property to stay concealed, she crept forward until she reached one of the large construction vehicles, where she crouched out of the trespassers' line of sight.

It was the exact place where she'd found the locked fire-safe box yesterday, among the other rubble and debris the construction workers had piled as they cleared the barn site. And now there were strangers who appeared to be searching for something in her field. She knew she should have tried to get the safe open right away, but she'd been too busy. If there was money in the box that Aunt Brenda had hidden, the box was vulnerable in her tiny camper.

Coral shoved down the fear that clawed at her. She had to call the police without being detected by the intruders.

She made out two large figures standing over a spot they had their flashlights pointed to. A third person seemed to be doing something on the ground. The familiar sound of a spade hitting dirt, and then a rock, echoed off the machinery she hid behind. As their flashlight beams landed on each other, she took note of their features as best she could. Until one mark, a tattoo on one of the men's arms, made her pulse trip.

Bratva. Written in Cyrillic, the Russian word for *brother* was stamped on the man's forearm. She'd only seen a tattoo like that once before, on Trevor's arm as he signed their divorce papers. She'd googled its meaning and knew it was related to Russian Organized Crime gang activity. Since her ex-husband did under-cover work, it made sense he'd have it, and she'd never thought about it again. Hadn't needed or, heck, hadn't wanted to think about the kind of danger he put himself in on a regular basis.

Until tonight. She knew there had to be thousands of Russian gangsters with the same tattoo. A sudden deep longing for Trevor to be here, to help her, stunned her as much as terrified her.

She had to shake this and take care of what was in front of her. Trevor was long gone, her ex, part of her history. Right now she had probable criminal activity in front of her nose.

Three strange men on her property, digging. Her mind raced with possibilities. She fought against her shaking hands as she pulled out her phone and dialed 9-1-1.

"Emergency Services, what is your emergency?" The dispatcher's voice was calm, competent. And too loud, even pressed against her ear, with no chance of the men hearing it.

"Please send police ASAP." She whispered the farm address, her hand cupped over her mouth and phone in an effort to muffle her voice.

"I'm sorry, ma'am, can you speak up?"

"No." The digging sounds stopped, and her heart pounded in time with her fear.

"Did you hear that?" A man's deep, heavily accented voice reached her, and she stayed still, frozen as she prayed he wasn't talking about her.

"Yeah. Over there." Another voice. Flashes of light beams bounced off the ground surrounding her as they aimed their flashlights toward the machinery. They couldn't see her hiding behind the construction vehicle's huge tire yet, but she heard their steps as they approached.

Coral left her phone on so that the police could track her, send help. It wouldn't arrive in time, though. All she had left for defense was her rifle. She couldn't afford to speak to the dispatch operator again, so she turned the volume down as she set the still-connected phone atop the construction digger. SVPD was competent—they'd saved her life along with those of hundreds of patrons during the winter gala—and she had complete faith that they'd arrive as soon as they could. Problem was she had to defend herself *now*.

"I don't see anyone." The man sounded grouchy, as if being out here was beneath him.

"Quiet!" A strong, lethal voice. Its owner wasn't going to leave until they found her. Coral released the safety, unable to keep the click of the older rifle from sounding. She inwardly groaned.

The footsteps stopped, and she made her move. Standing quickly, she aimed at what she now saw were three men. She prepared to fire her rifle, its butt nestled in her shoulder, her legs propped wide.

"Stop. What are you doing on my property?"

Flashlights in her face but not her vision—she deliberately kept her gaze lower than she pointed the barrel, at the men's feet. She'd anticipated their action. A sense of power, albeit tiny, gave her confidence.

"Who the hell are you?" The cranky one.

"Answer him now. Who are you?" The one in charge, the one with the scary tone. The third man remained silent.

"You are on private property. You are trespassing. Turn and leave now or I'm calling the police." No way would she let them know she already had. If they took off for the main highway, they'd be easier for SVPD to pick up.

The men's dark laughter drew her up short.

"We never take orders from anyone else, lady." The angry man's voice was all she heard before a shot rang out. The whir of the bullet sounded next to her ear right before the loud clang erupted as it hit the digger's shovel right next to her head. She flinched but held her position. Without a second thought, Coral fired off two rounds, aimed at the legs of her trespassers.

Howls and grunts filled the air, but she didn't wait to see whom she'd hit. She turned and ran in the opposite direction, toward her parked car. She kept the keys under the mat. All she needed was enough of a lead to get in, lock the doors and take off.

Suddenly the car that was always right at hand during her working hours seemed miles away. Her flip-flops were no match for the loose gravel underfoot, and her thrice-weekly sweaty gym workouts didn't appear to make any difference as the sound of pounding footsteps behind her grew louder and louder, her pursuer closing in. It was one of the men she either hadn't shot or hadn't injured seriously enough to stop. His breath became audible, emphasizing how close he was. Unlike how her gasps for air felt, out of control and nowhere near giving her enough oxygen, his pants were deeper, more even. As if he chased down women on a daily basis.

Her worst nightmare came true when his hand grabbed her by her shoulder, which she wasn't prepared for. In the self-defense classes she'd taken at Trevor's insistence, she'd been taught that her long ponytail was most likely how she'd be grabbed from behind. Adrenaline surged with hope, and she twisted to escape, but a painful pull on her hair, followed by her feet going out from under her, made freedom a fleeting dream.

Was this how she was going to die? At the hands of some random killers, on a warm Silver Valley night, on the land where she'd learned to walk?

Images of her childhood were quickly engulfed by her last image of Trevor as she packed her bags and left what had been their only home together.

Her brain's attempt to review her life crashed to a halt as her body landed hard atop a pile of rubble cleared by the construction workers. Her head snapped back, and the harsh contact of her skull to rock took her breath away. She thought she might throw up. A moan escaped her as the sparks dimmed behind her eyelids.

"She's not so bad. We could have fun before we finish her." The mean one, with the heavy accent.

"Not a bad idea." The one she'd thought was in charge, but he sounded out of breath. Panting. She'd shot him, then. "But we have to get out of here now."

"Yeah, she probably already called the cops." A third voice with the same accent, but also something… familiar. She'd taken a huge whack to the head, and it was messing with her perception.

Her bearings leveled, and while her head pounded, she was able to open her eyes. One man stood over her, as if pondering what to do with her. Was she going to be tortured, raped, killed?

Their flashlights weren't on her for a brief few seconds as they argued. She took advantage of reaching to her side for the rifle, lying where it had dropped when she was knocked down. These didn't sound like the smartest criminals, but she knew they were deadly. They had weapons more lethal than her rifle. All she had to do was incapacitate them until the cops came.

A siren sounded, and she wanted to shout in relief. Until the flashlight was in her face again.

"Kill her now, before the police come. She's heard our voices." The leader, still sounding as if he was in pain. *Good.*

She didn't hesitate as she brought the rifle up and

turned onto her knees, shooting at the two men on the ground. But she couldn't see and didn't hear any groans or cries. She'd missed.

"Kill her now, Adam." The grouchy one.

"I give the orders." The leader. "We could have fun with her first." A belt being unbuckled, followed by the sound of a zipper sent a cold shock of fear through Coral. They wouldn't risk being caught by the police, would they?

"Wait. I'll take her out." The third, steady voice. It still reminded her of—*no*. It was the head injury playing tricks with her. She tried to see past the flashlight in her eyes, held up her arm to protect her vision. Only when the man held his flashlight to his face and his features came into view did Coral know she wasn't hallucinating. She *had* recognized a familiar voice. The only man she'd ever loved, the man who'd broken her heart, the man who'd promised to always be there for her but then left their marriage in favor of his career, time and again.

"Trevor?"

Trevor Stone never took his eye off the ball while undercover. *Never.* But as he fought to keep these thugs from harming Coral while processing the fact that he still had to get her out of here, he was distracted. The last several days, working alongside ROC gang members, he'd felt her nearby, as if the invisible thread that connected them had come alive again.

He'd known she lived here, knew this was the farm she'd inherited. He knew what one rogue ROC member had done to the barn last January and hadn't been able to fight his protective instincts toward his ex, years after they split. He'd volunteered for the mission, stupidly thinking that he'd be able to ensure her safety while not coming into direct contact with her.

What he could never have predicted was how he'd react when face-to-face with Coral again.

His hands clenched painfully tight, and all he wanted was to throw Coral over his shoulder and run for the Appalachian Mountains that surrounded Silver Valley. Take her far from this night, to a place where ROC couldn't touch her. And yes, away from seeing him again, especially like this.

The raw fact that she was about to be assassinated by one of the two lower-level ROC crooks was all that kept him focused. The complication that she'd just blown his cover, carefully cultivated over the past two years, was a sideshow. One he'd have to address, but later, after he got her out of here alive. When he was far from her, and knew she was safe.

"What did she call you? Who is Trevor?" Disbelief, suspicion, anger snaked across the ground as the two other men cried out, and he figured he had about two seconds to act.

"Stupid bitch took a hit to her head." He spoke as Grisha, the undercover identity he'd adopted to help the Trail Hikers, the secret government agency that he worked for, and his sole focus was to break up the ROC's hold on the East Coast.

"I'm not a bitch, and my head isn't that messed up. It *is* you, isn't it?" At least she'd lowered her voice. It wouldn't be a surprise to her to know he was still doing undercover work. How could she forget? It had been the death knell of their marriage.

Coral's initial appearance of frailty after the conk on her head had morphed into righteous anger. He didn't blame her, but he couldn't keep looking at her. Three long years without one glance at her, without her eyes on him, without the sound of her voice, threatened to destroy any focus he had left.

He gave himself a quick mental shake. If she didn't get them killed with her words, he was going to blow it with his inability to block out the distraction that was Coral.

"We have to get out of here." He addressed the other two men, both young and not the brightest, working for Ivanov, the ROC head honcho. "The cops are coming. You two take off. I'll meet up later. I'll take care of her, trust me." He nodded at the road, and the two men craned their necks to verify his claim. The sirens screamed in the night, and he saw the flashing lights move down the highway in the distance. He took the opportunity to lift Coral from her bent position and pulled her up against him, his arm raised as if he was going to strike her.

"Don't talk. Follow my lead. And don't say my name again." He murmured into her ear, his lips against her skin out of necessity. He couldn't risk the others hearing him. "Now yell when I move my arm, like I've hit you."

Coral's strangled gasp nearly threw him out of his reality as an undercover agent posing as a working ROC stiff. Her voice tried to drag his mind back to hazy, hot California days when they'd spent all day in bed, getting up only to eat. It wasn't fair that a single sound from her still did this to him. That the surreal connection they shared hadn't perished with their marriage.

"Kill her now, Grish." Adam was pissed, in pain from the gunshot wound, and wanted Trevor to prove he wasn't Trevor, that Coral really was suffering from a severe head trauma. ROC agents weren't high on trust, and Trevor, as Grisha, was new to their local group.

"It'd be stupid to do it here. She's easier to move while she can still walk. Let me take care of her, then I'll come back for you both. Stay low, don't use your flashlights. The police will stop at the farmhouse first. We've got time." He wrapped his arm around Coral's waist—she was thinner, but still steely strong—and half dragged, half ran with her to where he'd seen her car earlier in the day, when he'd made his own excursion out here.

Self-recrimination threatened to stop him in his tracks as he knew he should have made doubly sure she wouldn't be on the property when ROC came looking for Markova's treasure. But he'd run out of time to verify his source who'd told him she'd be out tonight. Even with her being here, he'd never have expected she'd catch them—usually his ROC associates were somewhat competent. Unlike these two.

Thank God for inept thugs.

When they were what he estimated was halfway to her car, he pulled out his pistol and held her tight with his other arm. "Hang on. I'm going to shoot at the ground, to let them think it's you." He quickly fired two shots at the dirt, making sure the bullets had nothing to bounce off, making it sound like he'd just eliminated a witness.

The sirens were close, and he saw the patrols turn into the long drive leading to the barn area.

"What are you doing here, Trevor?" Her voice shook, but he couldn't tell if it was shock or anger. Probably both.

"I'll explain later. Right now we can't be seen by anyone."

"But that's the police—I called them."

"I can't be spotted, and for now you're with me." He had no way of knowing which officers were reporting, and he couldn't risk being taken into custody. Only two SVPD officers were cut in on his deep undercover work.

Now the woman on his arm was one more added to the list of people in the know. The woman he'd never forgotten, whom he'd still go through hell and damnation for. His ex-wife, Coral.

Don't forget she's your ex.

"Where are your car keys?"

"In my car, under the mat."

"Is there still a back way out of here, through the woods?"

They were even with the car, and he indicated she should get into the passenger seat and he'd get behind the wheel.

"The road's still there, but right now there's a huge pile of debris from what was left of the barn after the explosion. The workers started moving it there this week." He felt her gaze on him through the darkness as he drove without headlights toward their escape.

She pointed at a side road, not more than a dirt path.

"You'll have to drive around the pile of burned-out barn. And then how about you let me out, and I'll wait for the police to get those other two men. You can go ahead on your own, Trevor. I don't want anything to do with this."

"I don't want you to have anything to do with this, either, Coral, but neither of us have a choice. You've been identified by ROC—Russian Organized Crime."

"I know what ROC is. They took out my barn." No sense of martyrdom, only resignation. Coral's ability to deal with whatever life threw her way had always impressed him. He'd had to fight to learn adaptability, first in the Marines and then working undercover.

"Then you know they play for keeps." He reached the eight-foot-tall heap of charred wood and stones and drove around it, the ground bumpy and uneven off the gravel road.

"You mean like you said you did?" Slam, right to the heart of where they'd left off, why their marriage had failed. He'd never held up his end of their commitment. The divorce had been his fault, as had the irreparable harm he'd caused her.

He had to get her to a safe place and then get the heck out of Dodge. Before the black hole of emotions sucked him under again.

Chapter 2

Trevor shoved the car into gear and floored it, shooting them through the night and away from the scene just as the SVPD patrols arrived, their lights flashing across the fields.

"Grab my phone." He spoke as he maneuvered around the barn's foundation and deep into the cornfields. "It's in my front jeans pocket."

"What the heck for?" Coral was ornery as ever, but she complied. Driving in the dark through the damp fields was hard enough, but it was nothing compared to having her hand in the vicinity of his crotch.

She plucked it out and held it to his face. "I'll need your finger or your code."

He gritted his teeth. He couldn't take his hands off the wheel, but no way in hell did he want to give her the four-digit code. No. Way.

Don't want her to know it's your wedding anniversary?

"Trevor."

"Hold it up to my hand, my index finger." Her scent reached his nostrils as she leaned in, and he was immediately grateful for the rough ride, the unexpected turns and roadblocks. It gave him something else to focus on—anything other than Coral.

Her fingers grasped his and pressed his pad to the phone's button even as he turned a tricky left curve that led to the road behind the fields, to their freedom from the current situation.

"Got it." She began to tap on his screen.

"Go to recent calls and hit the first number. Then put it on speaker."

Within seconds he heard his Trail Hiker boss's voice in the car.

"What do you need?" Claudia Michele's smooth tone revealed nothing—not her identity nor Trevor's. Standard agent protocol. Her calm demeanor was due to her years of experience in the Marine Corps. A retired two-star general, Claudia was the epitome of a professional. Trevor trusted her with his life.

"I need SVPD to not follow the car that's left the barn venue area." He gave a quick description. "I'm driving it, and I have Coral Staufer, the owner of the barn complex, with me." Hell and damnation. Claudia knew who Coral was and that she was Trevor's ex. Claudia had been the one to warn him to take care around Coral. To not get in over his head, emotionally, not with the gravity of the ROC case weighing upon him.

Too late.

"Are either of you injured?" Claudia was brusque, ready to dispatch whatever help they required.

He risked a quick look at Coral, who shook her head in two short jerks.

"No. Not seriously. Coral looks to have a bump over her eye that needs examining. She's conscious, and there's no evidence of nausea. I can't stop right now, anyhow."

"Go to our established rendezvous. The team will report there as able." By *team* he knew she meant herself, Silver Valley PD chief Colt Todd and several other agents, many who also worked as SVPD officers, some who held down normal civilian jobs when they weren't on a TH mission. It took all types of talent to work undercover ops, and this particular threat from ROC had stretched their abilities to the limit.

"Got it." Done with the call, he eased onto the main road and was able to give Coral a nod. "You can disconnect."

She did and then tossed his phone on the dash. "*I* can disconnect? You show up in my life just when it's going well, bring these horrible men with you onto my private property, and you're telling me what I can do?" Her lagging energy didn't match the harsh words, and he recognized it for what it was—delayed shock and anger.

"If a burned-out barn and falling-apart farmhouse are your idea of 'going well,' then this is just another bump in the road." He slipped a glance at her, saw her jaw drop before she clamped it shut with typical Coral ferocity. Guilt scraped at his conscience, a constant whenever it came to his ex. "This is hard, I know.

And you're trying to have control over the uncontrollable right now. I'm sorry you've gotten mixed up in this mess, but I can't change it. I will explain all of this when we get to the safe house."

"Safe house? I'm not going anywhere with you. You're the undercover agent, not me. We got divorced over it, remember? And that woman you were talking to, who said to meet there? Count me out of any overnight with you. I'm going back to my property as soon as the police have those men in cuffs."

Her anger triggered an assault of memories he couldn't stem. So many disagreements from their past raced around his mind, vying for his melancholy. They'd packed an incredible amount of conflict into the few short years of their marriage.

"Believe me, if I had a say in the matter, you'd already be tucked back into your little camper and I'd be headed out of Silver Valley." He glared at her for the split second he'd allow his eyes off the road, now well lit and traveled. They had to drive west through Silver Valley and past Harrisburg to get to the safe house, on the other side of the Susquehanna. He'd have preferred a nearby mountain hideout, something adjacent to the Appalachian Trail that ran through Silver Valley, but ROC had used the Appalachians to conduct human trafficking. The enemy knew the area too well.

"How do you know about my camper?"

"Besides seeing it tonight?"

"I had zero lights on. There was no way to tell it was there or that anyone lives in it. You obviously didn't know I was there, I'm assuming, or you wouldn't have agreed to show up with your thug buddies."

Admiration for the woman he'd had to leave behind too many times flared deep in the center of his chest. Coral had just escaped being brutally raped and killed, to bounce back with her usual pluck.

He'd missed this so much, the constant tension between them, being with someone who knew him well enough to call him on his BS. It killed him that her jeopardy was the price for their reconnection.

"I surveyed your property earlier this week, on my own, and then again this morning." He'd imagined her in the camper but couldn't be sure she lived there full-time.

"I never noticed you." She sounded mystified.

"I made it a point that you wouldn't. The other day I was dressed like a bicyclist and rode up the farm path, circled around the main drive where your event guests come and park, drank some water, pedaled back out. This morning I looked like a construction worker and only stayed for a few minutes, took some photos. Which my buddies don't have, so don't worry—they probably didn't even notice the camper." He'd thought she'd gone to her parents' for dinner, as his brother had told him she usually did. His brother Ray was good friends with one of Coral's older brothers. He never should have trusted hearsay, which was what anything not verified by him or another trusted source was.

Because of his failure to dig more deeply into Coral's personal life, he'd almost gotten her killed tonight.

You were hoping to avoid her.

"I love how you call those criminals your 'buddies.'" From her grim tone, she felt the exact opposite. "I know you're undercover, that this is what you've always wanted to do, but haven't you gotten yourself in pretty deep this time? ROC has been in Silver Valley for at least the past year. They have feelers out everywhere. They're going to figure out who you are, and then where will you be?"

"Leave the undercover challenges to me, will you please? As you said, it's my job." And had been since he'd been courted by Trail Hikers as he left the Marine Corps. He'd joined the Marines to get experience and his foot in the door of government law enforcement employment. Since the darkest day of his life as a teen, when the older brother he'd idolized had been mistaken for someone else and gunned down by a gang in downtown Harrisburg, he'd wanted to serve and protect. "I'd never think of telling you how to plan a wedding buffet."

"How long is it going to take to get to this safe place?" She switched subjects.

"Another forty minutes."

"Where on earth is it? I thought we were headed into the mountains. Are we going to Maryland?"

"No, it's in Pennsylvania, but farther north." They were headed in the opposite direction of Maryland, in fact. "It's a nondescript place on the river. Nothing unusual. That's the point."

"I have to be back tomorrow for work. I have a big event next weekend, the first on my property since I lost the barn." Never one to simply drop her objective, she came at him again. He had to extinguish any glimmer of belief she still harbored that she had a say in when she'd return home. Otherwise the next hours and possibly days would be torture for her. And him, too. The reality that he wasn't willing to let her out of his sight, not after the near disaster in the farm field, sank in.

"Look, Coral, there aren't going to be any more events run by you if you're in ROC's crosshairs. These people don't mess around, don't leave any chance of being identified behind, and that includes you. This could be over by morning, or it could take days, even a week. But know that it will pass. We're going to get them all. There is an endpoint."

There will never be an end to your feelings for her.

He figured he'd have her back to her place by tomorrow noon at the latest. Unless his accomplices had heard her call him by his given name and were able to figure out who he was, under the Grisha disguise.

He swallowed against the taste of bile that rose in response to his most primal fear. The thugs didn't know Coral's name, but they'd easily figure it out, discover it from correlating the barn's address with her business. They'd come back to make sure he'd finished her off, even if they believed the story he was going to give them.

They're going to be arrested. He mentally repeated the mantra, but nothing would soothe him until Claudia or Colt confirmed that the men had been apprehended.

"You're going to tell them you killed and buried me, aren't you? Or will you say you dumped my body in the river?"

The image of her beautiful body floating lifelessly into the strong current of the Susquehanna made bile surge into his gut as his cheeks heated and sweat poured from his temples. He gripped the steering wheel, forced the unwelcome vision away.

"Whatever I tell them is my problem." He hated having her in the thick of this and vowed to get her out of it ASAP. But first, he had to get her to the safe house.

"No, it'll be my problem when they get out of jail, Trevor. You said it yourself—they leave no evidence behind. I've heard both of their voices, and I have a good idea of what they look like from the flashlights." Bravado mixed with fear in her reply and forced him to push his apprehension aside, if only to offer her an ounce of compassion.

"Trust me on this, Coral. If they get apprehended by SVPD tonight, and I have every reason to trust that they will, SVPD and FBI will work to keep them incarcerated for as long as possible. Normally a minor crime like trespassing wouldn't be enough to detain them, but since you were assaulted and threatened with worse, a good case can be made to not allow bail. The fact that they speak with Russian accents and have the tattoos to prove their connection to ROC doesn't hurt, either. They truly don't have a leg to stand on." He had enough evidence from the short time he'd worked alongside them to put them and their ROC supervisors away for a good long time. The only reason many of the ROC players in Silver Valley were still at large was because he, and the rest of the team tracking the ROC case, needed to figure out what they were doing. Tracking their movements was imperative, and that couldn't be done if they were all in prison.

She snorted in disbelief, and he wondered if it was an act. Was she as uncomfortable as he was with being this close to one another after so many years apart? Not that *uncomfortable* was an accurate descriptor. *Hyperaware* was more like it, especially of the undercurrent of physical attraction between them.

He immediately felt like a jackass for thinking with his dick in the midst of an op. Coral was more beautiful, more desirable than ever. And he'd almost watched her die tonight, because he'd messed up. His intended mission, to grab what could be the case breaker with a couple of ROC handlers, had turned into a nightmare when Coral showed up.

"You were supposed to be at your parents' for a family dinner tonight. I expected you'd stay over." It was hard to admit he'd been keeping tabs on her. As part of his job.

"How the hell do you know that? Are you listening in on my conversations? Just how long have you been creeping around my business, Trevor?" Since they were on a smoother road, he allowed himself to take a long look at her, soak in her feminine profile. He winced when he saw how large the lump on her temple was.

"I've been making sure you'd be safe."

"It was Jon, wasn't it?" Her oldest brother, his brother's best friend, was an SVPD officer and an obvious choice to have given up the goods on her whereabouts. "You got to Jon, and he ratted me out."

It was more complicated than that, as one of the SVPD detectives who was also a Trail Hiker agent had actually gotten the information from Jon. It corroborated what Trevor had already heard from his brother. Nothing Coral needed to know.

You still should have double-checked.

"I haven't seen any of your family since we split, Coral." It would have been too painful, another reminder of their unsuccessful marriage.

She shifted in her seat, clearly agitated. They entered Highway 83 and within minutes were on their way north, crossing the Susquehanna.

"Have you heard they're shutting down TMI?" Coral was still an expert at changing the subject to suit her mood. She looked out her passenger window as she spoke, and beyond her silhouette he saw the familiar red lights atop the nuclear power plant's stacks. Three Mile Island had always dominated their lives growing up, even more for him, as his father had been a nuclear engineer there. It was his father's career that had moved the family to the other side of Harrisburg right in the middle of high school. There'd been no way to predict his brother would be dead less than a year later, the victim of senseless gang violence.

Just as there'd been no way to predict he'd meet Coral not in Silver Valley, where they'd both grown up, but in Southern California, at college.

At his prolonged silence, she turned to face him. The bridge's lights shone on her right eye, which appeared almost swollen shut. He couldn't help the hiss that left his lips.

"I didn't realize you took such a hit to your eye."

Her hand came up to her temple. "It wasn't my eye, it was the side of my head. There's a huge lump here, and the blood's dried, so I doubt it's a concussion. I don't feel sick or anything."

The nausea whirled in his gut again. Funny how it didn't seem to matter how much time had passed since

he'd left the worry of how his job affected Coral behind. Within minutes of their imperiled reunion, it'd
all come back, only worse.

Was a soul connection a progressive thing, like ill-
ness or addiction? Because he felt worse than he had
the night he'd left her, right after they'd signed the divorce papers. He'd never been so low.

Until tonight. When he'd thought the ROC contacts
were going to hurt her, all illusions he'd harbored about
being over her had shattered. He tightened his hands
on the steering wheel, refocused his mental energy on
the tactile motion. The tried-and-true method to break
a dark chain of thought worked, but not without a lot of
resistance. He'd worn grooves into his soul over how
much he'd hurt Coral.

No more. He'd make sure she was taken care of tonight.

"You need medical attention." Despite what he'd
said to Claudia, if Coral needed an ER, he'd drive to
Harrisburg Hospital now. And take out any ROC member who showed up to find her.

"Seriously, I don't need a doctor. I mean, when I
took the hit, I did see some stars, but it went away very
quickly. And didn't you say we have to stay under the
radar? I can't imagine walking into a hospital or ur-
gent care looking as rough as we do right now would
be anywhere near unnoticeable."

For the second time in the drive, he felt called out.
He'd actually forgotten that he was dressed in his best
ROC thug gear—black pants, black T-shirt, bandanna
and tattoo, and he was a mess from the digging. His tall
frame next to Coral's petite, battered face would raise

all kinds of questions. Inquiry Trail Hikers and other law enforcement agencies—FBI, Treasury— couldn't afford in the op against ROC.

They were so close to bringing Dima Ivanov down. The head honcho for East Coast ROC, Ivanov had been a thorn to LEA nationwide, but especially on the eastern seaboard. FBI, Treasury and ATF had all been frustrated by the ever-moving target. Ivanov's number two, Anna Markova, was incarcerated and awaiting trial. But Markova wasn't sitting idle in the county prison. It appeared she was running a group of her own from ROC, right under Ivanov's nose. The many underlings who still ran a skeletal drug operation in Silver Valley could be rounded up, but LEAs including FBI and CIA wanted no less than to bring both Markova and Ivanov down by putting them both away for good, with no hope of outside contact ever again. Which meant they needed the information that only came from monitoring ROC operations. Trevor had arrived in Silver Valley in time to join the op to monitor the thugs working for Markova.

And just in time to save Coral's life.

"You're doing what you always did, Trevor." The level of jaded disgust in her tone didn't match how her eyes still glowed with enthusiasm. Well, the eye that wasn't a slit.

"What's that, Coral Bell?" The old nickname came out of his mouth of its own accord. He silently slapped himself upside the head. This was the problem with being around her again. It was getting too familiar, too quickly.

She didn't answer him at first. The silence stretched on between them as he left Highway 83, shot across

Highway 322, and continued northwest on Highway 15, the route that followed the Susquehanna River upstream. Moonlight caressed the water in slivers of pale light, and he was hit with a yearning to be anywhere else with Coral but in the middle of a TH mission.

"You still zone out, go into your undercover world. No matter if I'm sitting right next to you. A lot of our marriage was spent like this."

She made the observation with a quiet, calm voice, as if she were still discussing TMI or the weather and not eviscerating his soul. He thought about the bullets he'd taken over the years, the knife wounds, the punches and jabs. The hits had hurt enough to temporarily erase the pain only Coral was able to dish out to him, but nothing cut as deeply as her tongue. How could he have forgotten how deeply her words drove into his very marrow, how they reminded him that she deserved so much more than life undercover?

Claudia had warned him that working near his ex might be tough. At the time he'd disagreed. He'd been a fool to convince Claudia that he'd be able to handle this mission and any of its possible consequences. Yet thirty minutes into plan B and he was ready to pull the car over and jump into the river. Or worse, jump into a canoe with Coral and take them both wherever the current led. Far away from his past and his decision to leave the only woman he'd ever loved.

He'd let go of fairy tales long ago.

You thought you let go of Coral, too.

Coral blinked as quickly as she could against the tears that pressed on her lids. It wasn't easy, as one eye pounded like hell, in sync with the headache from the blow to her head. She'd lied about the bump being no big deal, but she wasn't throwing up and she didn't feel sleepy, so the pain didn't mean she had a concussion.

It was nothing compared to how much it hurt emotionally to see Trevor again, and to see him shut down into himself while she was right next to him. Right after she'd been attacked and narrowly avoided being raped or murdered, all because of some undercover op he was involved in.

And he'd had the nerve, the absolute *gall* to call her by the pet name she'd once adored. When she'd basked in the afterglow of what had always been spectacular lovemaking.

Don't go there.

She was such a dang fool, still able to conjure up memories best left in the ashes of their marriage. A sob tried to force itself past her dry throat, and she coughed to cover her sniffles. *Do not let him see you cry.*

"I'm not unaware of your presence, Coral. I have a lot on my mind, is all." Gruff and bare, just like Trevor's view of the world.

"You always did." Why did she have to sound so mean, so caustic? She didn't have to react to his callousness with her own. Otherwise, what had the last three years of healing been for? Digging her fingernails into her palms, she looked at him.

"I'm sorry, Trevor. You've saved my life, and all I'm doing is baiting you. I don't mean to, and then, bam! The words fly out of my mouth as if you never…"

"Left?" He finished her sentence as he drove. "Yeah, I get that. I'm the worst version of myself with you."

The worst version of himself. Great. So at least they agreed they'd be better off apart. Still.

Three years hadn't changed a thing between them.

Heavy silence descended, and she watched as he turned off the main road and onto a gravel drive that paralleled the river but was high above it. She estimated the drop to the river to be around two hundred feet. Only when the gravel path opened onto a larger parking area in front of nondescript ranch-style house did she realize they were done with this part of their journey. The traveling phase.

Now to spend the night in a strange house. Together.

Trevor cut the engine and looked at her. "We weren't followed, so know you're completely safe here. No one's coming after you, and you can let your guard down."

She'd never be safe, not with Trevor close enough to touch—or worse. Her body still missed his. As she reached for the door handle, his arm shot out. Familiar fingers wrapped around her wrist, and his face was inches from hers. His hair, longer than she'd ever seen it, curled at the edges under the black bandanna. He was dressed nothing like the Marine she'd married, yet when their eyes met, there was no question that this was the man she'd once vowed to be with for the rest of her life, in sickness and in health. Until death did them part.

Stormy blue eyes that she couldn't see save for the glitter of his focus on her made her want to scream. How had her nice, quiet life been blown up all over again in the space of an hour?

"Coral. Wait."

She refused to look away from his gaze, but the movement of his lips distracted her. They were still full, but with deep lines on either side of his mouth that hadn't been there only a few years ago. Whatever he'd been doing, work-wise, had taken a toll on him. Wonder at how much sleep he got each night arose before she stomped it back with a mental boot. Trevor's well-being was none of her business.

"I—I don't want to be with you here. I want to go back home." And she did. With a ferocious pang she didn't think possible for a humble camper trailer, Coral wanted to be back in the aluminum-framed structure, under her sleeping bag, listening to cicadas and the occasional coyote. She'd take a bear rooting through her plastic patio storage chest over this. Anything but being next to the one man who'd ever broken her heart into jagged pieces that had taken years to glue back together. Who had caused tears of regret and made her ache at memories of their happier times.

He let go of her arm but didn't move any farther. They kept looking at one another. So much passed between them, and yet, nothing was said. Did he remember their good experiences at all anymore? Or was he as frustrated as she that they'd been thrown back together like this?

"I know you want to be back at the barn. Trust me, I want you back home, too, doing what you want to do. It's my job to keep us both safe, away from the bad guys, though. So for at least the next twelve hours, probably longer, we're stuck together. You can deal with twelve hours, can't you?"

Twelve hours. Half a day, but it would be mostly at

night. If she managed to sleep through it, it wouldn't be so bad. "Until lunchtime tomorrow, then?"

He sat back in his seat, yanked off the bandanna and ran his hand over his head. He'd grown his hair out. Her fingers wanted to tug on where it turned into chestnut curls at the nape of his neck. She shoved her hands under her thighs.

"I can't promise that, but yeah, that's a good estimate." His Adam's apple did a little jump. The way it had when he'd told her that his missions and deployments weren't dangerous.

"You're lying."

He turned and faced her, eyes wide. "Jeez, Coral, now what?"

"You're not being truthful. I need to let my parents know I'm okay. They'll hear about the police at my place. They'll worry. You can't make any promises about how long I'll have to be here, can you?"

He let out a long sigh, and she bit back a grin. He'd always played the exaggerated-martyr card when she called him out. Except this wasn't anything remotely humorous. Their lives were at stake; she did believe him on that point.

"No, I can't promise anything, but I do have experience with similar scenarios. They usually resolve themselves within twenty-four hours."

"Even with ROC involved? And what exactly were you digging for out next to my barn?"

He unlocked the doors and shoved his open. "Get out."

Anger rushed heat into her face, and she got out of the car. It was more effort than normal with all the aches and pains she'd picked up only an hour before. He was already several strides in front of the car, and she caught up to him only as he stepped onto the small front porch, his back to her. Going by his stance, he was done with any discussion. Familiar resentment reared.

"Oh no, mister. Your old ways don't work on me the way they once did. Turn around and look at me when I'm talking, Trevor. You can't just blow me off like you used to."

They'd climbed onto a wraparound porch, but he didn't open the front door. He sighed with an exaggeration she'd once thought was charming, his way of showing his human side. All it did now was make her want to chew nails. When he turned to face her, exhaustion weighed on his expression, his mouth downturned and eyes squinting under the harsh lighting.

"We're not having this conversation out here, or even inside. The less you know, the better."

Chapter 3

Logic and fury fought for her common sense as they stared at one another. Damn Trevor and his tired look.

"Whatever." She shrugged with an insouciance she'd never have in Trevor's presence.

His hand touched hers, so lightly and quickly that she could have imagined it. "This isn't easy for either of us, Coral."

She blew a stray strand of hair from her face and grimaced when she realized it was stuck to her cheek by dried blood. "I need to get somewhere that I can clean up."

"Follow me." He turned and followed the porch around to the back of the structure, where he stopped in front of a very slick-looking flat metal door.

She fought not to stamp her feet as she stopped next to him. Acting like a child wouldn't solve anything, and what other choice did she have at this point? They were both beyond tired, and she suspected there wasn't going to be any rest, not immediately. Hadn't the woman on the speakerphone said she was sending a team to meet them? So some kind of meeting was inevitable.

Trevor leaned over a keypad next to the door and positioned his eye over some kind of scope. The door itself was covered by a screen door typical of the modest river homes they'd driven by. But once open, it revealed a flat surface that was barely recognizable as an entryway. The security devices were to the right of the door, underneath what looked like a hanging planter.

"You need a retina scanner to get in here?" She'd only seen them in television shows and film. "Who exactly do you work for, Trevor?"

He didn't answer but lifted his head from the scope and keyed several digits into the pad. As if by magic, the panel slid open with a powerful thud when it settled in place, revealing it was a kind of pocket door. She estimated it was at least twice the width of her palm, so about eight inches thick and made of stainless steel, from its apparent weight. Trevor stepped to the side and motioned for her to cross the threshold.

"After you."

She stepped into an interior that definitely did not match the plain old river house exterior. The immediate entry opened onto a contemporary office space, complete with shining desks all topped with expensive-looking computers. A large screen dominated one wall, larger than any television or monitor she was familiar with.

The sound of the door sliding back into place was

her only warning that Trevor stood right behind her. She whirled and immediately took a couple of steps backward when she realized how close they were. Her foot caught on one of the slick rolling office chairs, and she began to fall.

"Whoa!" The cry ripped out of her throat, but not before Trevor's hands had her by her upper arms. He righted her, kept her from cracking her head for the second time in one evening.

Pulled up against his chest, she realized that once again she was too close to him, too near the undeniable scent of his masculinity mingling with field dirt and leather. She looked up into his eyes and saw the wariness that held his deeper emotions in check. Trevor never had been one to share his heart with her, not unless he had to.

"Good catch. You always were good with your reflexes. Thanks." She shrugged out of his light hold before either of them had to come up with a reason for him to let her go.

"Not so fast." He had his hand on her elbow as he guided her toward the back of the work area, where he led her through a door to a simple but comfortable living space. A modern kitchen was to the right, the stainless steel appliances and sink gleaming under track lighting. An ample dining table sat between the kitchen and a small den that had a leather sofa, two easy chairs and flat gas insert fireplace.

"Here, let's take a look at your injuries." Trevor stopped in front of one of the cabinets over the counter and pulled out a large first aid kit. He opened it and extracted supplies as if he'd done it countless times before.

"This isn't your first rodeo with all of that, is it?" She nodded at the kit, but the small motion made her head throb and reminded her why Trevor wanted to check her out. Or maybe the pain hadn't ever stopped, but she'd been too distracted by Trevor and the fact that he was not only with her but had taken her to someplace in the middle of nowhere for who knew how long.

He doused a large sterile gauze bandage with peroxide and turned to her. "You know I had advanced first aid and injury training in the Corps." He smoothed her hair back and gently tilted her head so that he could access the lump near her temple. "This might sting."

"Might?" She gritted her teeth against a howl of protest as he deftly dabbed at the injury. "How bad is it? Will I need stitches?"

"No, I think I can patch it up here. But you're right—it's one hell of an ugly lump. You're very lucky. Temple injuries are often far more serious."

"I told you it was swollen on the outside. Isn't that the determining factor for concussion risk?" She heard herself babbling, but it was her only defense against his nearness, and the kindness he was showing her. If he were being a jerk, she'd have more reason to keep her guard up, to hide her heart under the zillion locks and keys she'd put in place during and after their divorce.

Since the divorce. It was true; she'd continued to keep an invisible shield around herself—anything to protect her from the hell that leaving Trevor had wrought. Her lack of dating since they'd parted was probably why she felt her internal sex sparklers going off.

Trevor appeared unaware of her dark thoughts as he worked on her wound. "Let's keep our fingers crossed that it doesn't start bleeding again tonight. If we can get it to scab over and use ice to get the swelling down, you'll be good." He put antibiotic ointment on a cotton swab and applied it liberally to the entire area. "I'll bandage this and then get you a bag of ice. It's amazing what a simple cold compress can do for the ugliest injury." He opened a couple of bandages and set them on her temple. She thought she deserved an award for remaining calm and not revealing how affected she was by his nearness.

It had to be the aftershocks of the attack, combined with seeing her ex so unexpectedly, that was making her so aware of him. Sure, she and Trevor had always had a great sex life, but steamy time between the sheets only went so far. Once the marriage was over, the emotions spent, it didn't matter how attracted you were to one another. Sex couldn't cure all.

Maybe your emotions aren't spent.

"When you said we were going to a safe house, I pictured something more, more…"

"Rustic?" He snapped the plastic lid of the first aid kit closed and put it back into the cabinet. Without stopping, he moved to a lazy Susan–type cupboard and pulled out a plastic quart-size bag and then walked the short distance to the monstrous refrigerator, where he allowed the ice dispenser to fill it. "That's the whole point. We don't want anyone thinking this is anything but an old, worn-down river house." He wrapped the bag in a crisp linen towel and then held it to her eye. Grasping her hand, he moved it to where his was. Their skin contact was brief but not short enough. Little sparks of heat zipped up her forearm, and she quickly motioned him away from her.

"I've got it. Thank you."

"Keep that on there as long as you can stand it. I know it stings, but it'll make all the difference by morning."

"You said *we* don't want anyone to think this is a safe house. Who's we?" She grimaced as she pressed the ice to her face, the cold soothing and painful.

"The people I work for." He went back to the refrigerator and opened it, peering inside as if the most interesting meal were on one of the pristine shelves. From her vantage she saw the top two shelves over his shoulder. Stacks of healthy items—milk, eggs, juice and yogurt—caught her attention. Her stomach growled.

"I thought you might be hungry." He flashed a grin.

"I can't believe I'm hungry this late, after almost being…" She was too spent to be worried about the impolite noises coming from her stomach.

"Believe it. You've been through a grinder tonight." He straightened up, holding a carton of eggs and a hunk of cheese. His brow lifted. "You still like cheese omelets?"

"Sure." Nodding would hurt too much, and saying more was dangerous. She didn't want to fan any more chaotic emotions by allowing her thoughts to escape her mouth.

Letting Trevor make her a meal was a safer option.

Cooking for her was a regular part of their routine, once. When he'd get back from his months-long deployments, and they'd stay in bed all night and into the next afternoon, Trevor was their chef. He created whatever she wanted, but her favorite remained a simple cheese omelet.

Coral couldn't stay here and watch him cook for her, though. It was too much to observe his masculine form moving with grace and ease over a stove as easily as it had to kill the enemy. As smoothly as he'd made love to her.

Stop. Right. Now.

"I need to use the bathroom. Which way do I go?"

"Down the hall. Your room is the second on the right, and the bathroom is en suite." He never turned away from the counter. Was he feeling the weight of their shared history, too? And if he was, were his thoughts as sexy as hers?

"Thanks." She kept the ice on her eye as she made her way to her room. Whoever Trevor worked for had a lot of funding, that was certain. She'd assume it was CIA but thought he'd have at least told her that while they were married. Before they'd signed the final documents that ended the commitment she'd made so freely. So foolishly. Tonight wasn't the time to beat herself up over her misspent youth, though, so she made herself stay in the present, away from the memories that still stung.

Snapping on the bathroom lights, she looked at the simple but, again, thoroughly modern and functional fixtures. Her reflection was pathetic. Her shirt was torn, revealing a lacy bra strap that was streaked with Pennsylvania yellow clay. The ponytail she'd worn was gone, and her hair hung in greasy lengths around her face, down to her shoulders. She looked like she'd been dragged over dirt, thrown against the ground and had taken several hard hits.

You have been.

"Now or never." Lowering the bag of ice, she wasn't prepared for the impact of her eye's ugliness. It was amazing she could still see at all through the tiny sliver of her swollen lids. She turned to the side and tried to see the temple injury that Trevor had treated, but peripheral vision was beyond her.

What was within reach was the shower, which she had to have. It'd be pure heaven to get all this grime off her.

Three sharp raps jarred her right before Trevor's voice sounded through the door. "Don't even think about taking a shower—you can't get your eye wet. The cut could get infected."

This was too close to how it'd once been between them. As if he'd read her mind, knew her thoughts.

"I'm going to take a bath."

"Don't wash your hair, Coral."

She opened the door and glared at him with the swollen eye. Maybe its monstrous appearance would scare him off. It hurt to focus, but Trevor was a hard sell once he decided what was best.

"I'm not a little girl, Trevor. I can wash my hair without getting the cut wet, trust me."

"Come eat your meal first. A few agents are on the way who are going to need to ask you some questions."

She opened the door fully. He stood in the center of the hallway, his expression unreadable. It didn't make him any less attractive, and she allowed the wave of desire to hit, wash over her and spiral deep in her gut.

What choice did she have—she'd never *not* find this man desirable. Her singular choice was to ignore it and keep going.

Shoving past him, she walked as calmly as she could to the kitchen, where she slid into the seat in front of the omelet. "Thank you for doing this."

Her fork cut through the flaky, tender egg to the gooey cheese, and she would have blinked back tears if both her eyes were functioning properly. Instead she allowed her good eye to stream and dabbed at it with her napkin. Trevor wasn't in front of her—she could hear him cleaning up in the kitchen.

He set his dish on the place mat across from hers and sat down. When he looked at her, she kept her gaze even with his, refusing to give an inch. Because if she gave the tiniest bit of ground back to what she'd once felt for him, she'd be digging her own grave.

Trevor had forgotten how expert Coral was at shutting down her emotions. She'd have made a damned good operative if she'd been called to it and not to the world of event planning. Her career choice wasn't something he knew a lot about, but he knew she made a big difference in people's lives. She'd once told him her gift was helping people celebrate their best versions of themselves.

"Do you want anything besides water to drink? There's whatever you'd like, from tea to hot chocolate." He'd filled a large glass with iced filtered water for her and saw it was almost empty.

"No. I can't deal with caffeine this late, and even if I could, I think it'd upset my stomach." She picked at the remaining third of her food. At least she'd eaten most of the eggs.

"It's natural to feel a little queasy when you eat for the first time after having to fight for your life, no matter how hungry you are. But we need to keep an eye on it—it could be a sign of concussion."

"It's not from my head, trust me." Her lower lip jutted out, and her white teeth dug into it. Whether to stop it from trembling or to keep her from saying something she thought better about, he had no idea.

"You can't know that. It's easy to mistake one symptom for another when a cocktail of adrenaline and endorphins is wreaking havoc on your insides. Adrenaline from the attack and endorphins from the pain."

Her eyes, always that mesmerizing shade of amber, glowered at him. Even the bad one seemed to radiate with her inner fire, swelling and all. "Save the mansplaining, Trevor. I know what endorphins and adrenaline are. You have no idea what I do or do not know anymore. I'm not the woman you left three years ago."

"No, you're not." And he didn't want—couldn't—take the time to discover how she'd changed. What had made her all the more beautiful, while her eyes reflected a sadness he knew he'd put there.

"Why are you back in Silver Valley? You had to know that taking a mission back home might mean you'd run into me."

He had figured the risk was worth it. When Trail Hikers had become entwined with the FBI operation to bring down the East Coast ROC group, he'd known it was a mistake to even consider coming back. At least for his heart. But he'd never have forgiven himself if he let any other agent come in and prowl around Coral's decimated property. It was bad enough that he hadn't been here in January. He'd never know if he might have been able to prevent Markova from bringing down the barn. And he'd never shake the chill that had jolted through him when he'd heard of the explosion, then read the detailed reports. It was a miracle that Coral was still alive.

"You're being quiet again, Trevor."

"Sorry. You're right—coming back here, near you, was something I had to do for my job. Once we're undercover, it's not so easy to switch around postings, like in the military. I couldn't take the chance of blowing my cover by *not* coming here." He lied with such proficiency it should have concerned him. But it was a facet of his job he'd had to embrace. It didn't feel like a professional tool when he used it on Coral, though.

"I blew your cover back there, by calling you by name." Concern made lines appear between her brows, deeper than they'd been. They'd both changed, aged since the divorce. A punch of regret landed on his chest. This was the woman he'd wanted the privilege of growing old next to.

"Trevor?"

He shook his head, as much from his thoughts as to emphasize his denial. "Those men didn't hear you, and if they did, they weren't sure what to make of it. They were thinking of only one thing in that moment, trust me."

"Raping and killing me?"

Her words cut through him as if he were still back

in her farm field, hearing the thugs proclaim what they wanted to do to her.

"Over my dead body."

"Yeah, well, you easily could have been killed by me with my rifle." She arched her unswollen brow.

"With the birdshot you had in it? Doubtful."

"You don't know it was birdshot." She sat up straight, defensive. This was better, having something concrete to talk about.

"If it was buckshot, both of my companions would be dead. As it is you've given one a decent leg injury and the other several surface bruises from what I can tell. Good job, by the way."

As he spoke, he was aware of how she watched him, how easily they communicated with one another. It didn't seem to matter where they were relationship-wise—lovers, friends, married or divorced. Their body chemistry melded perfectly and enabled them to understand one another with minimal words. He'd never had this with another woman before or since Coral.

You haven't given any other women a chance.

"How much longer do I have to stay here again?" She looked at her wrist, where instead of the fancy watches she'd adored in California, she wore a fitness band that she tapped on. Her good eye widened. "I can't believe it's only midnight. It feels more like tomorrow night."

"Time is odd that way." He heard the security door slide open and looked at the monitor over the refrigerator. "We've got company."

Coral's head turned as she followed his line of sight, and she gasped at the agents pouring into the safe house. "I didn't notice that before. How many people are coming in here?"

He stood up and grabbed both of their plates. "You weren't meant to notice it. It only turns on when it needs to, when the security system detects someone on the porch or nearby the house."

"Would it do that for a bear?" Her question reflected that she was more focused on the workings of the highest level of security money and military technology could provide and not their incoming visitors.

Before he was able to figure out what was happening, a huge laugh erupted from his center. "No, a bear doesn't match a human profile. And that's more than you need to know, frankly."

He was grateful for the excuse of cleaning up so that he didn't have to examine how long it'd been since he'd had a good belly laugh. No one tickled his funny bone like Coral.

As he scraped the plates and rinsed them, the party entered the kitchen. Coral rose from the table and gingerly stood, looking unsure of herself for the first time tonight.

Trevor loaded the dishwasher as his team filed in, including his boss, Claudia Michele. She was the founding director of the Trail Hiker agency, the secret group he'd worked for since he'd left military service.

"Claudia." He met her steel-blue gaze, noted the lines around her eyes. The ROC op was taking its toll on all law enforcement agencies, from the lowest-ranking uniformed police to the highest level.

"Trevor." She turned away from him almost immediately and strode over to Coral. She stuck out her hand. "Coral Staufer. Nice to see you again, although I'm sorry for the circumstances. I don't know that you remember me. I'm—"

"Claudia Michele Todd. I know you. You've been at the barn for the galas the past two years. You and your husband."

"That'd be me." The tall middle-aged man whom Trevor respected stepped forward and shook hands with Coral. "Colt Todd."

"Silver Valley PD chief of police." Coral added his title, and Trevor had to admit he was impressed. Silver Valley wasn't a tiny town, and it sprawled into the suburbs of Harrisburg, which at recent count was around a half million people. The odds of her knowing this many people in her few years back weren't high. But she'd met them at her events and remembered. Coral's steel memory hadn't lessened since their divorce.

Stop thinking about the divorce, about the marriage, about Coral or anything else not related to the op.

"Yep." Colt nodded, his usual no-nonsense self. "We've got a few more here with us from both SVPD and, ah—"

"The agency that we all work for," Claudia filled in smoothly. She looked at Trevor, who shrugged. He wasn't going to tell Coral any more than he had to about what he did or who he worked for.

Claudia turned to Coral. "I assume you know nothing of whom Trevor works for?"

"That's correct." Coral's defenses were back up. She had her arms crossed in front of her, and if her eye wasn't so messed up, he knew its brow would be a mile high. "But I have to say he's not spending time with the most savory characters, judging from what I saw tonight." That earned a chuckle from everyone present, except Trevor. He'd never be able to laugh about what could have happened tonight. It was validation that he'd made the right choice by taking this mission.

Another agent may have seen the op as the most important objective, and Coral would have been killed. His heart skipped a beat. Everyone sat down around the table to debrief, but his thoughts weren't on the mission for the millionth time that night.

He'd sacrificed the op's conclusion for Coral's safety. In all his years of Marine intel and undercover work, he'd never put the mission anywhere but first place. And yet tonight he'd done just that—shoved months, years of painstaking undercover work aside to protect Coral.

Just as with their divorce, he had no regrets about anything that kept Coral safe and far from the world he lived in.

He'd always made an exception for her.

Some things never change.

Chapter 4

Coral looked around the huge farm table. Until five minutes ago, she'd never met most of the people assembled—or if she had, only briefly—save for Trevor and a high school classmate. Trevor was in his own category, a file she'd labeled "ex" and tried to ignore on a regular basis since she'd left California. Not only had her mental manila Trevor folder been opened tonight, the emotions that assaulted her proved that everything had been shaken out of it, the shards spilling over her in a kaleidoscope of pain.

Her hands trembled and she sat on them and forced herself to pay attention. The sooner this meeting was over, the sooner she'd go home. Back to the life that had become her safety zone, where the only reminder of Trevor was her memories.

She recognized SVPD detective Josh Avery, whom

she knew from high school. He was set to get married at the barn to Annie Fiero, another classmate, this August. Fortunately they'd agreed to have the event in an outdoor tent if the barn wasn't finished by then.

"Normally we'd have you give your report directly to SVPD, Coral. But since your safety is premium, we've brought the team that's working this case to you." As police chief, Colt took the lead, but she noticed that Claudia sat at the head of the table with ease. She'd place odds on Claudia being the person in charge of the op, since she'd been the one Trevor had called from the car. It was clear Claudia had the power to tell SVPD where to send their units.

"Hey, Coral." Josh spoke up, jerking her from her observation. "Sorry to see you under these circumstances, but I'm glad you're okay."

"You can say I look like hell, Josh. I know this eye is scary."

Some of the other agents appeared surprised by how they spoke to one another. Josh cleared his throat.

"Coral and I know one another from high school. I saw her again at the gala in January. Annie and I hired Coral for our wedding reception in August," Josh said, filling in everyone.

"Is there anyone else you know at this table?" Trevor's careful tone caught her attention. She took her time looking at each person.

"No, I can't say that I do. Why does it matter?" Coral heard how tough she sounded, the lack of finesse, but she didn't care. Her head hurt, and she wanted to be back on her property—as long as the bad guys were secure either at SVPD or the county jail.

"Because we're all working for various levels of law enforcement, Coral." Claudia took over and confirmed what Coral had guessed—the sharp woman with the silver bob was the most senior person present, no matter whom the other people worked for. And she seemed to be Trevor's boss, too. So was she some bigwig from the CIA or FBI? Not that Coral needed or wanted to know. Okay, maybe she was a little bit curious.

You don't have a need to know.

"I think I get that, Claudia. And trust me, I was married to Trevor for over five years, and I understand the need-to-know concept. I don't want to know what all of you do, or who you work for. No offense." She waited for her words to sink in. "I'm grateful that Trevor was there, undercover, to get me out of a pickle. And I'm happy to know that SVPD took care of the bad guys, right? They've been arrested and won't be back to visit anytime soon?" She looked at Colt and then Josh, who both gave quick nods. Neither picked up on her attempt at humor, though. It made asking what she most wanted to know difficult.

"But?" Claudia smiled as if she knew what Coral was about to say.

"But I want to be back home as soon as possible. I have a business to run and a barn to build. I've called my folks to let them know I'm okay, in a safe place with the police, but that's all I can tell them for now."

"You've been a pillar of the community, the way you've taken the barn tragedy as well as you have, Coral." Colt's praise surprised her. No one from SVPD had spoken to her since right after the explosion, when they'd transported the reported ROC woman to jail.

"That was an awful night, but it wasn't a tragedy—no one was hurt."

"Absolutely. But it doesn't lessen the burden that's been placed on you and your event business," Colt continued. "We're going to do all we can to get you back right away. First, we're all here to debrief tonight's events and to ask you some additional questions about what you may have noticed going on at your place."

"I can say I haven't seen anything out of the ordinary this entire spring or summer. Just a lot of construction, and I did have run-ins with a few groundhogs. I know my staff pretty well, and I've made sure any new hires were vetted by other trusted business colleagues." The heat of Trevor's gaze burned the side of her face, but she refused to look at him. She wasn't the young woman he'd married, nor the shattered spouse he'd left. She'd built a life and a company of her own in Silver Valley.

"We're talking about the barn and surrounding area, Coral." Trevor's tone had lost the patronizing note she'd detected earlier. In its place was no-nonsense, undercover agent brusqueness. "Have you noticed anything on the property that wasn't there before the barn blew up? Anything, from a box to a plastic container or bag—anything that might contain a data device like an auxiliary hard drive or USB memory stick? Or maybe a phone, tablet or computer that you assumed one of your previous guests or clients left behind?"

Trevor spoke as if they were talking about the weather, but her gut clenched as the image of the fire-safe lockbox reminded her of what she'd found. But it was most likely from Aunt Brenda, right? A private item, something her eccentric aunt had hidden away.

It wouldn't hurt to tell them about it.

"Nope, nothing at all." She didn't look at Trevor—couldn't. He knew her too well, would know she was lying. But if she told them about the box in her camper, they'd have to clear the area of it, and she didn't want all these people in her tiny trailer. More importantly, it'd invariably delay her return home.

Tell them.

Guilt tickled her sour stomach, and she shoved it away. She'd tell SVPD about the lockbox tomorrow, take it to the police station herself, once she had time to see if Aunt Brenda had left its key behind in the farmhouse.

"Are you sure, Coral?" Josh asked the question like the expert interrogator he was. He had a reputation among their high school classmates for being a poker face, and while she'd never seen him that way, now she understood why. Gone was the happy, in-love man who'd come by with Annie to make wedding plans this past spring. In his place was a uniformed officer of the law. Except, she noticed, he was in civilian clothes. She took in the people around the table again and noticed that none of them wore a uniform.

"Wait—are you all undercover? Is this really a guise for some CIA or FBI op? Because if it is, I go back to the need-to-know deal. I don't want to know about any of this." Please, just let her go home, and she'd never mention it again.

"You're already *in* it, Coral," Claudia interjected. The woman leaned forward on her folded arms. "We're not trying to make this harder on you—you've been through enough tonight, and certainly since the gala. But we're up against some very bad people. We can't afford to overlook anything, no matter how insignificant it may appear to you. ROC is lethal and ruthless. Anything we miss can mean another life taken."

If she'd thought she felt guilty moments before, it was nothing compared to the stabs assaulting her conscience now. Images of the fire box as it sat on her tiny camper counter flashed in her mind. She could tell them tomorrow, after she opened it and proved it was only cash stored away by Aunt Brenda.

"I'll be sure to let you know if I see anything odd. Is it possible for me to get back to the campsite tonight?"

Her question was met with a beat of silence, followed by Trevor, Colt and Claudia speaking over one another.

"Not so fast." Trevor sounded annoyed.

"Tomorrow night, at the earliest." Colt spoke with measured conviction.

"It could take up to a week." This from Claudia, and it garnered the others' attention. "I know you have a life and business to run, but so do we, Coral. We're in the business of protecting Silver Valley and in fact the entire East Coast from the ROC's criminal activities."

"But, I mean, you want me to stay for a week? Here?" Coral swallowed. "What should I tell my family?"

"Hold on." Trevor's hand reached for hers under the table, under her leg, and he squeezed hers twice. Their old language for letting the other know they weren't alone. It offered more than reassurance, though, as white-hot attraction ignited, making the intentionally platonic touch downright sexy. She bit her lip to keep from hissing.

"You are not going to be here any longer than you need to be." Trevor misinterpreted her discomfort as solely connected to being forced into a safe house, not being stuck out here alone with him. "We're not taking you back home until we know it's safe, either. We'll make sure your family knows you're okay, just busy. Our team is expert at providing ruses. And to be clear, we'll have undercover agents protecting your parents. At the first sign of trouble, they'll be out here with you." His eyes were on hers, but he wasn't letting her see all the way in—he remained guarded. Of course he did, he was with all of his work colleagues. But it was more. He was guarded against *her*.

She took a second to do an inner check of herself. As she suspected, she was holding back from Trevor, too, on a more deeply emotional level that had nothing to do with the lockbox. She had to keep her heart on lockdown, though, or risk being thrown back into the pit of grief she'd barely climbed out of once.

No amount of mental defenses stopped the quakes of awareness from rumbling through her each time Trevor looked at her or touched her. And the heat— how had she forgotten the latent chemistry between them? It'd never left.

"Let's keep this rolling if we can. Boss?" Trevor looked at Claudia, who nodded, her expression un-readable. Over the next hour, the team of LEA officials questioned her and Trevor down to the tiniest detail, in-cluding where she'd purchased the birdshot she'd fired at the thugs. Coral answered every question to the best of her ability. She wanted the bad guys locked up forever as much as they did.

But she never told them about the lockbox. It could be her aunt's, and she wanted to see if she had a key somewhere in the farmhouse—or what remained of it. Once she knew it wasn't Aunt Brenda's, she'd turn it over to SVPD.

Trevor would be long gone by then, she was certain. He'd be back undercover, or if this case wrapped up in the next day or two, he'd be on to his next op.

Myriad emotions assaulted her, from regret to sadness. None of which should have surprised her.

Leaving was what Trevor did best.

Trevor knew that Coral was holding something back, but he also understood that it was fruitless to badger her about it. He didn't know what *it* was, but from how she'd sat on her hands, how she'd evaded eye contact with him when she'd been asked if she'd observed anything unusual on her property, the hairs on his nape were at attention. Coral was spooked about leaving her camper behind. So what was in that camper that she wanted? He'd looked around the table at the time and suspected that Colt and Claudia probably weren't buying her story, either.

Once the debrief was complete and the medic had looked at Coral's wound, the team left with a promise from Claudia that she'd send more groceries within the next twelve hours if Trevor and Coral had to spend another night here.

"Trevor, can you come with me for a minute?" Claudia spoke quietly.

"Of course." Trevor looked at Coral, who still sat at the table. "I'll be right back. Help yourself to whatever you need."

She waved him off without speaking. He understood the exhaustion—it was creeping in on him, too.

He followed Claudia to the miniature command center, small only in size but not capability. She motioned for them to go into the one room with a door, with glass walls.

"Coral's been through a lot, Trevor, but if she knows anything about her property that she's withholding, I need you to ferret it out. As in sooner than later."

"Of course. She's not required to tell us anything she doesn't want to, though." His defense of Coral was immediate, as natural as squinting in bright light.

Claudia's gaze sharpened. "No, she isn't, but you know that we're only trying to find out for her safety as much as to solve our case, Trevor. If ROC, namely Markova, left anything behind before she was arrested, as she's told her thugs, then you know the deal."

"I do." The deal was more like a death sentence for Coral and anyone found on her property when ROC came back. Markova would send in more and more hoodlums to scour the fields around the barn's foundation.

"All we know is that she told them to check around the barn for objects she buried, but she didn't tell them what they were. She said they'd know it when they saw it." Trevor repeated what he'd read in the most recent TH reports.

Claudia's mouth tightened into a grim line. "Markova's not stupid. She's betting on her defense attorney to get her out, and she's biding her time. If her minions get her the information she's using to keep her leverage against Ivanov, she'll use it while she's still behind bars."

"Before we can get to it or figure out what it is."

"Correct." Claudia offered him a brief smile. "We'll get the information, Trevor—it's what we do best. I'm confident that we'll wrap this op up and have Ivanov's ROC reach into Silver Valley and most of the East Coast cut off at the knees. I don't want another innocent civilian hurt from this."

Trevor nodded. "I'll keep an eye on Coral." At least while she was here, no one could get to her.

"That's my other concern, Trevor. I don't need you going down an emotional rabbit hole with your efforts to keep Coral safe. I know why you took this mission, no matter what you say. If it was Colt, I would have done the same thing. But rules of the game don't ease up while you're in the midst of working out closure for yourself. You have to keep yourself safe, too."

"I know that. Besides, Coral and I took care of closure three years ago when we got divorced. I'm just looking out for her as my ex."

Claudia's knowing, compassionate smile was deadlier than the bullet from a .45. "If that were true, you wouldn't be here in Silver Valley, Trevor."

Trevor had no response. Claudia, as almost always, was absolutely correct.

And you're absolutely screwed.

After Claudia left he gave himself a few minutes to

collect his thoughts before he went back into the living area. Back to Coral.

Yes, he'd acted on instinct when he'd read the investigative and crime scene reports about the barn and learned that Markova was targeting Coral's property from prison. He was excruciatingly aware of Markova's profile, her background, her ability to kill with zero warning and even less conscience. The thought of Markova going anywhere near Coral, even if it was Coral's property and not Coral herself, had been too much for him to let go of, to ignore.

He'd had to get here, be here, for Coral.

He supposed he still carried guilt from the several months before the divorce, when he'd had to take mission after mission and had been home so little that when he was, Coral wasn't willing to be the eager spouse who waited patiently for him any longer. She'd deserved more, more than he'd been able to give her. And once he'd figured out that his undercover life was too risky for her—the bad guys were better and better at finding out personal details of agents, including their families—he'd had to let their marriage go. No matter how deeply undercover he went, he was always putting Coral at risk.

He'd done what any man who was accountable and had integrity would have done. The divorce had freed Coral and him from a life of constant worry.

But the final papers that they'd signed hadn't freed him from the heartstrings that still bound him to her. There was no such thing as *ex* where Coral was concerned. But there had to be, because he wouldn't put her at risk because of his job.

You already have.

* * *

He found Coral in the kitchen, her expression taut with anxiety under the soft pendulum lights.

"So I have to sleep here tonight, no question?" Coral stood at the sink, speaking in between gulps of tap water. She kept refilling her glass from the faucet.

"The water on the fridge is filtered and a lot colder."

"I like the way our local water tastes. The minerals are good for you, you know. Answer my question, Trevor." She leveled him with her most no-kidding stare, and even with the swollen eye, it still gave him pause. He sucked in a breath before he replied.

"Yes, you're staying here tonight. We both are. In separate rooms, of course." He didn't want her to think that he'd ever try to…to what? Take advantage of the situation? Because he couldn't deny that he'd been fighting his attraction to her all night. And hated himself for it.

"If this is such a great safe house, I'm sure I can stay here on my own. You don't have to babysit me."

"I'm not babysitting, but I'm providing an extra measure of security by being here. I'd have to stay here tonight myself, anyway. I can't be seen going to and from SVPD, or—" He stopped himself. Crap, he'd been about to say, *TH headquarters*. Coral didn't know what TH was, and she didn't need to know, either. Although he suspected she'd figured out more than anyone gave her credit for.

"Or where, Trevor, the agency you're working for?" She tilted her head back as she drained the glass. "I don't give a dang about who or what you're working for.

Thank you for your service and for saving my ass tonight. Now, if I have no other choice, I'm going to bed."

"You need to set your alarm as the medic ordered. Every two hours." The medic had agreed she didn't have a concussion, but they couldn't be sure, not without an MRI. And it was too risky to go to the ER tonight. Anger rocked through Trevor as he once again faced the reality that ROC's grip on Silver Valley and surrounding central Pennsylvania was steel tight and impenetrable. Except by TH.

"Trevor—what is it? You look like you want to eat a lion."

"I'm pissed off, is all. It's not right that ROC has been able to get away with all they have." And he was pissed off at himself for thinking he'd come here and protect Coral. He'd saved her tonight, but now she was in the thick of things. He should have had SVPD go to her camper and verify she wasn't there, and if she was, tell her to go out of town for a week or two. Josh would have done that for him, for Coral. For the case.

She walked up to him and placed her hand on his forearm, breaking him out of his self-recrimination. Her scent was a bare whisper of itself, stirring memories of long nights spent making love to her. It was enough to make him hard, which only made him mentally dig in and focus on keeping Coral safe—his attraction to her would only detract from that goal.

"Coral—" He took a half step away, forced her to drop her hand. The heat of her touch remained.

"They're not getting away with it any longer, Trevor. You're on the case, and it'll be over soon." Her eyes, one wide and searching and the other still a swollen slit, conveyed more compassion and understanding than he'd felt from anyone since…since he'd left her.

"Coral. I never wanted you to be involved in any of this."

"By *this*, do you mean life? You had no way of predicting ROC would blow up my barn then come prowling over it months later, did you?"

"No. I found out they were looking for something for Markova at your place, that she'd used the barn as a drop point."

"Markova is the woman who blew up the barn, who was arrested? I thought she was in jail."

"Just because someone's in jail doesn't mean they're not participating in criminal activity. She's still sending out messages, has her minions doing her bidding. And Markova's not even the number one in the East Coast ROC." He didn't know how much she knew from the news reports, and he wasn't going to worry her with the weight of the case. She didn't have a need to know, officially, for which he was grateful.

"Are you close to bringing down the whole group of them, then?"

"That's just it. We thought we were, more than once. But dismantling ROC is like pulling bubblegum out of hair. It's one tiny branch of their ops at a time. Meanwhile, more innocents have been killed, and we've had more victims ODing on the heroin they're dealing."

"You'll get them all, Trevor. I know you will." She yawned, stretching her arms over her head. His arms twitched with the need to tuck her under his shoulder, kiss the top of her head, massage her back as she purred like a kitten. It wouldn't end there, though. If he deliberately touched Coral, he'd take her to bed. If she'd have him.

Get a grip, man.

"You're exhausted. I know I am. Let's get some sleep and see where we stand in the morning."

"See you then." He waited for her to close the guest room door before he went to his room. Had he known how challenging being around Coral again would prove, he might have thought twice about taking this mission.

Sure you would have.

Chapter 5

Coral expected to have nightmares and insomnia about the previous six hours, but instead a warm bath had relaxed her and she dropped into a deep, restorative slumber. She had vague memories of Trevor waking her every two hours, but she'd gone right back to sleep each time. Now she woke to the smell of her favorite food.

Bacon.

She blinked, at first thinking she was back in California, still with Trevor, and then as sleep fled, she thought she was still in the camper, but this bed was far more comfortable, the sheets finer than any she'd purchased as a single woman.

Trevor.

The safe house.

The events of the past evening rushed back in, along

with her trepidation at keeping the lockbox's location and very existence from the LEA team. From Trevor.

A knock at the door sounded before she had a chance to get out of bed.

"Yes?"

"Can I come in?" Trevor's bright morning voice. He'd always been better at sunrise than she, ready to start the day.

"Uh, sure?" She pushed herself into a sitting position, the clean, thick cotton T-shirt she'd found in the bathroom linen closet enough cover for her braless breasts.

Trevor stuck his head in, and the scent of his soap along with the bacon streamed in full force. His hair was damp, and she couldn't stop her mind from wandering to the memories of so many early mornings with him, fresh out of the shower, and ending up back in bed and then the shower together after they'd made love.

Let. It. Go.

"Good morning. Breakfast is served when you're ready. Your favorite." He gave her a dazzling smile and she clutched the bedsheets, needing something to anchor her.

"You didn't need to do that. What time is it?"

He nodded toward her nightstand. "The time's always projected up onto the overhead from the unit on your table."

She looked up, and sure enough, there was 0735 lit up against the cream-colored ceiling.

"Wow. It feels so much later. I really crashed. Thanks for only waking me enough to make sure I was alive." She couldn't help the grin that tugged at her swollen eye.

"You needed it. Take your time, and when you're up, help yourself in the kitchen."

"I will. Thanks."

Trevor shut the door behind him, and she stared at the oak panel. Even on their best days, he'd never been one to wake her up or let her know breakfast was ready. He'd done other things for her, for sure, but to take pleasure in making her a meal? Completely out of character for the Trevor she'd known. Maybe he had word on when she could return home, or…

Trevor was definitely up to something.

She hurried through her routine, splashing water on her face and brushing her teeth with the new toothbrush. Whoever Trevor worked for didn't spare any expense when it came to the comfort of their agents. Or the stray civilian witness, like her.

After she donned a pair of loose-fitting shorts from the pile of unisex clothing, she took a long look at herself. The eye wasn't so bad, if she ignored the glorious streaks of purple and red. The swelling was down, almost gone—a miracle of the ice pack, as promised by Trevor. She'd pulled her hair back into a loose bun at the base of her neck, the only way she could manage it right now. The long, straight locks would hang too limply otherwise, and she knew the tug of a ponytail would aggravate her sore temple.

Why did she care what she looked like? If anyone but Trevor was in the kitchen, she wouldn't give it a second thought, not after what she'd been through.

But it was Trevor, and like a compulsion she couldn't

control, she wanted to put her best foot forward with him. Always.

Lying about the lockbox wasn't your best self.

Wishing for once that she didn't have an overactive conscience, she walked into the kitchen in bare feet, stopping short of going up to the counter. Trevor filled the space in front of the oven, expertly flipping pancakes off a griddle while sipping a mug of coffee. He must have sensed her nearness as he looked over his shoulder and gave her another wide grin.

Yup, he was definitely up to something. She didn't think it was a surprise trip to the zoo or beach, though, as it'd sometimes been when they'd been a couple. More like he wanted something from her. Something she wasn't willing to give up. Like when he'd told her that their plan for life after the Marine Corps wasn't going to be as they'd discussed. Trevor had made homemade butternut risotto, her favorite, and a peanut butter swirl cheesecake to appease her before he revealed he wasn't taking a calm, safe civilian job as an intelligence analyst in Fort Meade, Maryland, less than two hours from Silver Valley. She could still see the charm in his eyes turn to steely determination at her protests. It had been the loneliest place for her in their marriage, knowing Trevor wasn't willing to do what was best for both of them.

She wasn't the same woman he'd hurt, though. Having survived the butternut risotto meal, she'd get through the bacon breakfast.

"Hey, Coral. Ready for some of my buttermilk pancakes? There's some local maple syrup on the table.

We get all of our foodstuffs locally—a lot of it comes from an Amish farm up the road, in fact."

She walked over to the coffeepot. The hit of fresh caffeine was worth the risk of getting too close to Trevor. He'd left a tiny pitcher of cream next to it, along with one large bluestone pottery mug. Exactly how she liked her morning coffee—with full-fat cream, no sugar.

"This is amazing." After she swirled the ivory liquid into the hot brew, she went to the table, where he'd set two places. "Does it matter where I sit?"

"No—you pick."

She sat and enjoyed her first few sips of coffee. The strong brew fortified her, reminded her that the simple things not only mattered but were essential to her.

"Any news from your colleagues on if I can go back yet?" Why waste time tiptoeing around what she wanted? Trevor knew her well enough to understand she wasn't going to let up on returning home until he relented.

"About that." He placed a huge pile of pancakes next to her plate and took the seat opposite hers. "Claudia's okayed your return earlier than I thought she would. But only because the two men I was with are in custody, and that buys some time before Markova can send more out." His body language was casual, detached, except for his gaze, which he kept fixed on her. She steeled herself to reveal nothing, as much as she could with the purple haze mark that was her shiner.

"But."

His expression reflected her frustration. "You know there's a *but*. Of course you do." He placed his forearms on the table, looked her directly in the eye. "In order for you to return to your property, I have to stay with you. And you go back knowing that with zero notice you may end up back here, or another place we deem safe from ROC."

"I'll take whatever time I can have back home." She paused. "I don't like having a bodyguard." Especially not Trevor. They didn't need more time together, especially in her small camper.

"There's no way we're going to risk leaving you unprotected if any more of Markova's thugs come out there. And I'm not working as your bodyguard—I'll be out there undercover, observing the comings and goings on your property. I'm not thrilled about you being back there, but I respect your urgency and sense of responsibility. And fair warning—I'm basically there to catch the ROC when they come back. Because we have no reason to believe they won't. I know you, Coral. You're going to do whatever you can to get back to your property. I get it. But you're not doing it solo."

Coral's stomach zinged with apprehension. Undercover ops weren't her career of choice. She hadn't been able to stay married to an agent, and being this close to a live op was frightening. And the thought of more thugs showing up and assaulting her…

Get home before you worry about that again.

Trevor made perfect sense, and he was right—she wanted to be on-site to oversee the many moving parts going on from the barn and farm home reconstruction to her catering teams. And then there were the tent people, who put the event venues up the night before and removed them right after, weather dependent. And the decorators and serving staff weren't going to do their work without direction from her.

She'd taken the barn and a permanent place to run her business for granted.

Never again.

"But you being so visible, isn't that a problem? If ROC sends anyone else out, they're going to see you. Aren't you worried about being recognized?" Or maybe he wanted to entice them. The thought of being the cheese for lethal, criminal rats wasn't a place she wanted to take her thoughts, either.

He shook his head. "I'm not concerned about it. The jerks I was with last night have been arrested, and they'll be busy being interrogated for the next few days. They won't be allowed to speak to Markova. No one else in the area, in ROC, knows me. I was operating on the West Coast and in the Asian theater exclusively before I, ah, found out about this case."

"You mean before you found out that my barn had exploded." She slathered butter on five silver-dollar-size pancakes. He'd remembered she preferred several smaller pancakes to plate size. Shoving his unwanted attention to detail aside, she watched him as she savored the hot treats.

"No. Yes. Kind of. I heard about the barn from my brother, who as you know still lives here."

"I heard your folks retired to Arizona." His parents had suffered the loss of their teenage son, Trevor's brother, before she'd ever met them, but the pain of his death had undeniably changed them. She was glad to hear that they'd decided to try to make a happier life for themselves.

"Yes, about the time you came back to Silver Valley." He didn't say, *When we got divorced.*

"Okay, so you heard about my barn and house event. That was back in January. What made you wait six months to reach out to me? Why are you here now?" Not that she'd expected to hear from him, but she wanted him to tell her why he'd not even sent a text, an email.

She despised the part of herself that still cared. Really, how many divorced couples did she know of who stayed in touch?

"When reports started coming out—intel reports, not public news—that Markova was operating her business from her jail cell, I knew it would be a great opportunity to dip my feet into East Coast ROC ops. It's always good to expand my area of expertise as an agent."

"You're lying, Trevor. You had to know she was sending her people out to my property."

"Actually, I didn't know that, not at first. I came back to Silver Valley to help with the overall takedown. Act in my usual undercover capacity, infiltrate local drug and crime rings. It's all hands on deck here. I'm sure I don't have to tell you that."

"No, you don't. We've lost more than one high school classmate to ROC heroin, along with much younger victims. And the sex trafficking is unreal. They caught several groups of women being smuggled in from Ukraine a few months back. But it's bigger than all of this, isn't it?"

Trevor was being candid, the overt play to win her

over dropped. "Yes, it's a mess. We're making progress, we always do, but we need a huge break."

"So tell me why you're allowing me to go back this early. Really." She sipped the coffee and almost moaned in delight. Except that might make Trevor think she wanted more from him than hotcakes and fresh java. Which her traitorous body did, in fact.

Don't do this to yourself.

"I have to find whatever Markova's hidden on your property before she gets her hands on it again. It'll appear more natural if you're back there." His candid expression hit her like a brick to the stomach.

"Ah, there it is." She enjoyed flourishing her fork at him as if she'd stabbed and gutted prey, caught it in the act of sneaking into her pantry. "I'm enjoying this delicious meal, trust me, but you didn't have to go to so much trouble to get me to do what you want. And you don't have to stay with me, either. Come and search all you want during the day, all day. I'll be fine at night. I'm sure SVPD is going to have additional patrols going up and down my road. I can always stay with my folks temporarily, as much as it's a pain in the neck."

"Like hell." Low and lethal, it was the voice he'd used only once before with her. When he'd told her there was no chance of reconciliation because they'd let their relationship fray to the breaking point and he didn't have the time between missions to work on it.

And it still hurt, that tone—it went right to her solar plexus and made the fluffy pancakes feel like a ball of raw dough in her gut.

"You want two things, from what I'm hearing. First, you have to find whatever it is you were looking for last night. Second, you're basically using me as bait to get the bad guy."

"I'd never use a civilian as bait." He appeared conflicted, though. "I'd be there to protect you, yes. Look, I'm on the same page as you, believe me. I don't want to put us through anything we don't have to. It's hard being with one another after we've been on our own this long. But your safety is nonnegotiable." Charming Trevor was back, his eyes on her. "And that of your family, too. SVPD will beef up patrols in their area. We take nothing for granted."

Her body reacted instinctively to his easygoing, sexy-as-hell manner, and she stood. It was one thing to still have the hots for her ex but another to let her hormones lead her astray when she felt so vulnerable. Staying at the table with him was too close, too risky.

"Cut to the chase, Trevor. You're plying me with everything you know I like to eat, and you're using your best manners, for the most part. What is it?" Her voice shook with her want, and she turned to head out of the room, to go anywhere else. Tears threatened again, but they weren't from her wound or other injury.

It hurt how much she still wanted him.

He reached over and grasped her wrist, tugged her hand from her hip as he rose to his feet and hauled her against him. It wasn't a one-way interaction, though. The second the heat of his fingers touched her skin, she leaned in, needing the shock of his hard body and his blatant arousal. Her body ached for him, and whether it was because she was exhausted from last night or the nearness of her ex or a bit of both, it didn't matter.

"Coral." He reached behind her head, held her. "Do

you feel it, too? I've never stopped wanting you." He nuzzled her throat, kissed her jaw, her cheekbone, avoiding her huge bruise. "I don't ever want to hurt you again."

She responded by wrapping both hands around his neck and pulling his head down, placing her lips on his. The feel of his erection against her midsection had lit her desire, but the touch of his lips, the lips she knew intimately, took her want to five alarms.

"Your eye." He spoke against her lips, his mouth's movements making liquid heat pool deliciously between her legs. She had to have this man again, had craved his touch since she'd heard his voice last night. It wasn't something she'd ever get rid of, her desire for Trevor. So why fight it?

"My eye's fine. Stop torturing me."

Trevor's nice, charming routine disappeared. He went in for the full kiss, his tongue impatient and greedy. She got it—she got *him*. Trevor was a man who focused his laser-sharp intelligence on whatever his task was at the moment, and right now she was the grateful benefactor of his attention to detail.

His hand moved to her breast and squeezed, making a cascade of sparks shoot under her closed eyelids as her nipple strained with arousal against the cotton fabric. Trevor lifted her T-shirt up and exposed her breast, staring at it as if he'd found the Holy Grail. She certainly had from the way her body reacted to his lovemaking. She moaned and writhed her pelvis against him as his tongue laved her areola and teased its peak into a tiny rock. Her vocalizations were uninhibited, coming from deep inside her. From the place that only Trevor had found the way to.

Her hands needed to feel every inch of him, and she started by shoving them under his shirt, moving her fingers over his chiseled back, loving every sinewy bit. She moved to his front and splayed her hands over his pecs.

"You're incredible." She breathed the words against his skin as she kissed her way to his nipples, where she left tiny bites on each one, relishing the sharp intake of breath her actions elicited from him. Primal satisfaction increased her enjoyment, as she knew she made him as hot has he did her.

Coral continued her exploration, this reintroduction to Trevor, as she unbuckled his belt and unzipped his jeans, reached into his briefs and wrapped her hands around him, freed him from his clothing.

"Coral, wait." He had both hands on either side of her face, his eyes burning with an intensity that made her knees week. "Are you sure this is what you want? Because I haven't changed. I'm the same. My job's the same."

"I want you, Trevor. As you are, right now." She moved her hands up and down his hard length, watched his expression fight against the ecstasy she was promising with her strokes.

He didn't reply with words as he took her hands from him, turned her to face the massive dining table, and placed her hands on its edge. "Hold on." His breath was against her cheek, his body over hers from behind. "You okay with this?"

"Yes." Her reply moaned out of her, and she couldn't

remember ever wanting a man this much before. Her palms grew sweaty as she waited for him to make the next move.

She heard his jeans hit the floor, gripped the table with all her might. And practically panted for him, anticipating the moment he'd fill her.

He placed his hands on her hips and reached around her waist to feel her, his fingers working magic on her swollen, damp center.

"You're so wet for me, babe."

"Hurry, Trevor. Don't stop."

"Let me get a condom." His hands left her, and she looked over her shoulder to see him pick up his jeans and grab a foil packet from the pocket.

"You were counting on this?" It made it all the sexier, thinking that he'd been on the same level of awareness as she had. That behind his so-professional bearing he'd been as vulnerable, as needy as she. That he'd planned for the opportunity to be with her as he'd prepared for the ROC mission on her property. Her breathing became heavier, and her legs trembled with unadulterated need.

"Ever since I heard your voice last night, I knew I couldn't risk not being prepared." His voice rolled over her with its husky tone—Trevor's sexiest one.

Just as she thought she couldn't handle one second more of not having him, her insides and outsides taut with her need, Trevor was back up against her, moving her hips toward him as he brought their joining closer, closer—

"Now, Trevor!"

He entered her in one hard shove, and the waves of

her next climax started as though they'd been doing this all morning and not just in the past few seconds.

"Come for me, babe." His thrusts were as purposeful as they were powerful, and as she held on to the table, her orgasm ripped through her, making her forget all that had passed between them. Right now it was just her and Trevor, together, as they'd been so many times before. As she climaxed he continued moving, giving her maximum pleasure before he found his release.

Trevor's shout, followed by him laying his length across her naked back as his hot breath caressed her nape, told her that he'd been as blindsided by their passion as she had.

It made it easier to accept the fact that she'd just been with her ex, knowing he'd lost control, too. They'd always had this chemistry. It wasn't anything to feel guilty about—she didn't want more than this from Trevor and was certain he felt the same. They'd divorced for very good reasons.

But the sex—sex with Trevor had always been life affirming, had taken her to the mental state of knowing all was well with the world.

She'd missed this.

Trevor allowed himself the few minutes it took to catch his breath to lay against Coral as he held her waist loosely. He'd always loved being with her—Coral was a generous partner and as unabashedly open about sex as he was. It was one of her strengths, something he wasn't sure he'd ever articulated to her. She wasn't afraid to go after what she wanted, to get her needs met.

But this, this had been cataclysmic. His mind was

blank, reality pushed aside for a brief, blissful moment. He'd missed this, the sense of peace after being with her.

"You okay?" Her voice sounded as dazed as he felt. He let his arms open, used the table to push himself up before he turned her around and pulled her close to him.

"I'm more than okay, Coral Bell." The endearment slipped out ahead of his thoughts. He felt her body stiffen.

"Don't call me…" She drifted, her breath fanning over his chest as they stood in the same place where they'd had the debrief last night. She melted against him again, probably having the same thoughts he did.

This was a onetime deal, a way to get one another out of their systems. Why fight it?

He stood up and pulled her with him to the sofa, where he sat and tugged her down on his lap. Her eyes were closed, her lips full, her hair wild around her heart-shaped face.

"You look like you've been through it with your shiner." His fingers had a mind of their own as they traced her features, roughly combed her hair back. She opened her eyes and looked at him.

"We just were through it." Her finger pressed against his lips. "Shh…can we please enjoy this little time together before we get back to the reality of our lives?"

He stilled. "It sounds like you're already there."

Coral sighed and pushed herself up into a sitting position off his lap, next to him. Their thighs touched, both still naked. But the intimacy was all but gone between them. He felt her detach from him mentally and emotionally, as harshly as he'd felt the Siberian winter roll across the Russian steppe when he'd been in country trailing an FSB agent.

He felt her arm move, knew she was going to stand up and walk away, just like she had right before the divorce. When their need for one another had overwhelmed the necessity of their breakup.

"We're both practical people, Trevor. Pragmatic, with incredible chemistry."

She thought it was chemistry, and he wasn't going to argue. He couldn't. Because if he told her what his heart was screaming at him, that what they shared was more than sex or pheromones, it'd blow the fragile partnership they'd established over the past twelve hours. A relationship they both had to count on to get through the next several days or weeks.

He fell back on the familiar with her.

"I need a quick shower."

"I'll meet you back here after I get one first. Then the shower's yours." Coral stood, and he watched her saunter to the dining table, reveled in the pure poetry that was her body as she bent to retrieve her clothing and then disappeared into the hallway.

He leaned his head against the sofa's back, staring at the ceiling. Since he'd seen Coral last night, he'd had to fight to keep his head in the ROC game, and having sex with her had to be the most stupid thing he'd ever done as an agent.

It had to stop here. He was responsible for her well-being until they broke the case. If he forgot it again, it could be life-threatening.

* * *

They each took twenty minutes to shower and get dressed before meeting back at the dining table. Coral didn't think she'd ever be able to look at an oak table the same way again. Trevor walked in after her, and she saw his gaze hesitate on the gleaming blond surface, too.

"Trevor, I'm sorry I was so abrupt. I'm a bit out of sorts. That wasn't anything I'd planned. Being with you, like that again."

He was walking from the kitchen but pulled up short and closed his eyes for a brief moment. She wasn't sure if she'd hurt him or angered him, or both. When he opened his eyes, she had no doubt whom she stood next to. Trevor the agent. The man who didn't have time for distractions. Trevor had once told her that his feelings for her were detractors from his ability to focus on a mission.

"Neither of us planned on being thrown together like this, under such stressful circumstances. Sex is something that happens during missions. It can be a good release, pardon the pun." He stood with his hands on his hips, totally in charge of his inner world. Part of her itched to remind him that he was one kiss, one grasp of his erection from being the Trevor who'd just made love to her. She didn't like the side of her that was so needy for his attention, though.

"I see."

She still couldn't help wondering how many "releases" he'd had since they'd been apart but declined to ask. The less she knew about Trevor's current life, the better. And she was a big girl—she could handle a hot sex interlude with her ex without making it into something it wasn't.

You don't want your heart broken again.

"I knew you would." Trevor nodded. "It doesn't change the ROC op, though. I have to go home with you. We're running against the clock here, Coral. We need your cooperation."

"You still know me well enough to understand that I wouldn't jeopardize a mission because of my personal discomfort. I'm just not sold on why you have to stay with me in my camper. It's tight quarters by myself." There were actually six sleeping spaces in the trailer—a queen-size bed in her bedroom, two bunks in the front room and both kitchen benches turned into beds. They'd be in separate places at night.

"We can't keep rehashing this, Coral. Time's ticking." He looked calm, but she saw the telltale twitching of his jaw muscle. She was wearing on his patience. "I have to stay on-site with you until we find what we're looking for, because until we find the missing data, Markova will send in more backup to retrieve it, which means more danger for you. You'll be happy to know that it won't only be me out there, on the job. There will be several other undercover agents, too, working with your construction team."

When he put it like that, of course he could stay on her property. She'd have to deal with their sleeping arrangements, though, because Trevor was a large, muscular man. While the bed frames would hold his weight, they were inches short of his height. Except for the queen bed. She'd have to give him her room and take the front.

Truth was, she didn't trust herself sleeping so close to her ex. Not when every single one of her most sensitive parts was firing off sparklers, anticipating some kind of connubial reunion.

Nope, not happening. What they'd just shared was one time.

"Coral?"

"Yes, fine, you can stay with me. We'll make it work. It's short term, right?" Besides, from what she'd observed at the debrief last night, the top tier of LEA were on this. They'd break through soon enough, get ROC out of Silver Valley. "How long can it take?"

Chapter 6

Three days later Coral knew how long it could take. Weeks. The other undercover agents—she'd picked out two men and one woman—worked with the construction crew on the barn by day, and with large spotlights they searched the grounds and fields by night. So far, nothing had happened besides additional construction.

And getting used to Trevor being in the trailer with her at night. He'd insisted on taking the kitchen bench-seat bed, said he had to have full access to the side door that faced the barn.

She'd let him have that access to everything. Except the lockbox, which she'd immediately hidden upon returning to the camper. She'd tried every key on it that she'd found in Aunt Brenda's house so far, with zero luck. Aunt Brenda had had a huge key ring that hung inside the kitchen door, and Coral had counted on the key being there. The only place she still had to search was one particular junk drawer in the kitchen.

She lay in her bed, listening to the birds sing as the sun crept over the mountains. The canvas window cover next to her head was ablaze with light, the new day undeniable.

"We need to talk." If she hadn't been lying flat, she'd have hit her head on the low camper ceiling in surprise. She'd been trying to figure out how to get out of her bed and drive away with the lockbox to get a locksmith to open it without Trevor discovering her secret.

His eyes blazed with intent, and she sat up, swallowed.

"You're usually out in the field by now, aren't you?"

"Stop evading, Coral."

"Evading what, Trevor?" She drew on her anger, long simmering and so much closer to the surface of her consciousness since he'd exploded back into her life less than a week ago. Since their cataclysmic sex, from which they'd refrained since that mind-blowing episode in the safe house. It felt as though they'd been living together again for a decade.

"You've been cagey since the night at the safe house. There's something you're holding back. You've either seen something or found something that you're not telling me about."

He'd already dressed, in his usual battered jeans and white T-shirt. The perfect way to blend in with the construction crew, especially when he wore a hard hat. He'd told them he was her representative, a licensed historical barn designer. She'd laughed but then took it back when the construction workers didn't bat an eye at his explanation.

"You're being ridiculous. If I'd found something that looked like a computer chip or memory stick, of course I would have told you."

There could be a lot of USB sticks in the lockbox.

"Coral."

Heat simmered between them, and it had nothing to do with the case and everything to do with the attraction they'd both denied since they'd locked gazes as he'd expertly saved her from death at the hands of the ROC henchmen. She'd given in to it once, at the safe house, but couldn't do it again.

"Get out of here while I get dressed, will you, please?" Hopefully her expression didn't reveal any of her inner turmoil. No way would going to bed with Trevor again ever be a good idea, but her body was her most vociferous betrayer, humming with delight every time he was near.

His eyes narrowed. "Sure." He left with only the tiniest click of the screen door as he closed it. As soon as she heard his steady footfalls on the hard-baked summer clay, she sprang up and shoved on her clothes. Showers were her nighttime ritual so that she was able to get up and going more quickly in the morning. With the recent heat wave, they'd helped cool her off, too. Not only from the hot weather.

"Damn you, Trevor Stone." She shoved on khaki shorts, a bright pink T-shirt and her ubiquitous construction boots. Normally she worked in sneakers up and until a big event, trading her comfort for dressier attire only on the day of. But since both the barn and her house were under construction and she often needed to work between the two sites, the steel-toed accessories were mandatory.

They also were way more supportive on her feet, something she'd never have known. *Good comes out of everything if we allow it to.* Aunt Brenda's favorite saying echoed in her mind. Usually her aunt referred to broken hearts and relationships with her catchphrase, and she had said it to Coral upon her and Trevor's divorce, just weeks before Brenda had unexpectedly died.

At the time, Coral couldn't believe anything good would come from the mess she'd made of her life. But after three years here—before the barn exploded—she'd found a quiet peace and stability she'd never had in California, with Trevor.

You haven't had sex since then, either. Except for that hot union with Trevor at the safe house. That had to explain why she was all of a sudden so hot and horny for her ex, right? The lack of regular sex these past three years.

Her phone pinged with a text from her head chef, who was setting up in what remained of her farmhouse kitchen for the wedding this coming weekend. She climbed out of the camper and saw Trevor across the field, in a cluster of construction workers. A pang of guilt about the lockbox tugged, hard. This was perfect—she'd find the box's missing key at the house after she spoke to the chef, a new hire. Two birds and all.

Because she'd promised to always let Trevor know where she was going and when she was leaving, she sent him a quick text. The five-minute walk to the main house, her home, gave her time to organize her thoughts and tasks for the day. Her fingers were crossed that the new chef would be easy to work with.

As she approached the front of the farmhouse, the now familiar sinking pit that was her stomach issued its own pang of dismay at the sight of the gaping side of the house.

"Focus on the fresh lumber." She spoke to herself as she neared, used her mind's eye to see past the framework repair. The half of the house that included the kitchen had been spared, its plumbing and electricity still intact, so while she was without her bedroom and living room, she had a fully functioning kitchen and bathroom. She couldn't complain—it could have been a total loss for the house, as it had been for the barn.

"Hello!" She called out before she pushed open the back door, the smells of various dishes mingling in the air.

"Hi, Coral. I'm just finishing with the desserts and appetizers." Chef Mike Rodinsky smiled over his broad shoulder, the flash of white beneath his very full mustache a reassuring sign.

"You found your way in, no problem, I see." She'd given him a key only yesterday, under Trevor's watchful eyes, albeit from a distance. Trevor had immediately installed hidden security cameras at the house. One inside the kitchen and one outside, focused on the back door. Coral thought it was overkill—she'd hired Mike from the same school she'd used before, as a private contractor.

"Yes, I've been here since five." He said it offhandedly, as if beginning work at the crack of dawn was what everyone did. Coral's respect for the food industry had quadrupled since she'd started the business here in Silver Valley. While she knew her way around a pastry, she didn't have the background or desire to prepare complex menus for hundreds of people.

"I can see you've been here awhile already. This looks amazing." She took time to look at all of his dishes, then made sure he had enough ingredients to last through the wedding prep. "I'm not sure if your colleagues told you, but my business has a running tab at the local farm store down the road."

"Yes, at Elderberry Farms?"

"That's it!"

"I've already spoken with the owner, and they've agreed to deliver on Saturday if there's anything we forget."

"Fantastic." Chef Mike sounded genuinely happy about having such ready backup. She related to his attitude, as it'd been a relief to her to build a dependable resource list for the business. By the end of the year, she hoped to employ a full-time cook, as now she still managed with contract employees. It was time to expand.

"You're squared away, I have to hand it to you, Mike. While you keep working, I'll stay out of your way. I need to go through a drawer or two in here, and then you'll have the kitchen all to yourself for the rest of your shift."

"I appreciate that." He spoke quietly as he wrapped slices of maple wood–smoked bacon around plump scallops, securing them with a toothpick.

She knew he would, since she too needed quiet to do her best work. As unobtrusively as possible, she opened the junk drawer in the far corner of the kitchen and began her search for the lockbox key.

* * *

She was as stupid as Markova had said she'd be, this Coral Staufer. The woman was young, and her privileged American self had no clue that her new hire was, like Markova, a former Russian agent who had decided to take his future into his own hands.

He'd been working at the county prison as a custodian for almost two years, placed there by ROC as his first duty when he'd arrived in the US. His job was to clean the jail, sure, but also to pay attention, be on the lookout for any ROC member who became incarcerated. Misha was the go-between so that ROC ops wouldn't suffer from silly arrests.

When Anna Markova had been put away in the solitary cell, it'd made his two years doing what he considered the paltry tasks of the ROC worth it. He'd had his hours changed to the night shift so he could have lengthier conversations with her. It left him the mornings and early afternoons to do whatever needed to be done for the sake of Markova's vision. She promised him freedom from servitude to ROC. He'd escaped the clutches of the FSB, wanting a new life for himself, just like Anna.

But getting out of ROC was nearly impossible. Ivanov demanded a life pact from all agents, from the senior operatives in his inner circle to the drug dealers and pawnshop owners.

Right now, he needed to portray himself as an accomplished chef. He smiled as he wrapped a scallop with the slice of overpriced pork. What fancy tastes such young people had in America. It wasn't different for the Muscovites or some of St. Petersburg's wealthier families. But for his family, and most of Russia, food like this was a fantasy, something only seen on foreign cable television or the internet.

Markova had told him to obtain a job here so that he could watch the comings and goings of the event business that somehow had survived the complete destruction of its "offices." Between what he saw of the leveled barn and how damaged most of this house was, he didn't understand why anyone would pay this woman to host a party for them.

Coral Staufer dug through a drawer that he knew had several items she might want, from nails to postage stamps. He'd already searched what remained of her fire-damaged home, just as Markova had told him to, in case she'd found one or all three of the items Markova had told him to be on the lookout for.

Coral stopped midpaw and shot him a sharp stare. He quickly covered his scrutiny with a smile. "What are you looking for?"

"Oh, nothing in particular. I've been here three years, yet I still don't know where my aunt left everything. I've been busy with the barn catering business."

"I understand."

She paused, and he wanted to tell her to keep looking for whatever it was she thought she needed. By the end of the week, once he'd retrieved Markova's prized possessions, Coral would be dead. She'd have to be taken out, because she'd seen him, knew his face. If the FBI or CIA showed her photos of him as an agent—which he knew they had just as the FSB had dossiers on all American agents they knew of—she'd be able to ID him, even with the mustache he'd grown as part of his new identity. He couldn't have that—it would upset his plans with Anna.

Ah, Anna. The one woman who understood him, knew where he came from. The only woman he'd ever considered a relationship with. All he lived for was to do her bidding, to make her happy. And to help get her out of prison so that they could be together, forever. Without the constant heat of the ROC's breath on their necks.

Trevor walked along the edge of the barn's growing framework, trying to appear like the designer architect he'd said he was. As soon as it was clear that the construction crew was engrossed in its job, he went over to the mounds of rubble and started looking at it from different angles. It looked to all be a pile of the usual central Pennsylvania limestone, the boulders that existed under every suburban and rural land plot throughout Cumberland County. He searched for anything that the construction digger may have unearthed, anything that looked like a container sturdy enough to contain computer data. The thugs he'd worked with for one short night had been rudimentary in their approach, not quite sure of where exactly they were supposed to dig, but they'd made it clear that they were looking for a lockbox of some sort.

Which meant that Markova wasn't sending in her top buddies. Or maybe it hadn't been Markova who sent them on the mission, since she would have known precisely where to have them search. Perhaps they had really worked for Ivanov, and Ivanov knew that Markova had dirt on him.

Trevor's bet was on the latter. Markova was biding

her time in prison, waiting for her defense attorney to get her out. Right now she was imprisoned without bail, because of her obvious ties to the Russian mob. But it wouldn't last forever, Trevor was certain. She hadn't come up for trial yet and had pleaded not guilty to all charges on her indictment right after the explosion. The bad guys were good at getting sprung by slick lawyers, and ROC was famous for hiring the best, most sleazy attorneys money could buy.

Coral had gone to meet her chef up at the farmhouse. It was a stone's throw away but too far for Trevor's internal radar. He wasn't comfortable without her in direct sight. Not until they had ROC's entire operation shattered. He took a quick look at the security app on his phone that he'd linked to the cameras he'd put up at the farmhouse kitchen door and inside. Nothing unusual, just Coral and the chef talking over the work island.

He looked at the road that led to the house. Coral's return wouldn't be that soon. Before he could convince himself otherwise, he made for the camper. She'd been keeping something from him, and he couldn't stop obsessing about it. One thing he'd learned undercover was that details mattered. The way Coral had acted in the safe house when told about the possibility of Markova leaving something valuable on her property had seemed off. He knew his ex well enough to know she was a bad liar—maybe the worst. She'd been lying that night.

Guilt caught him off guard as he closed the distance to the camper. Why should he feel bad? If Coral had something to hide and it had anything to do with this case, he was saving her life by invading her privacy.

He'd worry about her reaction later.

* * *

Trevor knew he had to search the camper but still felt like the lowest of low going through the tiny drawers and one half-size closet, which Coral used to stack her seemingly endless supply of bright, tight tops and tanks. Her scent was all over the place. It was impossible for him to get a good night's sleep, not with her slumbering next to him, oblivious of his raging hardons and threatening blue balls.

His sexual frustration wasn't Coral's problem, though. They'd agreed to back off after their unexpected lovemaking at the safe house, and he wasn't about to break the pact. Although finding her silky stack of panties that included thongs was a sore reminder of how well they fit together. When he'd been inside her the other day, it'd been the single most erotic moment of his life. He'd told her their explosive chemistry and resultant sex were simply a by-product of adrenaline and the stress of the night before.

He'd lied. Sex with Coral was never simple or uncomplicated, because his layers of connection to her were unending. Didn't the past several days prove that? They'd been divorced, hadn't seen one another in three years and yet had picked up where they'd left off, still as hot and horny for one another as two teenagers with their first loves.

He slammed closed the drawer he'd searched through, looked around the camper from his spot on the floor next to the kitchen bunk. On his haunches, he used his flashlight to see if there were small spaces under the sofa or beds, a place one could hide a slim container.

When he found nothing on the floor or in the closets, he went back to the largest bedroom, where Coral slept. He'd insisted she stay in here, even though she'd fought him about it. She wanted him to have the largest bed, said she'd have no problem either in the front bedroom with the bunks or on the kitchen pullout bed. Once he'd explained that he needed to be next to the main door, she'd relented.

There was one additional door, between her room and the Lilliputian shower, and he cursed under his breath. The janitorial closet—of course. He'd blocked the spare entrance with a combination of broom handles and heavy boxes. If there was a fire, Coral could get out the window of her bedroom, and he had the other door. This way he didn't have to worry about ROC coming in that back door—not without making a lot of noise and alerting them both.

He pulled the boxes out of the narrow passage, stacking them on Coral's bed. His watch revealed he had five, ten minutes tops before she'd come back this way and do her usual late-morning business of reconciling receipts, double-checking orders, playing around with her serving schedule. He couldn't keep the tiny smile from his lips as he felt the swell of pride in his chest. Not for his late-arriving hunch about where she might have stashed anything she'd found, but for how she'd taken her gift of organization and made a living out of it. When they'd been married, her need for tidiness had often clashed with his desire to toss things on the floor and let all sense of control go when he was at home. His life first as a Marine and then as an agent required the utmost attention to detail while working, so attention to detail was the last thing he craved during off-hours, as rare as they were. Coral was what he'd pined for, what he'd needed. She'd been his sustenance.

Until he couldn't give her what she wanted and deserved. A safe, stable home life.

The boxes cleared, he moved a mop handle and broom from sitting slanted across the door, gaining access to the utility cupboard. His fingers hummed with anticipation as he opened the door to a couple of shelves. Filled with cleaning supplies, nothing else.

He swore loudly and wanted to slam the door shut, but in this dinky trailer he'd no doubt break it or the wall.

"Trevor?" Coral's shout sounded down the length of the camper, and he froze. He'd been so wrapped up in his search and resulting frustration that he'd failed Agent 101. He'd not heard the signs of Coral's return.

He eyed the stack of boxes from the small space to her bed, saw the way it all looked. Like he'd been tearing the place apart.

Dread filled his gut, and it wasn't from being caught. He'd been caught red-handed countless times in his work; it was a noted job risk and one he often had to peddle back from or forge through.

His dismay was that he'd broken Coral's trust and had nothing to show for it.

"What are you doing, Trevor?"

Chapter 7

Coral's voice was coated in ice, and the guilt at betraying her trust smacked him in the gut. He straightened as much as he could in the low-ceilinged structure. He had to take this head-on; Coral deserved that much.

"I'm sorry, I've made a bit of a mess of things."

Everything in a camper was made for optimal storage, and it had taken him longer than he'd expected to get through the first half of the vehicle, leaving too many of Coral's possessions exposed and out of order.

Her bright eyes were on him, blazing with suppressed fury. It should have underscored to him why their marriage hadn't succeeded, why it had ended. He'd infuriated her countless times before, usually for missing a meal with her or putting his work first. Instead, her ire poked holes in all of his theories about why they shouldn't have stayed together. Because even when she looked about to lop his head off, he wanted to be with her. He'd missed their exchanges, no matter how rough.

"You can come up with a better answer than that. What do you tell the people you spy on when they catch you in the act?" Coral wasn't thinking the same thought as he was, but he did see her pupils dilated in the brightly lit space. Was it the thrill of catching him at something so wrong, or was it that they just couldn't help themselves when they were this close and this emotionally charged?

You promised her the safe-house sex was singular.

"I'm not spying on you, Coral. I'm looking for Markova's data. Or whatever it is that she's buried here." If he didn't stay focused on why she was so upset with him, he was afraid of what he'd do—or more likely, what he wouldn't do.

He wouldn't keep his promise to keep his hands off her.

"*Buried* being the operative word, right?" She shook her head, and he stiffened. Braced himself against whatever she was about to dish out. "As in, underneath piles of dirt near the barn. Not in my camper!" Fists clenched as her arms crossed her chest, she was the picture of fiery indignation. Righteously so, he grudgingly admitted to himself.

But her immediate defensiveness got his hackles up, erasing the guilt, morphing it into something more primal. Needy.

"The lady doth protest too much, methinks." The quote escaped his mouth before he employed his mental filter. Did she remember how he'd read Shakespeare aloud to her when they'd dated in college?

"Well, the agent is spending too much time on my turf, I think." Pink patches on her cheekbones were never a good sign with Coral. It meant she was about to blow, volcanically. And he'd put himself—and her—in a position that wasn't going to be advantageous to either of them. He had been going through her stuff without telling her. He'd broken her trust.

"Look, this is about keeping you safe, bottom line. I know that having to share your living quarters with me absolutely is the pits, and that law enforcement has basically invaded your entire life." As he spoke he put himself in her shoes and realized how overwhelming the past four days must have been for her. How difficult it was right now.

"Do you know, Trevor?" Her bottom lip was trembling. His heart ached with the need to comfort her, but touching her right now was—*hell*.

It was all he wanted to do.

"I'm sorry." He held his arms open, giving her the chance to either take the two steps into them or turn and barrel out the tiny screen door. It was a standoff as she stared at him, her emotions racing across her expression. He recognized them because they were at war in him, too. Desire, regret, mistrust, wariness of the other's motives.

When Coral moved, it was with purpose and all of her strength as she flung herself on him and wrapped her legs around his waist.

He was ready for her, grabbed her bottom and only took a half step back from the momentum of her full-on sensual attack. Their lips met and the air in the camper evaporated, the sounds of the construction crew less than a quarter mile away fading into the oblivion that was his purely chemical reaction to her.

"Why'd you say you're sorry?" She moaned as she reacted to his caresses. "You know I can't resist you when you apologize."

"I'm sorry for it all, Coral. And I know I'll be sorry for this—"

"No, not now. Just this. I need you, Trevor." She gasped between kisses on his jawline, a soft bite to his throat. As her tongue licked along his neck, he growled in frustration, swirled them around and pressed her up against the minuscule kitchen counter. She groaned, tried to press her pelvis up against his. Her whimpers of frustration shattered his attempt to remain emotionally detached, to let this be another sexual act of closure between them.

He'd never have closure from what they shared.

"Where's your condom this time? If you don't have any, there's a box in my bedroom." She shrugged out of her top and bra as if her life depended on it, and the sight of her bare breasts ready and needy for him drove all thought from his mind. He allowed her to lift his shirt up and off, and she pressed her breasts against his bare skin.

"In my go kit." He reached behind him to where his toiletry bag sat on his bunk and grabbed it. As he brought the bag between them, Coral took it and nodded at him, her eyes huge and languid with desire, her lips swollen from his kisses.

"I'll get the protection, you take your pants off."

He complied, but not before he shut the side door completely and lowered the blinds. His body shook for her, and he wasn't sure if he was going to be able to hold off his climax long enough to please her, but he didn't want any interruptions, either.

Coral unzipped her pants and pushed them down, revealing bright pink lacy thong panties. He'd never tire of the sight of her lush cheeks, how full and round her bottom was. When she stood, she held the condom in her hand and smiled at him.

"Ready."

"I know you are, babe." He walked up to her, both of them naked, and grasped her wrists. He kissed her then, using his tongue to make her groan. She was all softness and sexy female musk, and he had to have her with all of his being.

"Trevor, please. Stop teasing me."

"No problem." He nudged her into a seated position on the bunk, then eased her shoulders back. He moved to her legs, spreading them wide as he watched her. "You're so beautiful, Coral Bell." Her reaction turned him on more than anything, seeing the comprehension in her eyes as she saw, accepted and welcomed what he was about to do.

When he lowered his mouth to her center, she let out a soft cry that was almost his undoing. But pleasing her was more important.

Sometimes you took one for the team.

Coral couldn't escape the delicious warmth pooling in her most sensitive spot, between her legs, where Trevor's head was buried. And she didn't want to be anywhere but here, with Trevor—this was everything sex was supposed to be, and everything it shouldn't be with her ex. She was determined to soak up every blessed second of it.

His tongue knew her too well, and her orgasm hit without any preamble. She pressed her hand over her mouth to keep her shriek from leaving the camper's walls. The sun's rays beat down on the roof, and the small AC unit had a hard time keeping up with the summer heat. It was nothing compared to the incendiary chemistry she shared with Trevor, and it was their attraction that made her perspire, not the weather. She accepted his expert strokes, the way his mouth moved over her most sensitive spot, and allowed the ecstasy to roll over and through her.

After he made her come a third time, she tugged on his arms, urged him to let her reciprocate. Having him in her mouth again was her biggest turn-on, knowing she made him feel as wonderful as she did.

Sliding off the bench and onto her knees, she switched places with him and knew from how his hands grasped her head, how his fingers ran through her hair, that her tongue was as adept as his. He grew harder in her mouth, and as she prepared for him to climax, he grasped her shoulders and lifted her up, off the floor.

"Coral, now. I have to be inside you." His erection was at its peak, and he needed release immediately. The fact that he wanted to be inside her as much as she wanted to feel him there only made it sweeter for her, more intense.

She wanted them to be together, too.

He took the packet from the kitchen table and ripped it open, his eyes never leaving hers.

"Let me." She took the condom from him and sheathed him, loving how she knew every inch of him, what he liked best and what drove him insane.

"Babe." His groan was more like a growl, and he pulled her up and over him, positioning her atop his length. Coral couldn't wait any longer and sank onto him, her fingers digging into his shoulders as she tried not to hit her head on the very low cupboard above them.

Trevor wasn't about anything at this point but having them both reach another climax. Not that she could stop one if she tried. His thrusts filled her, stretched her to new heights of pleasure. As his deep groans accompanied his climax, she pulsed around him and was thrown into another level of sexual satisfaction, her womb clenching as her orgasm rocketed through her system.

Coral knew she was going to regret this in about five minutes, but right now she chose to remain in the moment, her head against Trevor's shoulder, as they floated on the waning sensations from their lovemaking.

"I have a confession." She spoke to his left pectoral, just under her cheek. They were on the kitchen bench, and he knew they couldn't stay here all day, as much as he'd love to rock her world again and again.

"Yeah?" He was surprised he could speak after the mind-blowing orgasm he'd just experienced.

"I did find something in the pile of rubble next to the construction site. But I'm certain it's my aunt Brenda's."

"You're a postcoital buzzkill, do you know that?"

"Sorry. But I don't want you to be mad when I tell you the next part."

"Why would I?"

"I found it last week."

"What?" Adrenaline shot through him, and he sat up. And immediately smacked his forehead against a small overhead shelf.

"Ouch, are you okay?" She'd slid off him and stood next to the bunk beds, her naked skin glistening from their sex sweat. His arms lifted to reach for her, bring her back to him.

No. Coral's safety. The ROC op.

He dropped his arms. "I'm fine, but you're incredibly naive, Coral, if you're telling me that you've had something that could be Anna Markova's, on-site, in the very place where you sleep, and you didn't mention it to the authorities or me sooner." The post-sex relaxation was the only thing keeping him from totally blowing his cool over the threat of ROC coming after her again and finding her so vulnerable.

"I'm not stupid. If I thought it was what you were looking for, I would have told you." Her white teeth contrasted with her dusky-rose lower lip as she tugged at it. "Give me a minute and then you can jump in here." He heard the shower run, and true to her word, Coral was out within three minutes, hair damp and body slick from the water instead of him. Her movements were swift as she used a small microfiber towel to wipe down and quickly donned her clothing. A pity, seeing her dressed again, but also a miracle, as he could not trust himself around her.

Coral had become a major distraction to him solving the case. He squeezed by her and got into the shower, which he'd been using the last few days but still found surprisingly small each time he did.

After he was done, he dried off and joined her back in the kitchen area.

"Can I see whatever it is you've found?" He pulled his shirt on, stepped into his pants. "And why didn't you tell me sooner?" She wasn't going to get away with keeping this from him. He pulled on the thick socks that protected him from ticks, a local menace, and shoved into his construction boots.

"I knew if I mentioned it at the safe house that all of those agents would be in my camper, climbing over all my stuff. And like I told you, I'm certain it's my aunt Brenda's lockbox. Or, at least, I was. I've had a tricky time finding the matching key for it."

He stilled. "You have a lockbox? And you didn't mention it." The epithets that swirled in his mind were so close to his tongue. But they wouldn't make Coral any more receptive to him or more willing to share what she'd found.

"Where is it, Coral?"

"Here." She stretched up and pulled a duffel bag from the overhead storage shelf. He sighed. It had been right in plain sight of him. Placing the satchel on the small table, she offered him a slight smile.

"It's nothing, I'm telling you." She unzipped the bag and pulled out a run-of-the-mill fire-safe lockbox. Upon closer inspection, it had a lot of scratches and was banged up, no doubt from the rocky place it had been buried, and then from the hits it had taken when it was unearthed by the construction shovel.

"That's exactly the kind of container we've been looking for." A mix of anger and anticipation colored his voice. "But you haven't found a key for it? And you still think it's your aunt's?"

"I've tried many keys I found in the house, with no luck. But this morning I found these in the house's kitchen junk drawer." She pulled a large ring with at least two dozen small keys on it from the tote bag she used to carry her business documents.

"I've cleaned out and redone everything since I moved here, but I kept Aunt Brenda's junk drawer as it was, since there were so many household items in there that I knew I might need." She seemed as intent as he to put their mutual secrets over the lockbox and searching for it behind them.

He nodded, pointed at it.

"Let's get going, then. Get it open."

He watched her trembling hands as she tried each one of the keys. So many of them were rusted and appeared much older than the lockbox, so he wasn't surprised that none of the keys she first tried worked. But as the number of keys dwindled, his gut began to sink.

"Coral, if you can't open this, I think it's fair to conclude it's not your aunt's and highly probable that it's Markova's. I have to take it in to my team or have SVPD come out for it. It's dangerous to have this here. For all we know it has a GPS locator inside." Though he doubted it. Markova wouldn't be sending in the B-team thugs to prowl through Coral's property if she had a more exacting means of location. He didn't care about how the box was found but that Coral had had this box the night he'd come in with the thugs. Before, even.

He couldn't examine the pain that seared through him at the thought of ROC finding out she had one of Markova's hidden treasures. They'd have killed Coral on the spot, but then again, probably only after torturing her with rape and other physical abuse, as they'd threatened the other night.

"This is the last key." She spoke quietly, her initial confidence bashed by her lack of success. As she struggled to fit the too-large key into the lock, he grabbed the lockbox off the table.

"It doesn't fit, either, Coral. None of them do, because this is Markova's."

"You don't know that for certain." Her tone was heavy with defeat and something else—guilt?

"I have good reason to believe it is." He spoke through gritted teeth. How had they gone from intense sex to wanting to duke it out again, so quickly?

It had always been like this with her. Coral was an all-or-nothing prospect for him.

As was her safety.

"You'll let me know what's in it, if it's Markova's?"

"Of course I won't. You don't have—"

"A need to know. Of course I don't. But at least tell me if it leads you to solving the case."

"I—"

His words were cut off by loud banging on the door.

Coral looked at her watch and gasped. "We've been in here for almost two hours. I was supposed to check back with my chef right after lunch." She looked at him, desperate for guidance. "We can't let anyone see the lockbox, Trevor."

"And we won't." The knocking came again, and Trevor wanted to tell the dude to go pound sand. What he really wanted was to turn back time and keep Coral from ever getting this close to the danger of the ROC.

Chapter 8

Trevor looked at her grimly. "Give me the box and answer the door. Don't let on that I'm in here."

She gulped, tremors racking her body. They weren't the sexy kind of shakes from only minutes ago, the ones that Trevor's touch caused.

The pounding increased, and so did her anxiety. When Trevor slipped into the back room, she saw him draw his weapon from his backpack.

How had her quiet centuries-old farm property turned into the OK Corral?

"Coming!" Thank goodness she had her shirt and pants back on. She opened the door slowly, leaning forward. If she acted like she was in the midst of something else, he'd leave more quickly.

As she'd expected, it was Chef Mike. He stood on the tiny steel stoop instead of on the patch of indoor-outdoor carpet that delineated her makeshift patio. Alarm whispered to her, making her shiver. He was too close to the door for her liking.

Stay cool. You're overreacting.

"Hey, Mike. What can I do for you?" At least her voice sounded steady.

"I was going to text, but I thought it'd be easier to walk on down here. I know you're super busy with the barn construction." He flashed her a quick smile. She didn't think she'd ever seen the man have an expression other than focused and serious.

She stepped out of the trailer and took the two steps to meet him on the ground.

"Yes, texting me is always the best way to communicate." Not that she would have heard any alerts while she and Trevor were together, but Mike didn't need to know that. "I'm in the middle of a videoconference with prospective clients." The lie came so easily to her she wanted to cheer. Trevor had nothing to worry about—she could handle herself in any situation. Except the other night, which was an anomaly.

Mike nodded. "I understand that you're busy, and I won't keep you. I wanted you to know I've finished with all the prep for the event. Everything that can be frozen will be and heated up the day of. I have a couple more hours that I can give you if you'd like. I just need direction."

A gust of wind blew across the fields, and her hair went everywhere. She reached into her pocket for a band and quickly put her hair up. Chef Mike had to know she'd been having seriously rocking sex in the camper. She felt as though it was all over her face. She refused to be apologetic about it—about anything at this point. It was her property, her life, and this man worked for her.

"I think that's all we need to do today, Mike. You're still coming early tomorrow morning, right?"

He nodded. "I am. The desserts will need more refrigerator space than you have, though. I'm going to make them up at home tonight and bring them in coolers."

"Oh, I'm sorry to hear that." And she was. The barn's destruction had affected not only her venue and overall business, but the workers who wanted to put forth their best efforts for her and their clients. "Can I help? Do you want me to rent commercial coolers? I could probably find space in a commercial kitchen somewhere." She should have thought about getting an extra refrigerator until the reconstruction was finished.

"No, no, that's not necessary. My coolers are large, and the desserts are small." He gave a smile under his very bushy mustache, and she realized she hadn't seen him appear happy in the several times they'd met. Belatedly she felt contrite, seeing how he was doing his best to earn his paycheck under the circumstances.

"I really appreciate the extra effort." She thought of Trevor in the camper and wondered if he'd crept up to the door, his pistol drawn. For Chef Mike! It seemed so silly now. "See you tomorrow!"

Mike acted as if he hadn't heard her, distracted by the sound of construction equipment. "How much longer will your barn take?"

"They're telling me it's going to go into the fall, but I'm hopeful it'll be done sooner. I need my house finished before it gets cold, too." Small talk had its place, but Trevor was in the camper, wondering if Mike was a threat.

"Sure seems like a long time for you to have to camp out here." He looked at her, and she felt a shock go through her. Was it *interest* in his glance? It took all she had not to roll her eyes. For the last three years, she'd not so much as flirted with a man, buried herself in her work. Now that Trevor had stormed back into her life in the biggest, sexiest way, Chef Mike was trying to keep her talking?

Not that he was at all her type. Nice enough, but there was zero attraction on her part.

You'll never be attracted to another man like you are to Trevor.

"Oh, I don't mind camping out." It was tempting to tell him that Trevor was in the camper, and if Chef Mike was here at night, he'd see that Trevor had been staying with her. It wasn't like her to be so fearful around men, but she chalked it up to the last four days that had turned her life upside down.

Get him out of here.

She didn't want to keep talking to him, or anyone right now. She and Trevor had a lockbox to get open. "I'm really sorry, but I've got to get back to my videoconference."

"Okay, well, see you tomorrow, then." He turned, disappointment on his face, and with a jaunty half wave was out of sight. She hurried to the front of her camper to see whether he'd driven down here or walked. As he eased into a large pickup truck, she realized she didn't know a whole lot about him—or a lot of her current extended staff.

The past months since the barn explosion and losing both her business venue and her home had taken a toll.

She went around and back into the camper, pausing only to quickly knock and announce to Trevor that it was her returning. He stood up from where he'd perched on the side bench, his weapon nowhere in sight.

"I'm glad you put your gun away."

"It's a weapon, and we had no idea who was at that door." His eyes were troubled as he reminded her of the appropriate label for his .45. "You are too vulnerable out here, Coral."

She put her hands on her hips. "That was my chef, Trevor. My cook. And he wasn't wielding his knives, so I was good."

"Not funny. We're going to remedy this."

"I can't leave again, not now. I have an event at the end of the week. It's my biggest moneymaker since January. Unlike you, I don't get a steady paycheck each month."

"Whoa, what do you know about my paycheck?"

"I assume you're working for some government agency and that they pay much like the military—regularly."

He cocked his head. "You have no clue who I work for."

"Right. We've established that."

"No, what I mean is that I want to change that. Your event is on Saturday. It's Tuesday, so that gives us a few days."

Suspicion crept up her spine. "A few days for what? I'm not leaving my property." Although she knew, as she'd already told him, she could go back and forth between her parents', or get a hotel room. Which would be more money she didn't want to spend, but she could put an insurance claim in. "The safe house is too far away."

"I'm not talking about leaving. You can stay here, Coral, but you need to have some training."

"Training?" But he was already on his phone, placing a call. As if she wasn't standing in the same room. She turned to leave, to go anywhere but be in the same space with Trevor, but his hand on her upper arm stopped her. He placed his phone along his thigh, and his eyes sparkled.

"What?" He had the same look she remembered from when he'd convinced her to go skydiving with him for her twenty-fifth birthday. Scared as a lost kitten, she'd done it but had her heart in her throat the entire time.

And loved every single second of it.

He smiled. "We're going someplace fun. Trust me."

Anna Markova waited for Michael Rodinsky with total faith he'd return. He needed her, wanted the freedom she offered. Which was why he'd so willingly accepted her offer of escape from the ROC's clutches. All he had to do was work a little overtime outside of the prison job he held down in order to conduct ROC business as different agents were incarcerated. Dima Ivanov's reach was beyond the law in more ways than one.

But Ivanov's reach stopped with her. She wasn't going to spend the rest of her life working for him or

ROC. Her years with FSB, trained by former KGB agents, had gotten her into ROC and the United States. Now she wanted total freedom from it all.

First she had to get out of jail.

She'd been stupid to allow herself to be captured by the local authorities the night she'd burned the barn to the ground, but it'd been worth it. She'd hidden some of her secret information in the Silver Valley library as needed, but the one librarian had stymied her plans and made her life difficult. To see the Silver Valley employee and her bodyguard, whose agency she still hadn't identified, lying there, so vulnerable under her power, had been the best time she'd had in years, if not ever. But that was months ago, when she'd been free of this county jail.

When she heard the familiar creak of the wheeled bucket, she allowed herself to relax in the solitary prison cell. As she sat on her bunk, the thin mattress no match for the steel coils beneath it, he appeared.

"Good evening." He spoke in their native tongue. His bore the accent of the rural areas, while hers was pure Muscovite. Russian allowed them to speak a bit more freely without concern of being overheard by the guards. Or her plans discovered.

She nodded. "Hello."

As he moved the long-handled mop back and forth over the concrete floor, he spoke in low tones.

"The woman is back at her property. She lives in a camper trailer in between the farmhouse and barn."

"Tell me something I don't know." The derelicts who'd been arrested by the local police had wound up in county jail, and the information had been passed on to her.

"She has a man living with her. He works with the construction crew. I interrupted them earlier. I had zero luck flirting with her. We won't get to her that way."

"Were we able to get anyone working on the construction team?"

"No. It's just me, and she expects me to stay in her kitchen. Since she thinks I'm a chef."

Anna laughed at this. He was no more a chef than she was a waitress, attorney, teacher or any of the myriad other disguises she'd employed over the years. Her FSB training came in handy working for ROC, but she wanted to be free of ever being beholden to any man.

The offshore bank account information she'd stolen from Ivanov's most trusted accountant, after she'd screwed and then drugged him, was her golden ticket. That sad, unrealistic tale by the Western writer Roald Dahl came to mind, the one about the chocolate factory. The Brits and Americans were so hopelessly naive and believing of a happy ending. Anna knew there was no such thing.

But there were better finishes than others, and being on her own, under a new identity, was preferable to dying as one of Ivanov's hired thugs. Or worse, at his hands.

"This man who's with her, what does he look like?" She had her concerns since the two accomplices serving time with her had been working with a third man, one they'd told her was solid, also one of them. He didn't know anything about the mission; she'd made sure all they used him for was his brawn and digging power. But she couldn't be too careful.

Michael shrugged. "Typical American—too tall and strong to know what to do with it. He's some kind of specialty architect, hired to make sure the barn is re-built according to historical specifics."

"Keep an eye on him. Have you seen any other signs of the police or undercover agents?"

"No. It's all construction and cooking at that place, trust me." He wrung out the mop, and she saw the tired lines around his eyes. Their business was a tough one.

"You still want to go with me when this is over, right, Michael?" She purred his name, the way she knew he liked it.

He met her gaze. "I will go with you, Anna. You will do nothing alone anymore."

"You don't know how good that makes me feel." She lied, but he thought she'd agreed to spend the rest of her life with him. *Let him.*

"We have to get this wrapped up, though, before Ivanov gets any clue of it." Michael had worry lines between his brows. The deep concern seemed so out of place as he mopped the floor in his janitorial over-alls that she smiled.

Ivanov wasn't the worry Michael thought he was. ROC's leader still didn't know about her private, sep-arate operations going on in Silver Valley. He'd not been pleased when the barn blew up and she'd been arrested. No matter, as he'd forked up the money for her defense attorney. The man was a bottom-feeder but smart and knew his way around criminal law. Except he hadn't managed bail for her, not yet. Something she wasn't happy about.

"Let me worry about Ivanov. I need you to get to the data boxes."

"There are only two? You're certain?" He didn't forget a thing. Which was why she'd kill him as soon as she was done with his usefulness.

"If I told you there were two, that's how many there are." She kept her tone casual, a little rattled that he'd read her so easily. She'd best find some other people to back her up, especially if she had to eliminate Michael sooner than later.

Another thing she wasn't too concerned about—scouting for more help. Between her figure, which was still decent, and her wits, she was getting what she needed from the prison population and even one of the guards. In a few short days, she might be able to find the data on her own, where she'd left it in three separate places. Two of the lockboxes were easy enough to find, since she'd buried them in the ground near the barn's foundation. She'd used a blowtorch to melt the January ice and snow. But the third and most important data container was nearly impossible to find without her guidance.

The opening and shutting of prison doors echoed down the corridor, and Michael looked over his shoulder, then turned back to her. "I have to leave. I'll come back in two nights."

"See that you do. And if you can get me a message sooner, that you've found the boxes, I'd be most obliged."

He smiled at her. "I won't let you down, Anna."

* * *

Trevor considered it a major win that Coral had agreed to come with him, in the middle of her workday, with the construction crews at full speed on her property. She'd matured and grown past many of her youthful traits, as had he, since they'd first met in college, but she'd never stopped being a control freak.

Which was why he knew she'd be a perfect coagent. Temporarily, but he saw no way around it. She wanted to be at the barn, near her event tent and the farmhouse kitchen. He wanted to have her in the safe house until ROC was out of Silver Valley. Getting her a brief indoctrination into Trail Hikers was a safe middle ground, if Claudia agreed to it.

It wasn't something he hadn't already thought of, but he'd stalled, hoping the case would crack before Coral needed to be more prepared. Of course, if the case had already been solved, he'd be out of here, on to the next ROC op, probably closer to New York City.

Turmoil threatened to overwhelm his thoughts, and he expertly compartmentalized it. He'd not been as happy doing the TH ops with ROC, had thought about how he could transfer to a desk job, doing the intelligence analysis he'd originally trained for as a Marine.

But he didn't want to kid himself. Even if he did make the career change, a lateral move, it wouldn't fix the fact that he had to leave Silver Valley and allow Coral to have her life back. Without him. Great sex aside, their time together was over years ago. She deserved better than the man who'd crushed her heart. She deserved better than him.

He turned off Silver Valley's main pike into a commercial business development and risked a glance at Coral, who'd been quiet for most of the ride.

"This is the only answer, Coral. If you can have even a fraction of the training that I've experienced, you'll be more equipped to handle what could go down at your place." And he'd rest easier, his conscience wouldn't constantly be haranguing him, if he knew she could work through a tough situation. Without him, in the event he was taken out. And after he left her, again.

"I can't believe the FBI or CIA, or whoever you work for, would allow me, plain Jane civilian, to be trained even for a few hours. Do you mean you're taking me to a shooting range?" She looked out the windshield at the nondescript redbrick buildings, each with a different logo but all the same profile.

"Something like that." She'd know soon enough that he didn't work for either of the agencies she'd mentioned.

He pulled into the appropriate parking space and put the car into Park while leaving the air-conditioning on for a bit.

"Keep an open mind and answer Claudia's questions truthfully. That's all I ask." Her eyes widened at his words. A man could live forever in her liquid gaze.

You want to.

"Claudia—as in the woman running the op against ROC? The woman I met at the safe house? I'm the last person she wants to see, Trevor. I'm a civilian distraction from your mission, aren't I?"

He couldn't keep from chuckling. "You're making this easy for me, Coral. This is a very good idea. I don't know why I didn't think of it sooner." As more time passed, there was a better chance of Markova sending more thugs to the property. Short of forcing Coral to remain at the safe house, which would make them both miserable, this was the ideal solution. For now.

"Think of what?"

He wanted to kiss her, reassure her the way normal lovers calmed one another down. But he couldn't, because he wasn't in a position to give her any inclination that what they'd shared this morning and at the safe house was more than hot sex between two people who'd once loved one another.

Liar.

"I think you're going to like what you're about to see, Coral. Before we go in there, though, I want you to know that if you decide it's not for you, no problem. If anything frightens you, makes you think you want no part of it, fine. I'm only trying to find a way to give us both what we want—your safety and ability to keep running your business."

"Thank you." She tilted her head. "Something else is on your mind. Spit it out, Trevor."

It still gobsmacked him how easily she read him. Thank God she'd never been on the other side of a weapon pointed his way. He'd have been a goner.

"I don't want what's passed between us to affect your decision, one way or the other."

"Do you mean the sex?" A raised brow, the quirk of her lip. So tough, so incredibly vulnerable. Guilt gnawed at him. What the heck was he doing, bringing her here?

Her hand on his cheek stilled him. "It's okay, Trevor. We're doing what a lot of divorced couples do. We probably would have hooked up right after we signed the papers if you hadn't left so abruptly."

He'd had a mission, had people whose lives depended on him. He'd had to leave but didn't want to. Walking away from Coral had been the worst day of his life. A day he never wanted to repeat, which was why he told himself they had to have this conversation.

"I've heard that, too. About the closure. Glad we're on the same page. Let's go." His ability to sit with the truth, the reality that they'd never again be together in a relationship, was short-lived. Coral agreed with him that they were no more than friends at this point, that the sex didn't signal anything deeper—or more stupid, like reconciliation.

As they walked to Trail Hiker's smoky-glass commercial entrance, he wondered why he didn't feel a shred of relief.

Chapter 9

Coral had a hard time believing that a place like what she soon learned was Trail Hikers headquarters existed in her own backyard—almost literally.

It was clear it was no ordinary business headquarters when Trevor used a retina-, hand- and voice-detection unit to get into the building. There were tiny camera lenses above the entrance, and she assumed they utilized facial recognition.

"This is a first." She spoke her thoughts as they walked in a plush reception area. Trevor stopped and looked at her.

"As in the first time you've been here?"

"No, as in it's the first time I've gone to a place where you work." Even when he'd been a Marine, he'd worked in the equivalent of a vault.

He blinked. "Yeah, I suppose you're right."

"Trevor?" A man dressed in a nice business suit addressed him.

"Hey, Bill." Trevor and the man shook hands, after which Bill turned toward Coral.

"You're Coral Staufer. Bill Peyton." He held out his hand, and she shook it.

"Nice to meet you."

"Welcome to Trail Hikers. I'm the receptionist today, and we're going to walk back to Claudia's office. You'll be asked to sign several forms, the first of which is going to be a nondisclosure contract. Is there any reason you'd refuse to sign it?" Bill's eyes were bright, his countenance pleasant, but Coral got the feeling that he was as trained and expert at taking out bad guys as Trevor. The man had huge, muscular hands and appeared to be in top physical shape under the well-cut suit.

"Ah, no, I don't think I'll have a problem with that. But to be frank, I don't want to know anything that's going to keep me in the middle of things any longer than I have to be. Does that make sense, Bill?" The entire time she spoke, she felt Trevor's gaze on her, his body heat unavoidable as they stood next to one another. He'd always had a higher-than-normal internal temperature, even when they'd come back to Silver Valley for the holidays. While their families wore Christmas sweaters, some hand knit by her mother, Trevor never needed more than a dress shirt. He'd told her that the delivery nurse warned his mother when he'd been born that he'd always "run hot." She bit her lip, annoyed that she was still so lousy at keeping the memories at bay.

"I understand, Coral, and I think you'll be more comfortable about all of this once you speak to Claudia. If you'll both follow me." Bill led the way to a large door that, when slid open, revealed it was several inches thick and made of steel. Coral knew Trevor was undercover and worked with sensitive intelligence, but this seemed overkill.

Of course, she had no idea whether this was FBI or CIA, nor how dangerous their work was, overall. The ROC was probably one of many cases.

Claudia sat at a bank of several computers in her very slick, contemporary office. As soon as Coral and Trevor stepped over the threshold, the door slid shut with a definite click behind them. Coral looked over her shoulder—Bill had disappeared.

"Good morning, folks. Please, take a seat." Claudia motioned at the two posh but also modern chairs in front of her desk. Trevor waited for Coral to sit before he joined her.

"Hello, Claudia. Thanks for agreeing to this." Trevor spoke with quiet sincerity.

Coral wondered what exactly *this* was.

"Of course. It's my job to support my agents in the field, and you're in the thick of it right now, Trevor." Claudia landed her gaze on Coral. "As are you, Coral. How are you doing?"

Coral shrugged. "I'm good, really. But it is a little, ah, cramped to have Trevor at my place all the time. And I haven't been able to convince him to let me stay on my property alone. I'd even be willing to go to a hotel and come back during the day, if that makes your work easier."

Claudia waved her hand dismissively at Coral's mention of a hotel. "A hotel won't change the fact that you're being targeted by ROC for what they believe you may have. They'd still come after you, and by staying anywhere but on your property, you'd only put other innocent civilians in danger."

"Wait, is this why you brought me here?" She looked at Trevor. "Am I going back to the safe house? Don't I have a say in this?" She wanted to know who the hell they worked for, too, but first things first.

"Why don't you let Claudia explain before you fly off the handle?" Trevor spoke in even tones that made her fingers curl into her palms. She had to choke back her shouts, fueled by the anger triggered by his smug attitude.

"Coral, I'm always most sorry when an innocent by-stander, which was you in the case of Anna Markova's explosion and attempted murder, gets caught up in one of our ops. You didn't ask for this, and yet your entire life has been uprooted."

"It's not been easy, but I've managed okay." She wasn't going to burden this powerful woman with her concerns.

"Yes, of course you have." Claudia typed on one of the many keyboards, then looked and pointed to the screen behind her, where Coral saw a typed outline. The subject was *Trail Hikers*.

"Trevor brought you in to see if you'd be interested in knowing more about what we do here. It can be helpful to understand all of what's going on with the ROC case on your property, to help you deal with your anxieties and the business setbacks that have been un-avoidable since the gala."

"So this is what you need me to sign the nondisclo-sure agreement for?"

"Partially, yes." Claudia nodded at Trevor, who opened the file she'd seen Bill hand him.

"Here you go. Take your time to read it." Trevor handed her a sheaf of papers and a pen. Coral read through the contract and then quickly signed and dated it. She handed it to Claudia over the desk. "I take it that you're the witness?"

Claudia smiled. "I can be." As soon as Claudia's signature was complete, she gave Coral a long look. "So, about who we are and what we do. We're a covert government shadow agency that employs many, many highly trained personnel. They're undercover agents, administrative support, IT, engineers, intelligence. We even have some food specialists who ensure our agents on more prolonged missions get the nutrition they need if at all possible."

Claudia paused to let her words sink in, and while Coral appreciated it, she grew impatient.

"Okay, so you're doing super-secret stuff. I get that part. What else do I need to know?"

Claudia continued. "We're not working for any other US government entity. We report directly to Congress and the White House, depending upon the gravity of the case and its potential to harm the United States. I can't emphasize enough that no one locally, unless they're sworn in as a member of Trail Hikers, knows what we do. Few know of our existence."

"Let me guess—you picked the name Trail Hikers

to be able to pose as some kind of Appalachian Trail travel organization. To draw the least amount of local notice."

"Exactly. If anyone goes to our initial waiting area, all they see are brochures about extended hiking opportunities in the area, with the contact information for a local Appalachian travel company."

"Abi's Appalachian Adventure Agency, which is located next to Annie's grandmother's yarn shop, Silver Threads?" Both Abi and Annie were acquaintances she knew from the local women's business league. Abi was married to an SVFD fire fighter, Annie to an SVPD cop. "I know the place. So now you're telling me that Abi is part of Trail Hikers?"

Claudia shook her head. "I could tell you that, but honestly I'm not going to confirm or deny who is and isn't in Trail Hikers. If you agree to what Trevor's proposed, you'll be informed on a need-to-know basis who is a TH or not. Trevor doesn't know all the TH agents. No one but myself and two archivists know. It's for their safety."

Claudia was affirming, almost encouraging in her approach. Trevor seemed on edge, and Coral sensed he wanted her back at the safe house soon, where he'd be assured of her safety.

"So what do I have to do to keep from going back to your place in the woods, Claudia?"

Claudia smiled. "So Trevor hasn't offered to explain his grand scheme. Trevor, how about you pick it up from here?"

Trevor's flushed cheeks revealed his consternation. Coral bit her lip again, but this time it was to keep a smile from splitting her face. Claudia was incredibly astute and obviously knew Trevor very well to call him out so accurately.

He cleared his throat. "You're absolutely right—I want most to take you back to the safe house and leave you there until this op is concluded. I don't trust Anna Markova, even locked up in prison. She's pulling her usual antics from her jail cell, using the deeply ingrained ROC network that Ivanov, the ROC head honcho, put in place as early as two years ago. Ivanov is methodical in his approach to taking over the business commodities in an area. While he initially moved in with human and drug trafficking, he established people at all levels of our local government bureaucracy. There are people working in the high school, the hospital and even the prison."

"But they're doing legitimate jobs in each of those places?"

"Yes, they have to be. They're undercover, in effect. Inserted to keep communications fluid and unhindered by something like Markova's arrest."

Coral's stomach flipped, and she clutched her chair arms to remind herself she was safe, in a very secure location with Trevor. She wasn't at risk at this moment.

But Silver Valley was at risk. Big-time.

"There's more, Coral," Claudia interjected. "We have reason to believe that Markova is planning to take over ROC. She's continued to run her part of ROC from prison, which is keeping the heroin shipments into Silver Valley moving. They were disrupted greatly this past winter, right when the gala explosion happened. But once ROC figured out that the rail system wasn't a good way to get heroin in here, they switched back to private transportation. We're having a rough time anticipating deliveries."

"Which explains the uptick in ODs." Coral murmured her worst fear. "But what do you want from me?" She looked at Trevor. "You have the box I found." Turning back to Claudia, she felt contrite. Guilty. "I found it before Trevor and the thugs showed up at the barn site, but I really thought it was my aunt's and that I'd find the keys in the kitchen drawer where she kept everything of importance to her. But we tried all the keys earlier today, and none worked." She looked at Trevor, then at the floor near his feet. He'd come into the reception area with the lockbox in his backpack— where was it?

He gave her a lopsided grin. "I passed it to Bill when we arrived."

"Oh."

"Speaking of which," Claudia interrupted, "we've already got the results." She turned one of her monitors around for them to see. "The lockbox you found appears to be one of two, as she marked it, no doubt to aid her helpers in finding all of the data. It's one memory stick's worth of a spreadsheet that appears to be a listing of overseas bank accounts. Markova was clever—she has information on all the accounts, but none match. In other words, we need the rest of the information she hid."

"Whose accounts, Ivanov's?" Coral asked, and Trevor nodded.

"Exactly. So the other columns with data like passwords and monetary value are in the other box." He spoke aloud as he stared at the long list of numbers on the screen.

Coral swallowed, her face hot. "I had no idea... I'm so sorry." Her desire to keep the lockbox from Trevor, convincing herself that it was Aunt Brenda's, seemed so weak and wrong. "This is a global crime ring, isn't it?"

"Yes. And while we see a slice of Ivanov's reach in Silver Valley, as you can surmise from this list, whatever we do here will impact ROC's ability to operate effectively worldwide." Claudia used a laser pointer to highlight one line. "See this account number? It's the only one we've verified so far, since we don't have all of the other information, but it's valued at almost a billion dollars, and it's in a small bank in Switzerland."

It was unbelievable to Coral. She looked at Trevor with new eyes. He met her gaze and nodded. "This is what I've been working on."

She swallowed. "What can I do?"

Trevor expected to feel relieved, jubilant even, when and if Coral agreed to pitch in on the case. Because then she could at least gain some basic Trail Hiker training, enough to allow him to live with himself. He should have never allowed her to go back to the camper in the first place. If he'd done the right thing, she'd never have had to face those thugs, never have the indelible memory of her life being threatened or the threat of being raped.

He should have contacted her ahead of showing up with the ROC agents and warned her off. Coral was stubborn but not stupid. She'd listen when it came to her life.

Instead of a sense of accomplishment, all that filled his gut was dread.

Stop with the regrets. Move forward and change what you can.

"Coral, there's a lot you can do, but the biggest thing would be to get the hell out of Silver Valley until this passes."

"Since we've already discussed this, and you know how important it is to me to keep my business going, what's my next option?"

A sliver of admiration worked its way into the dread. "It's up to Claudia."

"Coral, from what we know of you, from what Trevor's told us and the background check we were obligated to conduct before you even walked through the front doors, you've never had any formal military or law enforcement training. Is that correct?"

"Yes." Coral shifted forward in her seat. "Nothing official. Trevor took me out to the firing range a few times when he was still in the Marine Corps. And we went skydiving a couple of times. Is that the kind of skills you're asking about?"

"Yes. Have you ever flown a plane?"

Trevor spoke up. "No."

"Yes, yes, I have." Coral talked over him, her spine stiff in the chrome-framed office chair. She looked at Claudia, flat-out ignoring him. Good thing, because he was pretty sure smoke was coming out of his ears. Coral, a pilot?

"When I first came back to Silver Valley, I needed

something to get my confidence back. I had the barn, the event-planning business, but I wanted to do something that never in a million years I'd ever considered. I have the worst sense of direction, and my aptitude to fly a plane, at least on paper, was nil. I took lessons down in Carlisle and got my private pilot's license. I considered saving for my own plane, but it's more of a hobby, nothing I need for my day-to-day life. As I've already mentioned, since the explosion and fires after the gala, I can't afford to fly. I do hope to get back to it someday."

Claudia's grin was a rare sight. "Coral, you're better suited for the next few days than I thought you'd be. This is great. You're going to enjoy yourself."

"What exactly am I signing up for? I have no desire to do the kind of work Trevor does. Not long term, anyhow."

"That's fair. We're not recruiting you to be an agent. That would take years of preparation, experience and training. Trevor suggested that you'd benefit from one of our mini courses, where we put you through several of our course challenges. Physically, that includes a very difficult obstacle course, hiking on the AT—Appalachian Trail—for an extended period with minimal equipment and extreme water workouts. Mentally and psychologically, we have a few exercises we offer, and of course there is additional weapons training."

"The defensive-driving course is another one I think Coral could use." Trevor couldn't stop himself from interjecting. Chances were that he and Coral would have to get away from her property again and use either one of their vehicles. If something happened to incapacitate him, he wanted to know that Coral would know how to maneuver through a firestorm of bullets if need be.

The thought made him sick.

"Yes, well, that's definitely available. We are looking at what, only four days, though, before your next event." Claudia looked at a computer screen that Trevor couldn't see. He knew she was probably scrolling through the TH training schedule, seeing which classes and times Coral would fit in best with.

"Is Trevor doing the training with me?"

"That would be a negative." He'd want to kill every instructor who threatened Coral with either certain death or torture as part of the class.

"Where will you be while I'm doing this for the rest of the week?"

"Doing what I've been doing. Playing the part of historical architect and designer. Keeping an eye on your place."

Puzzlement drew her brows together. "This was your idea. You want me to get this training, but you're not going to do any of the classes or exercises with me?"

He shook his head. "If I'm with you, I'll get in the way. It wouldn't be fair to you, either. You deserve to see it as a new agent would without me butting in and telling you how to do things." He looked at Claudia to back him up.

Claudia nodded. "Trevor's correct. As much as we will do everything to keep you out of any contact with ROC, we can't promise that you won't face the bad guys again, not if you're going to remain on your property. As for your upcoming event—give us anything you need completed while you're in training. If you can handle the event planning in the evenings after class, you'll be good to go. In the meantime, you need to know that ROC agents are notoriously unpredictable as far as their tempers and emotional maturity go. What is absolutely certain is that they have no compunction about putting their victims through unnecessary pain and suffering before they pull the trigger."

"I'm facing more than death is what you're telling me. That doesn't sound like such a good deal. I'd like to avoid all of the above." Coral addressed Claudia.

"Agreed. Trust me, if we get the smallest bit of intel that Markova's sent in more people, I'm pulling you off your property. This training is to make all of us more comfortable, frankly."

"Bring it on, then." Coral looked like she'd take out the meanest ROC member on the spot, given the necessary skills and weapons.

Trevor's insides warmed like a marshmallow against a sizzling fire. Coral's emotional strength had always buoyed his own. And turned him on in so many ways.

He couldn't stop the memories of their first skydive, where he'd been free-falling and she'd had an instructor jumper she'd been attached to. It'd allowed him to watch her expression as it went from abject terror to wonder to an adrenaline-fueled exultation. She'd vowed to jump again the minute her feet hit the ground.

They'd gone home and made intense, very passionate love that afternoon, and he'd thought he'd never been happier. It had been the last year of their marriage, when their relationship was becoming strained but they both thought they had a lifetime ahead of them to made things right.

Until they'd destroyed it.

He'd been the one who'd caused their breakup. He knew he'd never have Coral as his again, but they could have these days, this op, as their final memories together. He'd keep her out of the worst of it and get her to the safe house before the takedown.

He knew it could go to hell in an instant; ROC cases often did. He didn't know when, so he was going to make the most of these few days with Coral.

They'd be their last together.

Chapter 10

When Coral and Trevor arrived back at the camper, she immediately opened her laptop to the event spreadsheets. She had a few hours to organize what needed to be done before Saturday's event, and she wasn't going to be around during normal working hours to inform her staff and contract workers of the myriad details that had to be covered before the wedding dinner. More importantly, diving back into the familiar kept her from obsessing over what she faced at Trail Hiker's training facility tomorrow and the two following days.

"You didn't waste any time getting back to it." Trevor walked past her.

"I can't afford to. You heard Claudia. I'm at TH's beck and call for the duration, but especially for the training days." She'd signed the nondisclosure agreement as well as several other documents that gave her temporary security clearances, as needed, and all the benefits afforded any TH contract employee. She'd nearly wept when she'd realized that all of this, the huge responsibility of his government's trust in him, had always been on Trevor's shoulders. If she'd known, would she have been a better partner to him?

"Don't you think you need to eat first?" Trevor was in the small kitchen area as she worked at the kitchen table. The same place where they'd made love—no, had incredible sex—only hours before. It was as if a switch had flipped since then, the way Trevor was treating her. With respect and a sense of pride, she sensed. But not as a lover.

She should be glad that the sex option was off the table, pun intended. But she still felt it every time their eyes met, every time she looked at him. Standing in the camper over her counter made her imagine all the ways they could enjoy themselves, naked, in the kitchen.

This had to be the first part of her training—ignoring her personal feelings for the sake of the job. For the first time, she had compassion for what Trevor must have gone through during the last years of their marriage.

"I'm not really hungry. I lost my appetite when I realized that I won't have a minute here or with my event team, except at night, once I begin my three-day training period. The wilderness instructor said I should plan to sleep out with the class from Thursday to Friday. Luckily the new chef hire has everything prepped, so I won't be scrambling as much on Saturday morning." She tried to suppress the shudder of distaste that ran up her back. Glamping it in the trailer was one thing, but being outside with only a bedroll didn't appeal to her.

"You don't have to do any of it that you don't want to." His tone was noncommittal, carefully neutral.

"Oh, but that's the kicker, isn't it? I didn't want to be involved in any of the ROC garbage, and yet, here I am, almost six months after they blew up my home and barn. No one in Silver Valley asked for ROC to come in, but they're affecting life here in the worst ways. And let's face it, if I don't volunteer to help, who will? I'm the best candidate, as I'm single, no kids who'd lose a parent, you know. The usual."

"There's nothing usual about you putting yourself in danger. That's what law enforcement is for."

"And you're all stretched to the max. I'm under the impression that everyone from SVPD to TH wants ROC brought down like, yesterday." She closed the calendar app on her laptop. "I don't get it. Actually, I don't understand where you're coming from, Trevor. You were all about me getting to the TH office and agreeing to the training. And now you seem against it. Care to elaborate?"

He didn't look up from the cutting board, where he was chopping what looked like all the remaining veggies in her refrigerator.

"My hope was that you'd get some basic evasion and self-defense tactics. Brush up on weapons firing, maybe some lessons on how to survive another face-off with ROC agents." His voice was low with the weight of his thoughts.

"Isn't that what I'm doing?" Honestly, for as much

as they knew one another's bodies inside out, Trevor was still a mystery to her.

"No—you're getting more in-depth training than I expected. I'm not the boss. It's Claudia's call on how much you'll be allowed access to, and it looks like she's not putting a limit on it."

"It's not like I'm going to be a Trail Hiker agent, like you. You know me, I'm the last person to do undercover work."

"Which is why you're perfect for it, in fact." He halted in his chopping. "I've told you how nondescript, ordinary-looking people make the best undercover agents. While you'll never be ordinary, you fit the descriptor of an average woman from Silver Valley. You wouldn't be my first pick to be an agent."

"Because you know, or knew, me and don't think I have what it takes? Or are you feeling as though by getting this training you're not going to be as valuable to my protection?" She'd been thinking aloud again, had failed to use the filter that would have kept the provocative words as they belonged—silent.

He paused in his meal prep, and she saw him take several deep breaths, his chest rising and falling under his simple T-shirt. The silence grew in the cramped space, and she had to work at not trying to fill it with small talk. In that moment she realized that's what she'd always done—filled their time together with chatter. And sex. They never had taken the time to share their deepest thoughts—not after graduating college and beginning their very separate, individual careers.

He looked at her, and his eyes were full of remorse, his expression grim. "I never should have come here."

A shot of pain sliced through Coral's heart, and she closed her eyes against his declaration. "Here" didn't mean Silver Valley, but *her*. He wished he'd never come back to where she was. Her mind fought for purchase, one measly thought to hang onto that would keep her from losing her crap right in front of Trevor.

He regretted seeing her again? Making love? Involving her in his work? All of the above, most likely.

She'd let it happen again. Somehow, she'd allowed a crack in the brick wall encircling her heart. And her feelings toward Trevor, emotions that were better sealed away, had leaked out.

She had no one to blame for her vulnerability but herself.

Footfalls sounded, and then he was next to her, his weight settling on the bench, too close for her to maintain the essential physical boundary she needed to convince her brain that she only shared good sex with Trevor, nothing more. When his hands covered hers, she opened her eyes and looked at him. "No, Trevor. Stop it. I'm fine. You're only being honest."

But he didn't budge, only looked at her with regret pooling in his eyes. "I didn't mean that I regret seeing you again. This time together has been beyond what I ever thought being with you again could be. What I regret is that I didn't come out here ahead of the ROC op and that I didn't tell you to go away until it's all over. It was a big mistake on my part, and I unnecessarily involved you in a lethal mission."

She stared at him, needing with her entire being to believe him but not able to, not fully. Having her heart broken by Trevor the first time had been enough to last several lifetimes.

"I appreciate you saying that. I also need to tell you something."

"What?" She felt his body tense, saw the muscle on the edge of his jaw jump erratically.

"What we've done, um, at the safe house and here—it was a two-time deal. I have to say it again, for both of us. We can't have sex again, Trevor. It's too distracting." As she spoke she gathered momentum. "I need to be able to focus on the little training I'm getting, and then we need to make sure we're aware of our surroundings out here at all times. I can't be worried about your needs." Or hers, for that matter. But this was about keeping Trevor shut down emotionally from her. Because it was impossible for her to maintain her mental distance from him if he kept looking at her with those sexy eyes, smiling in his easy way.

His crow's-feet deepened and it took her a minute to realize he was smiling.

"What's so funny?" She spoke to his back as he slid off the bench and resumed his spot in the kitchen.

"You. Us. Isn't that what I used to tell you when I was in the middle of workups for deployment? Or after I got out of the Marines and had to prepare for my first jobs with Trail Hikers." She watched his hands make short work of a zucchini and wondered what he was going to do with it. "It's a weird feeling to be in your shoes for once, Coral. And I have to say, it doesn't feel great. You must have thought I didn't care anymore."

Her mouth suddenly parched, she grabbed her water bottle and drank from it. She suspected her sudden craving for water was more about her insatiable thirst for Trevor and a need for distraction than true dehydration. "None of that matters now. We've been through it all. This is our chance to work together as, as—" Stymied, she halted.

"Friends?" His hands dropped the zucchini into a hot fry pan, and the sizzle drowned out her groan. She'd been a lot of things with Trevor—his confidante, lover, spouse. But true friendship? With no sex?

"Friends don't—"

"Have sex. I heard you the first time." He cracked eggs into one of her two cereal bowls, then whipped them with a fork. "It might not be so bad, being friends. Work colleagues."

She sighed. It would be an absolute disaster. Not because she didn't think they could learn to work well together. It was the risk of getting to know Trevor at another level, a place they hadn't often traveled in their marriage.

It meant trusting herself that she wouldn't be the one to cross the boundary she'd set down. Surely she could keep her hands off Trevor for as long as it took to find Markova's two remaining treasures. And she'd be grateful that she had, because as soon as the op was over, Trevor would be on his way again.

This time the pain that hit her middle was more familiar. She'd already survived Trevor's leaving once, and it had been rough. If she wasn't careful, it would be worse this time.

Trevor was impressed that Coral had Gruyère and a decent assortment of farm-fresh veggies in the camper's fridge drawer. When they'd been married, she'd been more of a bagged salad woman.

"Finish whatever you need to do for work after dinner. These omelets won't wait." He brought the two concoctions to the bench table; the aromas of the sautéed vegetables mingling with the melted cheese made his stomach growl.

"You're the one who's hungry." Coral half laughed as she cleared her spot and accepted his offering. "I hate to admit it, but I do like this side of you. You never used to cook—when did you have time to learn?"

He retrieved two glasses of water from the kitchen, replaced her reusable water bottle with one and sat down across from her. "I had no choice. I lost my best cook when we divorced, and work as an agent is too demanding to rely solely on fast food. Don't get me wrong, I eat my share of it when I'm on the road, but I enjoy a healthier meal whenever I get the chance. Eggs and omelets are a no-brainer for me."

She licked melted cheese from her lips and sighed in satisfaction. "This is incredible. I don't know the last time anyone's cooked just for me, save for you at the safe house."

"I'm glad you like it. The training you're doing won't be that difficult, not over only three days, but it's still demanding."

"Mmm." He watched her devour the omelet and fought with whether or not to ask her the question neither of them had yet broached. Before he lost his nerve, he plunged in.

"So, how many men have you dated since the divorce?"

Coral's eyes flew open midchew and her nostrils flared. When she began to cough, he realized she was choking.

"Are you okay?"

She nodded, holding up her hand in a "wait" gesture as her face reddened and she sounded as though she were hacking up a lung. He waited, knowing from his extensive first aid training that it was best to allow her to clear her windpipe on her own. But he mentally went over the Heimlich maneuver, just in case.

"Here." He handed her her glass, and she took it, sipping.

"Sorry." Her voice rasped. "I'm fine, it was just the wrong pipe."

"No, I'm sorry. I didn't realize that was such a touchy subject."

"It's not. The truth is that I've had a few dates, but ah, none of them, you know, got very far."

"You haven't had sex since?" He hated how his tone revealed he was thrilled with this news.

"Not counting yesterday and the safe house, no, not since I left California." She blushed but maintained eye contact, letting him know she wasn't ashamed about her choices.

He stared at her, tried to keep a silly grin off his face. Her sex life was none of his business, at least up until this past week, and she wasn't his possession. He'd never want any woman who cleaved herself that tightly to him. Especially Coral. Knowing she chose him and wasn't afraid to show it had always been a big part of his attraction to her.

"What about you, Trevor? I imagine you have a lot

of opportunity depending upon where your assignments take you. And I noticed several women at Trail Hikers, in the classes that are in session. Have you ever worked with a female agent?"

"I've worked with many female agents, and you know I served alongside women in the Marine Corps."

"But you were married to me then. Now you're free and single."

Single, yes, free—never. Not from her sultry expression, her laughter, the way he always felt as if he was the only man in the room when they were together.

"Trevor?"

"Sorry. Daydreaming. Like you, I had some dates." Unlike her, he'd had sex. And had never been able to stop comparing other women to her. "But to be fair, I've been working undercover to develop the best skill set to be able to blend in with ROC all over the world. This recent gig here, in Silver Valley, is a big career move for me."

Her face fell. He wanted to ask her why—was she disappointed it wasn't all about her? But it wasn't prudent, not when they were still on this new turf of friendship only. Unknown territory for their relationship.

"I'm happy for you, Trevor." She sure didn't look it. "You deserve to go as far as you want in this business."

"I knew I needed to expand my repertoire with ROC, and it's been a career priority for a few years now. But then I heard about your barn, read the classified documents on Markova, and the choice was made for me."

"That Silver Valley was where you needed to be?"

She'd finished her meal and held her water glass as if it was a martini, regarding him like a long line of blockheads she'd swiped left on. "For your progression with Trail Hikers?"

"Yes."

"Tell me something. Is your whole career working with TH? Or do you go back and forth with other agencies?"

"Just TH. I could always apply for a job with the FBI, or any state or local police department. They aren't as keen on contractors, though. The neat thing about how TH is set up is that I can decide to quit at any time, or turn down an op, with no repercussions. Career progression with TH is on a case-by-case, contract-by-contract basis. It allows for transfers, too. If I wanted to get out of operations and work in intel analysis, for example."

"You'd never be as happy as you are out in the field, though." Not a question. As little as a few months ago, Coral would have been correct. Anything not in the operational setting seemed boring. Now, after so many nights on the run with whichever gang he was pretending to be part of, taking an assignment with regular hours and having at least a day a week off appealed to him.

BS. You're imagining what you could do if you and Coral decided to make a go of it again.

He shook his head slightly to clear his mind of the unwanted interrogation from his conscience. Coral stood up from the table, taking his body language to mean something else.

"I'd expect no less from the Trevor I know." She cleared their plates and retreated the eighteen inches to the sink. "I'll handle the cleanup. If you want a shower, I'd suggest you take it now, because I'm going to spend time under the hot water."

"You never run out of it with the flash heater."

"No, but we could run out of water. There isn't a whole lot left. I'll make sure another tank gets delivered tomorrow." She squirted dish soap under the stream of water at the sink. "Go ahead, I've got this."

He read the invitation for what it was. She wanted to make sure they didn't cross paths any more than necessary, now that she'd laid down the no-sex gauntlet.

What Coral didn't know yet and what he'd lived with, was that life undercover, whether for three days or three years, often left the players with no control of how closely they worked together. As much as he intellectually agreed with her platonic plans, his experience led him to believe that he couldn't absolutely promise he'd never touch her, never kiss her again. When all hell broke loose, Coral was always his source of strength and comfort. His heaven in the midst of insanity.

What he'd told her held true. He should never have come back home to Silver Valley.

Coral made good on her promise to enjoy a long, hot shower after dinner. As the water streamed over her, she missed her house bathroom and the stronger water pressure, but this would do. Trevor had insisted she stay in his vicinity, and it was easier to shower here than track back to the farmhouse.

It hadn't been easy talking to Trevor at dinner about her lack of a sex life since the divorce. And from what he'd admitted, he'd not been any luckier in love—although he'd pointedly not given her a straight answer. The intense pain of regret would have made her sink to her knees if the stall weren't so small. It was none of her business if or how many women he'd been with. But it didn't make it any easier to stomach.

He'd been clear about not finding someone to have a serious relationship with. So maybe he'd been lonely, too. At one point during her recovery from the divorce, she'd have relished the thought that Trevor was as miserable as she was. It'd been so easy to blame him and his work for their failed marriage.

But tonight, as she ran her bar of soap over her body, wishing it was Trevor's hands, profound sadness placed a heavy weight on her chest. What had they done to one another that neither of them had been interested in finding love again?

As she turned off the water and dried her dripping hair, a loud thump hit the trailer. She froze, her mind frantically searching for a cause. Since she'd been out here, she'd dealt with a fox or two, but nothing that would hit the side of the aluminum camper with such force.

A brief knock sounded on the thin bathroom door, and she couldn't help but long for the protection of the steel doors at the safe house and Trail Hikers headquarters.

Stop it. It's something obvious, nothing to fear. But she wasn't so sure.

"Coral, you okay?"

She cracked the door, tried to show Trevor she wasn't afraid. "I'm fine, but what was that? Were you just outside?"

"No. Get dressed—I'm going out to find out what

it was." As he spoke, three more thumps sounded, this time closer to the back bedroom area where she slept.

"Someone's throwing rocks at the trailer. Trevor, please wait for me."

"Stay put. Go ahead and call Claudia." He was gone before she had a chance to stop him. The fatigue of the day and their emotional conversation fled as adrenaline surged. She cursed her clothes as she pulled a T-shirt and jeans on her wet skin and shoved her feet into hiking boots. Why couldn't she have already completed the Trail Hiker training? Maybe she'd have a weapon that was useful, at least.

Making her way to the front door, she grabbed the only protection she had besides Trevor—Aunt Brenda's old hunting rifle. She took the time to load the bird-shot cartridge and promised herself she'd get a permit to carry a concealed weapon after this. A handgun was far more maneuverable than the antique rifle.

Before she opened the door, she quickly called Claudia using the speed dial she'd updated this afternoon at TH headquarters. Claudia listened to her description and urged her to do as Trevor had told her and stay put until help arrived.

"I can't wait in here, Claudia, I'm a sitting duck!"

Several loud pops in rapid succession startled her— definite gun fire—and she heard Trevor's muffled "get down!" She forced the phone into her front pocket, finished loading the shotgun and, locked and loaded, prepared to join Trevor in the darkness that swallowed the camper.

Chapter 11

Coral might not have much training yet, save for the shooting range time with Trevor years ago, but she'd watched enough police procedurals to know she didn't want to be the victim of her own stupidity. It was imperative that she manage her trembling limbs, control her reaction to the stressful situation and take her time egressing the trailer. Carefully looking through the door's tiny window blinds, she saw nothing unusual on the makeshift patio where less than a week ago she'd enjoyed nightly glasses of wine. The trailer's interior and exterior lights were off, giving her good cover. She sent a silent thanks to Trevor for extinguishing them as soon as he heard the first *thump*.

Coral eased outside, shotgun in hand, and moved alongside the edge of the camper, conscious of each crunch upon gravel or dirt. Her ears strained to hear

Trevor's steps, or better, his voice. All she wanted was to reach him, to be in a place to offer backup. And to get the heck out of here with him, as needed.

Her gut clenched on instinct, and she knew they were going to have to flee. Getting out of a pursuer's reach was rule one according to the Trail Hiker intro video she'd watched earlier today.

Silence stretched for what felt like eons, long enough for the crickets and cicadas to blossom into song, as if the danger had passed. Trevor and the shooters, wherever they were, had to be standing still.

A shot rang out in the dark, and she held her breath, fighting the urge to run into the night and see who Trevor had fired at. The thought that it could be Trevor who'd been shot occurred, and she moved to the corner of the trailer, the shotgun nestled in her shoulder, safety off. As she edged the barrel around the camper, another shot rang out, and a split second later her rifle jerked to the side, butting her chin. She bit down on her tongue at the unexpected contact. Coral knew how to absorb shotgun kickback, but she'd always done it from firing a round straight out in front of her, not because someone had been shooting at her.

The barrel had been hit. It would have been her if she'd been inches past her current spot.

"Stay back!" Trevor's voice. He didn't have to tell her to be quiet—she knew enough to know that one person had to be lead and it would never be her. She was merely an informed civilian who knew how to fire a weapon or two, not a highly trained lethal agent like Trevor or any of the Trail Hikers.

Still, it took all of her self-control to obey his command, knowing that at least one shooter was out there, aiming at Trevor. She'd underestimated her personal connection to her ex and wasn't ready for the sheer terror that washed over her in a cold deluge of awareness. She didn't want anything to happen to him. The thought of a life without him was unimaginable, even though they'd always be apart.

Shouts echoed in the dark, and she had a flashback to the other night, when she'd been out here alone.

You're good. Trevor's here.

"Go get the car. Drive back for me." Trevor's voice was low, steady. "Don't hesitate or slow down, just leave the door open. I'll jump in."

She ran for the car, glad the keys were where she always kept them under the seat. If she'd had to go back in the camper, it would only give the thugs more time. There was no doubt in her mind that the ROC had come back, and they weren't going to leave either her or Trevor alive. Only a dedicated criminal would bother to get their attention, entice them out of the camper then try to pick them off.

They had to get out of here, and it was up to her to help them make their escape. The grass was wet and slippery from the dew, but this time she was prepared to run. Instead of the flip-flops she'd worn the night before, she wore hiking boots. It was far easier to navigate the uneven ground, her only obstacle the limits of her own speed. It took seconds to reach the vehicle.

Go, go, go. Keep moving. It took all of her focus and energy to stay on task, to not scream with the fear and frustration roiling in her gut.

The car door opened with a tiny creak, and she

prayed the sound wasn't audible to their attackers. She slid into the driver's seat and fumbled for the keys. Keeping the rifle across her lap, the butt in the passenger seat until she got Trevor, she pushed the passenger door open. As she turned the engine, another shot sounded right before the engine purred, and the deflection of a bullet hitting the front side of the car made her jump.

Resolve gave her strength, added fire to her determination. "Not on my property, you losers!" She spoke the words to herself, wishing she could yell at the top of her lungs. Instead she channeled the surge of adrenaline into driving around to the back side of the camper and then, with a deep gulp of air, flooring it around to the vulnerable, exposed side. Where Trevor lay on his belly, his weapon aimed at the low hedge of volunteer soybean plants that had cropped up, the seeds blown in from neighboring farms. Too late she realized that if she could see Trevor, so could the enemy. She'd left the headlights off, but the sky was clear and the moon full, illuminating the white trailer like a beacon.

It wasn't difficult maneuvering the car to where she knew she had to be, but she wasn't fast enough. To her horror she heard more shots and then saw Trevor's body jerk back. She couldn't keep the scream from erupting, her entire being attuned to him.

"Trevor!" She was next to him and saw his head through the open door. "Trevor! Get in!"

Please, please let him be alive.

"Trying." He gasped. "They…" The air wheezed in and out of him. "Got my hand."

She looked toward the spot where she'd seen two

shadows, where the gunfire had come from. A pair of dark shapes were running toward them. They'd close the distance within thirty seconds, tops.

Acting on pure instinct, she jumped into the passenger seat and slid out the door, onto the ground next to Trevor. She was not leaving without him.

"Can you get up? I'll help you."

He struggled with one hand held against his chest, but he got to one foot and then she shoved him with all her might into the passenger side and shut the door. Peering under the car's chassis, she saw and heard the thugs' feet as they closed in. They were too close; she'd never make it out of here in time.

With seconds left until they were upon them, Coral had no other option but to shoot offensively.

Springing up from the ground, she rested her rifle on the hood of the car and took aim. Using the steady squeeze that Trevor had taught her on a hot day in Southern California, she fired off one, two shots. She had one round left before she'd have to reload. It was only birdshot, but it'd do if she made contact with her targets.

A yelp pierced the night, followed by a loud thud. But the remaining figure kept running. She saw a black ski mask and recognized that the figure had stopped midstride.

He was going to shoot her or at Trevor in the car. Without hesitation, she aimed at his legs and fired. As if on a slow-motion reel, the attacker dropped to his knees, seemed to hang there for eternity, then finally dropped to the side. Coral gasped, wondered if she'd killed the man. And then a loud string of the filthiest epithets she'd ever heard cut through the muggy air. The other attacker answered back in low, guttural grunts. They were both down—objective achieved. She'd analyze what she was hearing later; right now getting out was the primary goal.

Coral ran around to the driver's side, got in and slammed her door shut as she moved the stick into Drive. There was no time to see how Trevor was or to wait for his instructions. She knew where she had to take them.

Back to the safe house. It was a straight shot there once she got out of Silver Valley and past Harrisburg. No map needed, and Trevor would tell her the specifics once they got closer.

Flooring the accelerator, she drove back around the camper and then out toward their escape, using the trailer as a shield between the car and the shooters. She'd hit at least one of them but knew that birdshot pellets weren't enough to stop a large man, much less a trained assassin. She had no idea who the men were, but they'd wanted to do harm.

Only when they were on a main highway and out of the range of handheld weapons did she realize she'd almost forgotten about Trevor. The exhilaration of getting them out of there had caused the adrenaline surge that her brief training had described.

"Trevor, you okay?" She looked at him, expecting an appreciative gleam from his eyes. He'd be proud of what she'd done, right?

But Trevor's form was still, his eyes closed.

Fear sliced through her. It was her worst nightmare. Trevor's wound had been fatal. She couldn't have stopped the primal scream that ripped from somewhere deep in her chest if she'd wanted to.

"No! No, no, no! You stay with me, Trevor Stone."

She reached across the console to feel the side of his neck, but in her agitation she jerked on the steering wheel, careening them onto the gravel shoulder. Gasping, she used both hands to get back on the road. Growing up in a winter snow area had taught her not to hit the brakes, and as soon as the vehicle broke from the skid, she slowed down and stopped the car in the next pullout, about a mile up the road. She put the gear into Park and began to triage Trevor.

Her fingers touched the clammy skin of his throat, and she pressed more deeply than she intended, desperate to feel a pulse.

"Please, please, please." Time stopped. Fate couldn't be so cruel as to give her this short, tempestuous time with Trevor only to take him away forever, could it?

Sobs broke out of her throat, and she didn't bother to wonder about whether there was a wild animal in the car with them. She recognized her tortured cries as her own.

Trevor's ears hurt, and he tried to remember who'd boxed him. As the mists of unconsciousness cleared, he recognized that a high-pitched cry had made his eardrums ring, not some thug's fists. The pitiful sound had a familiarity about it, and he knew it was a woman, but the only woman he'd been around long enough to hear cry was Coral.

Coral.

He opened his eyes, ready to take on whoever was hurting her.

"What the—" His voice was his, but a little weak around the edges as he sat in the passenger seat of Coral's sedan. The camper, the shots, the thugs. His hand throbbed like the devil, and he held it up. And immediately lowered it, not needing to see the bloody mess he knew it was. Or to pass out again.

"Trevor? Trevor!" The scent of her hair reached his nostrils before she filled his vision, her eyes luminous under the dash light. Which hurt like hell as he squinted against it.

"Babe. Can you tone it done an octave?"

"I thought you were dead! Let me look at your hand."

"It's fine. Please, leave it."

She ignored him, and he closed his eyes against the risk of seeing his hand. Her fingers were warm, and he swore he felt water drop onto his messed-up skin. Coral was crying over him?

He had to protect her.

Coral sniffled. "It's a surface wound, I think." Her fingers were on his wrist, and after a bit he realized she was taking his pulse.

"I'm alive, remember?"

"Shh. I'm checking you for shock. You taught me First Aid 101, *remember*?"

He did. When they were college students, he'd practiced on her to be able to pass the EMT training he'd completed to be more prepared for the Marines, and also to pull in a few extra dollars. His favorite part had been when they'd been at an abandoned, private strip of beach on a gloriously sunny day, so typical of Southern California.

"I remember the time you pretended you were drowning so that I could bring you in and practice CPR." She'd run into the ocean, ignoring the frigid temps of the deep Pacific, just to help him out. But when he'd reached her, they'd been in water to his chest, just over her head. Coral had been at his mercy to keep her above water, which he'd done with a deep kiss that he told her was the training substitute for a lung fill. He still felt the imprint of her fingers on his erection, and the thrill that had shot through him when she'd asked if having a hard-on was part of EMT training. Her bright pink bikini bottom had been no match for his eager fingers or her impatient writhing. He'd grasped her ass and—

"Trevor. Really?" He opened his eyes to her bright intensity, her hair wild around her face. Looking past her obvious distress at his faint, she emanated a sense of connection he'd never felt before.

She still cares for you, man.

"What?" Feigning innocence was weak but all he had with her staring at him so openly. With such comprehension. Another reason to not work with his ex—she knew him too well.

"This isn't the time to get yourself overly excited." Her heat was gone, the dash light clicked off and she restarted the car. Dang, she'd seen his erection. He felt like a teen, unable to handle his most basic reflexes.

There was nothing basic about how he felt about Coral, though.

"Sorry. It's the—"

"Let me guess, the adrenaline?" She interrupted him with a throaty laugh, and he smiled into the darkness.

"Caught." He watched as she pulled off at the next exit, lost in his memories of them that day at the beach. Except—

"Coral, where are you going? The safe house is another thirty miles north."

"I'm taking you to Harrisburg Hospital. You appear to have only a surface wound, but you passed out. I don't see any other bullet injuries. Did you hit your head?"

"I'm not hurt enough for an ER. Turn back around."

"No can do. We lost the thugs back at the barn, and we don't look as rough as we did last week when we had to go to the safe house."

As she spoke, he narrowed his eyes on his side mirror, where he noticed headlights closing in—the same ones that had trailed them off and then back on the highway. He used his good hand to flip down the passenger visor and access the mirror to verify his suspicions.

"Son of a…" He wanted to put his fist through the window.

"What?" The high-pitched note was back in Coral's voice.

"We're being tailed." Damn his weakness, the one freaking thing he had no resistance to.

"Here." She floored the accelerator as she arched her pelvis up out of the seat and pulled her phone out of her front jeans pocket. "Call Claudia back."

He grabbed the phone and looked at the face. "Wait—pick up your speed and don't stop until we're at the Second Street exit." At least if they were in downtown Harrisburg, he'd be able to get them to the main police station.

"We're going to the hospital." She drove like a demon, passing every other car to the left without hesitation. He loved it.

"No, the police station. I'm not seriously hurt, Coral."

She snorted.

"I'm serious—I have a phobia to blood."

"I'm waving the BS flag on that. You took care of my eye like a pro."

"It's my own blood that I have an issue with, not anyone else's. Please keep your eye and focus on the road, will you?"

Putting the phone to his ear, he listened.

"Hello?" Claudia sounded a bit annoyed that she'd had zero comms from them. But she'd used Trail Hiker advanced tech gear, so she knew their GPS location within seconds of answering Coral's call.

"Boss."

"Tell Coral that's us behind you before you kill someone on Route 15 into Harrisburg."

Relief splayed across his chest, and he wanted to shout.

"Coral, slow down, that's a TH vehicle behind us." He waited for Coral to comply before turning his attention back to Claudia. "Sorry about that, boss. There was no telling who was on our six." He looked out the side window. "Uh, how much of our conversation have you heard?"

"Enough to guess that you passed out when you saw

your hand bleeding." There was no recrimination or judging tone to Claudia's reply. "Actually, as much as I know you hate that, it was a good scenario for Coral to work through."

"That's what I like to be, a training dummy." He shifted in his seat. "Did SVPD catch the jerks who were shooting at us?"

"Oh yes."

"So it's TH four, ROC zero."

"Not exactly." A grim note entered Claudia's voice.

"What is it?" He glanced over at Coral, who he was sure was listening but couldn't make out the entire conversation. He had a premonition he wasn't going to want her to know everything.

"We've got a big problem, Trevor. I'll tell you at the hospital." Claudia ended the call, and he stared at the phone, holding it in his uninjured hand.

"What's wrong?" Coral knew him too well; there was no use hiding his apprehension from her.

"Claudia's got some news for us but didn't want to tell me on the phone." His gut ratcheted into a tight coil. TH used the best scramblers and encrypting technology available. There were few adversaries who'd be able to break through their communication defenses.

But Claudia was concerned, obviously keeping something from hitting the cellular towers and being intercepted.

He only knew one adversary worthy of her concern. Russian government agents—specifically, FSB-trained agents.

Markova.

Chapter 12

The drive to the hospital was anticlimactic after Coral realized that Trevor's wound was superficial and Claudia confirmed it was TH agents who had followed them, not ROC thugs. She'd made this drive once or twice with her parents when either of them needed her for an outpatient procedure.

"Go ahead and park. I'll walk with you from the lot." Trevor's complexion was still too pale for her comfort level under the city streetlights. Downtown Harrisburg was a ghost town this time of night, adding to the sense of them being alone against the world.

"No. You need to get looked at sooner than later." She was certain his wound wouldn't need more than a few stitches, but she wasn't a medical expert, and for all she knew he had another bullet wound somewhere he hadn't told her about. "Here you go." She pulled up to the automatic doors marked Emergency Room and put the car in Park. The door locks clicked open, and she gave Trevor a smile that hurt her cheeks. Hopefully he wouldn't notice she was forcing it.

"I don't like this." His gaze was on her for a brief few seconds. "Here." He handed her his pistol. "Keep this with you until you park and are sure it's safe. They won't let you bring it into the hospital—there's a security checkpoint this late at night. Pick a spot as close to the elevators as possible."

As he spoke, someone rapped on her window, and she turned to see a uniformed officer.

"You cannot park here, ma'am." The man spoke through the glass.

She rolled down the window and offered another smile. "I'm sorry, Officer, I'm dropping off my friend who's been hurt. I'm going to move the car right away."

"Now is best."

"Yes, sir." She rolled the window back up and looked over at Trevor. "You need to get out now."

"I am." He winked. "You're doing great, by the way."

Exasperated, she let out a slow laugh. "Go get your stitches, will you? I'll meet you in the ER. Give me about five."

He slid out of the car and gingerly stood up, taking a few halting steps toward the doors. Maybe she should have walked with him—

The blare of a horn behind her forced her gaze to her rearview mirror. An ambulance with flashing lights had pulled up, and she had no choice but to drive away.

She did have the satisfaction of seeing a hospital

worker in scrubs greet Trevor with a wheelchair. The way her ex plopped his large frame into its seat revealed that he wasn't as tough as the stern face he'd displayed for her benefit.

Although his bravado was also for him, she figured. It kept him going and not passing out again at the thought of his own blood seeping from the gunshot wound.

Trevor had a fear of his own blood. In all their time together, he'd never mentioned it, and she'd never had reason to suspect it. He'd gone into war-torn provinces in Afghanistan and sustained other minor injuries, not unlike the one tonight. But he'd never told her about his anxieties over blood. Another layer of Trevor she hadn't excavated during their marriage, and another reason why their relationship had failed. He'd never trusted her enough to be completely open with her. To be fair, she hadn't shared everything with him, either. How lonely she felt when he was gone, how she hated being in her twenties but spending most of her time alone, without him. She'd wanted him to think she was as strong as he was and didn't want him to see her as anything but one hundred percent behind him and his career choice. It was what a good partner did.

There was a lot she still didn't know about him, and it made her sad. Driving around the spiral ramp, she went to the top of the parking garage before coming back down and determining the best location that would hew to Trevor's specifications—close to an elevator. She was almost at the bottom before she saw a family get into a car next to the stairwell and pull out, done with their hospital visit. They left behind a large empty spot, and she pulled in.

Trevor's pistol lay in the passenger seat, his advice to leave it behind echoing in her mind. Even if she somehow got the gun past security, she didn't have the right training to use it in a close space, so she shoved it into the glove compartment and turned the lock.

The parking garage was well lit and cavernous, with few places for anyone to hide behind. She let out a sigh of relief. Claudia had said it was TH following them on the highway, and to prove it their tail was nowhere in sight, but Coral was still shaken from the entire ordeal. The last thing she needed was to be worried about some loser jumping out at her.

She skipped the elevator and opted to take the stairs to the sky bridge level. The two flights up were quick, the night warm on her skin.

"Hello, Coral Staufer." A woman's voice sounded behind her, and she turned at the top of the stairwell. A slim figure dressed all in black leaned against a cement column just to the left of the sky bridge entrance.

"Excuse me?" If this was one of the TH agents who had followed them, she didn't appreciate the cloak-and-dagger routine.

The woman sauntered toward her, and only then did Coral spy the lethal blade in her gloved hand. Who wore gloves in the middle of summer?

A murderer.

Coral's mouth went dry, and she wished she'd listened to Trevor—kept the pistol in hand.

"You're not one of them." The woman was shorter than her by several inches, but Coral didn't doubt her athletic ability. It was evident in every curve of her compact body, in the way she walked like a cat on a high wire.

"'One of them'?" Coral heard how ridiculous, how weak she sounded and steeled herself to stand straight, not balk from this person. Although it was the knife blade she was focused on. What had Trevor told her? That knives were the worst weapon because they could pierce most body armor, go where a bullet didn't have a chance.

"Law enforcement. You're just the dumb socialite who had the bad luck to host a party last winter where the scum of Silver Valley showed up."

"Ah, sure." Coral wasn't about to correct her about her job description. "I'm afraid I didn't get your name."

The woman laughed, and the sparkle in her eyes was from the reflection of the halogen lighting, not because she had any level of joy in her being. Her eyes also revealed a void of connection. Coral knew she'd kill her without hesitation if she wanted to.

Since she could still feel her blood pounding through her veins, she was still alive. The woman wanted something else. Coral looked at her escape options. Running back down the stairs to the ground level, or past the woman to get to the sky bridge. She'd have to pass the woman to get to the bridge: not something she relished. If she turned and sprinted across the mostly empty parking garage, the woman's knife could still outrun her with one lethal flick of a wrist.

"You want my name, bitch? It's Markova." Anna Markova stepped closer, wielding the knife as if she were about to slice through a watermelon and not Coral's throat. Coral backed away but only inches as her back ran into the steel railing. Her gut tightened in primal fear. Markova had been let out of prison? Who had given her bond?

Capture the details.

"You've heard of me, then?" Anna Markova ran the blade down Coral's cheek, and she leaned as far back over the railing as her spine allowed. Markova's breath carried the scent of cinnamon, and her hair was freshly washed. In fact, her skin looked as though it had been scrubbed to the point of irritation.

I'd do the same if I'd been in prison.

"Stop looking around like a jackrabbit—you have no need to run from me tonight. Tell your boyfriend that you saw me, and if he's not around, tell the police."

"I don't have a b-b-boyfriend."

"Semantics. The man you're with has a big target between his eyes. Tell him that, and let this be a warning that next time I'm not going to let you go without a permanent reminder from me." Coral felt the cold blade against her throat, the pressure going from discomfort to pain as Markova's eyes glittered with emotionless satisfaction. "I'd suggest you find another man to shack up with, bitch. Now turn around and walk across the bridge before I gut you like the stupid fish you are."

Markova grabbed her by her T-shirt's collar and in a quick turn twisted her around to face the sky bridge.

"Go!" The kick to her butt was the hardest humiliation to ignore, as all Coral wanted to do was turn back around and take this vile woman out.

Wait until you've received training.

She walked to the other side of the walkway, and when she turned around, Markova was gone.

Her phone was still in her pocket—she could call Trevor, but he was being treated. TH and Claudia's numbers were in her phone, too, but why bother. She pushed through a set of doors and followed the signs to the ER. She'd tell them in person.

"I'm sorry, ma'am, you're not allowed past this point."

"I'm the one who brought him in. Trevor Stone."

"And your relation?"

"I'm his…his wife." Trevor jerked at the sound of Coral telling the ER nurse that she was still married to him, neglecting the *ex* part.

"Stay still, please." A doctor stitched the skin between his fingers and atop his hand. The trauma team had triaged him and determined the same thing as Coral had—he had a surface wound from a bullet graze. The stitches were necessary but he'd live.

"Sorry."

"Trevor." Coral stood at the foot of the gurney, her eyes wide and her mouth open, as if she'd run a mile. As he looked at her, he saw a trickle of red on her throat.

"What's that on your neck?"

Coral swiped at her throat and pulled her fingers away to look at the substance. "Blood. I was cut by Markova's knife."

"What the—" He sat up straight, unable to keep from bellowing. "Where were you? Where is she—"

"Sir!" The attending staff surrounded him, and he

was pushed back down on the bed as the doctor glared at him.

"Ma'am, let us take a look at that." Coral protested, but then she quieted and he assumed she was led out. The doctor resumed stitching, and Trevor wondered if he'd imagined Coral being there. Who was parading around saying she was Markova?

"Trevor." Claudia stood next to him, and unlike with Coral, the trauma staff all but ignored her. The director of Trail Hikers spent a lot of time in the ER with TH agents. The hospital staff didn't know about TH, of course, or what Claudia's true job was. They thought she was a hospital chaplain, something she'd applied for to be able to move around any of the local hospitals with minimal notice.

"I'm fine. But Coral's—"

"I'm over here, Trevor. In the next bed." Coral's voice sounded stronger than it had only minutes earlier. He allowed the gnawing in his gut to ease up.

Claudia's concern was etched on her grave expression. She leaned close to Trevor and whispered in his ear. "Markova broke out of county jail three hours ago."

Pulling back, Claudia smiled and looked like the hospital chaplain the staff thought she was. "That's a little prayer I repeat to myself when I'm going through a tough time."

"Thanks. I appreciate it." As he watched, Claudia walked around the curtain, and he saw her approach Coral's bed, heard the murmur of their conversation.

He couldn't do anything until the staff left them all alone.

"How much longer till you're done, Doc?"

"This is the last one." Trevor watched the doctor tie off the stitch and marveled at how the appearance of his swollen hand, tinged yellow from the disinfectant wash and bearing the ugly stitch marks, didn't faze him in the least. If his cuts started oozing blood, it'd be a different story.

You should have told Coral.

He should have, especially since they were living together through this case. Chalk it up to another failure on his part. He'd had so many that had added up to the end of their marriage, he'd stopped counting years ago.

"Thanks, Doc."

"The discharge nurse will be here in a bit to go over your care instructions. There's a gunshot wound right now, so it might take a little longer."

"Sure thing."

He watched the doctor clear the area and bit his tongue to keep from shouting out to Coral and Claudia, just on the other side of the room divider.

The doctor's sneakers squeaked across the linoleum, and as soon as the sound faded, the curtain snapped back. Claudia stood between him and Coral at the foot of Coral's bed.

"Okay, you two. Coral, tell us quickly what you saw."

"I was on my way in here. I parked two floors below the sky bridge. When I got up the staircase, a woman— she said she was Markova—came out of nowhere, with a knife. She toyed with me, told me to tell Trevor that I'd seen her."

"She called me Trevor?" He was a dead man walking if Markova knew his real name.

"No, she called you my boyfriend. She thinks you're

LEA, I think, and said to tell you there's a target on your forehead. 'Between his eyes' is what she said, actually."

"What else did she say, Coral?" Claudia's soft prompting was a clear sign of his boss's fury. The former Marine had never lost her military bearing and treated every TH agent as her family. When someone hurt one of them, she went for justice.

Coral leaned back on the pillows, the red slash on her throat in stark contrast to the white linen. He only saw a portion of the injury from where he'd sat up on his cot, and it was more than enough to make him want nothing but Markova's total apprehension.

"You're exhausted." His observation came unbidden, as did the wave of regret. Coral was an innocent in all of this. And he'd led her here.

"Let her finish, Trevor." Claudia kept the focus where it had to be—on the op and not his self-recrimination.

"She said that if Trevor wasn't available or around, to tell the police that I'd spoken with her. She wanted to make sure law enforcement knew she was out of prison. What I don't understand is how she was given bail, with her history? I'm not a cop or one of you, but I read the papers, I see the news. She's a threat to the community."

"She wasn't let out, Coral. She escaped from the county prison a few hours ago."

"Escaped! How?"

"Several guards were sickened by a smuggled substance. Not only at our county jail but across the entire East Coast. We believe it's ROC heroin laced with synthetics. She had to have had help on the inside, though. When the guards fell ill, someone helped her out." Hearing Claudia's grim report made the anger in Trevor's gut flare. ROC had to go, Markova being the first target.

Coral's face paled. "You're telling me that Markova was the one on my property, shooting at us?"

Claudia shook her head. "Doubtful. SVPD took two men into custody and found no signs of anyone else on your property."

Trevor had had enough. He stood up and walked over to Coral. "She wasn't on the property or we'd both be dead. Markova's a skilled assassin and doesn't leave witnesses behind."

Coral's gaze arrested him on the spot. "Then why did she let me go? She doesn't sound like the type of criminal to play around with a victim like she did with me tonight."

Trevor met Claudia's gaze. There wasn't an easy answer to Coral's question. The main issue for him was that Markova wanted to get to him and if it meant harming Coral, or worse, the former FSB agent would do it.

"What's important is that you get your throat looked at and then we all get back to work on your training." Claudia cleared the tension that the mystery of Markova's motive caused.

"You're still going to let me train after how badly I screwed up tonight?" Coral's incredulous tone scraped at his scars, the ones he'd grown to cover his self-hatred over how badly he'd treated her when they'd been married.

"You behaved with as much courage—more, actually—as any law enforcement officer." He spoke with the force of the conviction he felt from his heart to his toes. "It's one thing to act when you have all the training and equipment to back you up. You didn't have a whole lot more than your instinct to get us out of there, Coral Bell."

Chapter 13

"Visualize how you're going to take me out before we engage." Bill Peyton, the receptionist she'd met the first day, was the TH training instructor assigned to Coral for her brief but intense session. He coached her through their fight scene with complete ease. No weapons, just her fists, feet and wits. This was her last exercise, a test of what she'd absorbed over the past seventy-two hours.

Before her thoughts flooded in to distract her, she practiced the mental clearing technique of taking a conscious deep breath, letting go of any distractions on the exhale. Without further delay she began to attack her adversary. Bill had told her at the start of the three days that by the end she would be able to get through a scenario on instinct. Her mind was more elastic than she'd ever suspected, and this last test proved it.

The enemy was on the floor after she'd backed him up to a wall and taken him out with a flurry of practiced maneuvers.

Bill's grudging grin was all the reward she needed.

"I did it!" Her triumph wasn't like winning an Olympic medal, but more like a benchmark she'd never believed possible. Not by her, a woman with zero military inclination or background. She'd never even liked playing police or fireman as a kid.

"You did." Bill stood and offered his hand, which she grasped and shook.

"I did what you said I would. I never had to think ahead to the next move once we were in it."

"That's the objective." Bill's grin faded. "You're going to come up against adversaries with far more training, though. It won't hurt to have a weapon with you at all times as long as ROC has their sights on you and Trevor."

The chill of reality doused her jubilation.

"I know."

"Have you decided what it will be yet, Coral? A knife or pistol?" Bill couldn't be much older than her, maybe five years if that, but his eyes belied the chronological marker. He'd seen more than enough to give him the wisdom of how evil could play out in the real world. His bio, which she knew had been left mostly unclassified for her benefit, involved years of not only undercover work but active special forces missions as a Navy SEAL. The man was a walking survival savant.

"I still don't know, Bill. I need to talk to Trevor about it. He's going to tell me to use a .45, if I know him as well as I think I do."

"I'd agree with that, except you do seem to be more comfortable with a switchblade."

She nodded. "I do. I hate having to carry any weapon. And I wish I could go on this last class we just finished and feel confident that I'd take out anyone who got in my way."

"ROC agents and thugs will all carry a weapon, Coral. You can't let your reluctance or a false naiveté keep you from being prepared."

"That's it, then, isn't it?" She walked over to the table that held the dummy pistols and rubber-bladed knives. A firearm seemed the easiest, the most expedient, but she didn't trust her aim in the midst of a fight. "I'm going to get a switchblade, then."

"Good choice. Make sure it fits your hand and that you can readily employ the blade. Oil the mechanism regularly, but keep the handle clean of it for obvious reasons."

"Will do. Thank you, Bill."

"Thank you for your service, Coral. You're little more than a volunteer here, yet you've stepped up to fight one of the worst adversaries out there. Good on you."

She watched Bill leave the gym before she turned and went to the locker room that housed a state-of-the-art ice soak tub and sauna. Both were instrumental in getting her through the past couple of days of high-intensity physical demands on her body. But she couldn't hide out here forever in the training module.

It was time to work alongside Trevor and get rid of ROC once and for all.

* * *

"It's not like Markova to play cat and mouse with a target." Claudia spoke to Trevor, Colt and Josh as they waited for Coral to finish up her training. They were all to do a debrief before he and Coral went back to the safe house, where they'd stayed since he'd taken the bullet graze to his hand.

Since Markova had put her hands on Coral. The memory made Trevor unable to focus on Claudia's conversation, so he shoved it aside. It would be back, haunting him at his most vulnerable point. That's how it worked when someone you cared so much about found herself in criminal crosshairs.

"Markova would have killed her if she didn't think she still needed her." Colt looked at Trevor. "We're working hard to figure out what the missing parts of the data are, but without the other two components Markova hid, it's very slow going."

"I haven't found anything out at the barn, but I didn't have as much time as I needed. I have to believe we're overlooking something obvious, but I don't know what."

"Did you have Coral look for herself?" Josh stood up and paced the small conference room. "She knows the property better than any of us, and she'd be more likely to recognize something unusual. She did find the first box for us."

"Markova's going to go back to the site—it's a matter of time." Trevor looked at Josh. "Can you have a patrol out there 24-7 until we find what Markova wants?"

Josh nodded. "We've been out there since the first incident with you, and I wish I could commit more personnel, but we're so strapped. We brought down two more heroin dealers last night, but still no joy on who's running the ring."

"It has to be Markova." Trevor hated that she'd escaped, but even more, hated that he hadn't expected it from the former FSB agent. "She's been in charge, calling the shots from prison, no matter how closely we watched her. Now she's back on the loose, so there's no limit to how hard she'll push to get more dope on the streets."

"I think she's only going to stick around for the length of time it takes to get her boxes back, Trevor." Claudia interjected, and as she spoke, the door behind her opened. Coral walked into the room and nodded to their boss.

"Sorry I'm a little late."

"No problem, we were just getting to the important part of our briefing." Claudia didn't miss a beat. "It's imperative that we find the two remaining containers of information that Markova's so desperate to find. Is there any place you can think of that you haven't looked?"

Coral met each person's gaze before she answered. "I have thought about it, actually. I found the first box sitting on a pile of rubble. The mound consisted of the barn remnants and the extra earth the power digger dug up. It was easy to see the lockbox as it stuck out of the topsoil, not at all appearing like a typical rock. I think the second box wouldn't be far away. None of you know the layout of the property as I do, but when the barn was still standing, there were only a couple of places that Markova would have been able to dig a hole into during the kind of winter we had last January. Remember the night of the gala, how frozen it was?"

"She'd have needed a blowtorch to melt the ice that covered the ground." Colt folded his hands in front of his face, his elbows on the ebony tabletop. "There wasn't enough time for her to do it, either."

"Right. With sunset so early and the gala's cocktail hour beginning at five thirty, she had no more than an hour or two to hide her data." Coral paused, and a shock of recognition coursed through Trevor. She looked exactly as he'd felt that first time he'd taken on an undercover op. Passionate. Engaged. Cautious.

"Where are the few places she would have dug, Coral?"

Finally her gaze rested on his, and while he saw the woman he'd never let go, he didn't recognize this facet of Coral's personality. More detached, calculating and absolutely perfect for undercover work. Her newfound dedication to a different type of job didn't alter her beauty or how much he was attracted to her, though. It heightened his awareness, made him see that he'd been such a fool during their marriage. He could have trusted her with more of himself when he'd gotten in too deep with his ops. She would have been the source of dependable strength he'd needed.

She still could be.

"Here, let me show you." She stood and went to the whiteboard positioned in the corner of the room. Rolling it to where they all could see it, she drew a quick diagram of her property.

"When the barn was still standing, there was only at most ten feet between it and the storage building, here." Trevor watched her hand move across the board effortlessly, mesmerized by how at ease she was in this setting. How had he not seen it before, her natural ability to lead?

"And you found the lockbox in the rubble pile that's on top of this strip of dirt, right?" Claudia pointed.

"Yes, but there's more," Coral continued, her hair glinting red under the lights. She drew a rectangular box atop the patch of earth between the barn and other building. "This was where I had a covered walkway between the barn and storage facility. Since I had my commercial refrigerators in the storage building, I wanted an all-weather quick-access path for me and my staff during events. When the barn blew, it took the storage unit with it, along with the covered walkway. But Markova only would have had either where I already found the first box, or here." Coral picked up a red marker and circled a small triangular spot in between the two buildings and walkway structure. "The other grounds were covered with the barn's foundation."

"You think the other box is in the ground, still in that spot?" Colt sounded doubtful.

Coral shook her head. "No, not at all. I think they're in the super-big pile of scraps that was hauled away from the barn and is closer to the farmhouse. I've never bothered to look through it, as it looks like a huge pile of burned wood and it's several hundred yards from the barn, where I have my camper."

"We have almost five hours of daylight left." Trevor spoke up.

"And no resources to get out there. We're planning

to bring a halt to as much of the heroin sales tonight as possible." Colt frowned. "Unless you have some TH resources you can free up for us, Claudia?"

Claudia looked at her husband, and Trevor knew it couldn't be easy, being married to someone who was in the same challenging and often dangerous business. And yet he was envious of the glance the couple shared. It was entirely unique to Claudia and Colt and reflected how special their relationship was.

He wanted that with the right woman.

You have the perfect person to share your life with.

But he'd blown it the first time around.

"Coral and I will go out there and do what we can until sunset."

"Not on my watch. That's way too risky with Markova out there." Josh shook his head.

"I just completed the training you all said would help. And I won't do anything that I don't have to— I'll do whatever Trevor needs me to."

"Markova's not going to show up in broad daylight, not after showing herself to Coral at the hospital. She'll wait and come looking for her treasures at night. You can have several more TH agents ready by then. In the meantime, Coral and I can go back there and dig around." Trevor was anxious to get the two remaining boxes in his hands for TH analysis. "Coral needs to be there to work on her event."

"Take a metal detector, although I don't know how effective it'll be with the arson remnants." Claudia knew as well as they did that the rebar and other scrap metals would probably interfere with using the device, but it was worth a try. "And no questions about being out of there before dark, Trevor. You too, Coral." Claudia made sure to acknowledge them both.

"Josh and I will see what we can do to scramble a couple of units to be out there tonight. We'll call in extras from other county townships." Colt looked at Josh, who nodded his affirmative.

"So it's set? Coral and I head to the barn now and dig until we find the other two boxes or sunset."

"And report in on the quarter hour." Claudia stood up. "Be extra careful, folks. ROC is wound tight, and Markova isn't going to issue any more warnings."

Trevor saw the shiver that passed over Coral's expression, and his arms ached to hold her and hug away her worry. But that was what he'd have done to Coral, his partner and spouse.

Now, Coral was his colleague, and he had to demonstrate how much he trusted her.

"Coral, let's head out."

"It's in here, I feel it." Coral grunted as she used the short-handled spade to throw more of the debris aside. The refuse pile was at least ten feet high and as many feet wide and long. Enough dirt intermingled with the singed wood beams and rusting steel bars that it was evident the power digger had unearthed the first foot or two of ground under the barn. Sweat ran down her shoulders, across her back. She wiped her forehead with the back of her suede work glove and saw that Trevor looked as hot as she felt.

"I'm a believer in intuition, Coral, but in this case, 'show me the lockbox' works better." His shoulders bunched in sync with his biceps under his sweat-stained charcoal T-shirt, and she had to remind herself they were partners in the law now. Or at least, partners in trying to find Markova's hidden data. Coral knew she'd never be a real TH agent, and she didn't want to be. But to be able to work alongside Trevor as he fought to bring an end to an op he'd chiseled away at for the last two years was a privilege. She'd do her best to help and not hinder him.

They'd been at it for almost three hours and only had at best another ninety minutes to find what they were looking for.

"Keep at it, Coral. It's only a matter of time now."

She looked longingly at the metal detector. "If only that magic wand had worked."

His chuckle warmed her. "In my experience the tough cases don't get solved with anything less than a lot of hard work. I do wish it'd worked, too, for what it's worth."

"Humph." She sucked in her core muscles and dug in deep, determined to make some headway in this pile of rubble. A large, painful reverberation ran up her arm as the shovel hit something hard. Unlike the shards of wood and metal, whatever she'd hit didn't easily move aside. Leaving the shovel exactly where it had hit something solid, she knelt down and pulled as much of the scorched debris away as possible. She used the handle as her guide, clearing the area around it until she'd opened up a hole approximately eighteen inches wide and just as deep. Her flashlight illuminated the dark hole—and a metal lockbox the size of the one she'd already found.

"Trevor!"

The sun's rays had grown long across the fields, and when she looked up to ascertain he was next to her, she couldn't see his face as his body blocked the light.

"Did you find something?" His eagerness matched hers. They had to get out of here before nightfall, before Markova attempted another search. She'd be back with a team of thugs, and no matter how strong Coral and Trevor were together, they weren't fools.

"Yes. It's an exact duplicate of the first one."

"Here, let me help. It'll take too long to remove the top of the heap. I'll hold up the wood on top of the hole while you reach in and grab it."

"Great." She waited for him to brace himself on solid ground and insert his shovel into the gap she'd opened. As soon as it looked sturdy, she moved to get the box.

"Take it easy, nice and slow." Trevor guided her through the extraction. "It looks easy, but if this pile of junk falls on you, we'll have two things to dig out."

"Right." The smell of rot and decay mingled with the charred odor that she didn't think she'd ever be free of, no matter how many times the barn was rebuilt. Her flashlight in her teeth, she tried to stay steady and keep the beam on the box. Her hands were only inches from it, and she estimated she was in as far as her waist. Since she stood on a precarious pile of wooden slabs, sticks and rebar, it wasn't the most secure feeling in the world.

"You've got this, Coral Bell. Keep going in there, bit by bit. Once you've got the box, I can help you get out."

Trevor's voice served as her anchor, but her lack of firm footing unnerved her. His weakness was the sight of his own blood, and hers had always been small spaces. He knew this and kept talking to her, giving her comfort while remaining professional.

Her hands finally reached the box, and she grasped it on either side. "Got it!"

"Good, now hang on to it and back out the way you went in, nice and easy."

But her flashlight fell out of her mouth, and she was plunged into total darkness. Cold sweat immediately sprang out on her palms, and the box became difficult to cling to. She wanted to feel around it for the small handle on top but was afraid that in the darkness she'd slip and drop it. It'd be impossible to find in the dark without illumination, which meant going back out and in again.

The sunset was minutes away, and she couldn't risk a second dig for the box.

"I dropped my light!" The shout was the hardest thing she'd ever done, fighting past the panic that bubbled in her chest. TH training had introduced her to several ways to remain on task no matter how her body was reacting to a particular threat, and she mentally fought to see the list of techniques in her mind.

"Breathe. Count to five. Exhale," she whispered to herself, and at least the self-talk kept her from total panic.

You cannot panic now.

She wriggled her hips and used her knees to root herself and attempted to back out of the makeshift tunnel. Her booted feet were unable to make purchase, though, and within seconds the inevitability of failure engulfed her.

No. They had not come this far for her to blow the entire ROC case by having a freak-out under some charred wood.

"Keep it going, Coral. You've got this."

She heard Trevor's voice as if through a sieve and tried again to squirm out backward. Her skin scraped along the rough-hewn opening, the hem of her shirt riding up over her waist, her ribs. To heck with any cuts or bruises—they were all worth getting Markova's data figured out.

Jubilation filled her as she realized she was indeed backing out, inch by inch.

A sudden *bam* reached her ears just as her toe lost its purchase and she heard Trevor say words he'd learned in the military. Words that meant he was frustrated, angry or scared.

"Trevor!" But it was too late for him to hear her as the weight of the wood collapsed on her back. It wasn't so heavy as to stop her from breathing, but it was enough to trigger her panic response.

"No. One. Two. Three." She kept her eyes squeezed shut against the horrific inky darkness and refused to give in to the anxiety. "One. Two. Three." Regrouping, she ascertained that she still held on to the lockbox, a miracle considering how her entire body was slicked in fear sweat.

"Coral, hold on!" Trevor's voice, tinged with alarm, wasn't the comfort it'd been only seconds earlier. Before she had time to consider her remaining options, a huge tug on the waist of her pants had her moving, the lockbox coming with her. With her arms fully stretched in front of her in a classic flying pose, the security box in her hands and Trevor pulling on her waist and hips, she felt each and every scrape, every bump and hit of the wood and rebar.

It didn't matter. Trevor was getting her out.

With a last pull, she was clear of the rubble and fell onto Trevor as they both landed atop the refuse heap. The box fell out of her hands and hit her stomach.

"Oof." She breathed into Trevor's shoulder, near her right arm.

"You did it, babe!" Trevor rolled twice down the pile and was on his feet ahead of her, reaching down for her hand as she tucked the box under her other arm. "We have to make a run for it, though."

"What was that noise?"

"I can't be sure, but we're not hanging around to find out."

Back on her feet, she shook her head, stamped her feet, and nodded. "Okay. Let's go. Here, you carry this." She handed him the box, which felt much heavier than the first one.

He tucked it under his arm like a football and they ran from the woodpile, away from the barn's reconstruction, away from whatever or whoever had made the explosive noise. Into the night, which had settled around them as they'd retrieved the second of Markova's hidden data treasures.

As they ran she had no fear, no concern for her safety. She'd made it through one of her worst nightmares and was now running for her life, no stopping needed to soothe her panic.

She ran alongside the one man she trusted with everything.

Chapter 14

"Have we found out anything about the exploding noise?" Coral stood next to Trevor at the safe house as he worked to open the lockbox with the super-secret-agent tools he'd always relied upon. Steel picks and a hammer. They'd driven back to the safe house, as going to TH headquarters was too risky with Markova on the loose. Coral had run into the bathroom when they'd arrived and wanted to know if she'd missed a call.

"SVPD found a hole blown in the ground next to the barn's front." He hated telling her the rest. "It damaged some of the new framework."

"Was it Markova?" Coral didn't miss a beat, and he wondered how he'd ever missed noticing this side of her. The strength she'd exhibited over the past week was nothing short of heroic.

"No telling, as by the time the patrol reacted, there

was no sign of anyone there. My guess is on her, though, yes." He felt the last tumbler click into place, and he opened the box.

Coral's gasp echoed his *oh crap* thought. "Is that what I think it is?"

He made note of the timer, which had begun a digital countdown the minute he'd opened the lid. Several squares of C4 explosive filled the box, underneath which sat a plastic bag, in which were several USB sticks. Markova wanted to make sure no one but her would get the data.

Unfortunately for the former FSB and now ROC mastermind, Trevor knew his way around more than just rudimentary explosive devices.

"It's a bomb." The timer reflected six minutes and counting. He'd need every last second to defuse it. "Get out of here, and stay at least one hundred feet away from the house until I come out."

"I'm not leaving you alone, Trevor."

"Get. Out." He needed silence and total concentration to dismantle the deceptively simple bomb Markova had devised. "Take the phone and notify Claudia, Josh and Colt. Now."

Her footsteps sounded but then stopped and came back to him in rapid staccato rhythm. As he stood looking at the killing device, he felt her next to him, her hands lightly on his shoulder as she stretched up and grasped his face in her hands. Their eyes met, and he knew she saw the fear in his gaze. Not of the bomb or injury, but that he might never see her again.

Coral took one second to kiss him, quickly and hard,

before again turning and heading for the exit. This time she ran out of the building.

He hoped like hell that he'd see her again.

No, he would see her again. But first, he had a bomb to defuse.

Coral's fingers shook as she dialed each of the TH contacts and informed them of the situation. Claudia was the most adamant that Coral keep the faith.

"He's an expert at EOD, don't worry." The former Marine's honest assessment of Trevor's talents validated what Coral already knew—her ex was the best in the business as far as being an undercover agent was concerned. He was valued by his peers as well as superiors and subordinates and gave every mission his all.

As much as she knew this, it did nothing to calm the anxiety that had her heart racing and her breathing so shallow she leaned against a pine tree, on the edge of the woods behind the safe house. There was no way of knowing how far along Trevor had gotten with the bomb, no way of predicting if he'd be hurt.

Please, please, don't let him get hurt.

She gritted her teeth against her fear and faced a hard fact—splitting from Trevor hadn't been the worst thing that ever happened to her. Fearing his loss had been her nightmare scenario, whether they were married or divorced.

Coral didn't know what they exactly were right now, but it was in some limbo place between spouse, partner, lover and friend. An intangible space known only to those who've met their soul mate.

Trevor was her soul mate, no question. It didn't

mean they could spend the rest of their lives together. Quite the contrary. It was so painful to live with him knowing he faced death with each case, each time another bad guy popped up on TH's radar. But when faced with the grim alternative, Coral would pick the painful route each time.

Because a life knowing Trevor was forever lost and dead was not her definition of living.

As the minutes counted down on her watch, she estimated Trevor had two more to cut the correct wires and get out of the house. Would he come out in time if he didn't figure out how to beat the bomb?

An owl's hoots sounded, and she wondered briefly if the bird was alerting to a trespasser. Only when a large jackrabbit shot past her, oblivious to her, followed by the dusty sound of the raptor's wings as it took off after its prey, did she allow herself to lean against the pine tree more fully.

"Come on, Trevor." She whispered the prayer. Just as he'd encouraged her when she'd been trapped in the rubble pile, she willed her thoughts to aid his speed and dexterity as he worked over the lethal box.

A bomb. Markova didn't mess around, and Coral had to face the fact that if she'd wanted to kill her, Markova would have. Without compunction. Her gaze on the sliding steel back door, she forced herself to focus on the case. It was the only vestige of sanity she had left.

Markova had left two boxes behind, but no one seemed to have a clue as to where the third item was.

The explosion.

A hole in the ground.

The framework damaged.

If the bang had been because either Markova or one of her thugs was looking for the second or third box, that meant Markova was pretty dang sure she'd buried one of the data containers there. Coral racked her brain for mental images of the barn in its original entirety. The base had been made of limestone boulders and rocks, all found on the property as her ancestors settled in Silver Valley almost three hundred years ago. A wobble of emotion rushed her. It was humbling to know her source of income two centuries later, while not related to the barn's original life and intention, was sustained by property and a building her ancestors had procured and built so long ago.

A large *bang* shook her out of her attempts at patience. Her heart skipped a beat, and she fell to her knees. *No.* The sound of pounding feet sent relief through her. It had been a car door slamming, not an explosion. With a start she realized that Claudia and Colt were running toward her.

"Is he still inside?" Claudia reached her just as she got to her feet.

"Yes. Oh my gosh, I thought that your car door closing was the bomb going off." She sucked in a few deep breaths as Colt and Claudia stood on either side of her, facing the back of the house.

"How much longer?" Colt's voice was low and rugged.

"Maybe a minute." As she said *minute*, her efforts to remain calm extinguished along with the hope that she'd be able to somehow be with Trevor once again. The odds of him surviving this, of letting his determination not get the best of him and leaving the bomb where it lay on the workbench, running out of the house and saving his life…they were all stacked against him. Against her.

Against them.

Tears began to fall down her cheeks, and she let them, not caring what Claudia or Colt saw. It didn't matter. Nothing mattered anymore. Let ROC and Markova take whatever they wanted from her property. What difference did it make?

"Hang on, Coral. He can feel your will." Claudia's admonition jerked her head toward the woman.

"I—"

"She's right. I always feel Claudia's support with me whenever I'm in trouble. Stay focused on Trevor running out that door—" Before Colt finished, the back door slid open and Trevor burst out of the house, bolted over the back deck, rolled onto the ground and rose, running toward them. He held up a sealed plastic bag, and Coral screamed with relief.

"Yes!" She jumped up and began to run to him, but Colt's and Claudia's hands were on her shoulders, holding her back. What the—

"Run! As far away as—"

The rest of Trevor's words were swallowed by the humongous explosion that burst behind him, the sound wave pulsing across the half acre of property and making the trees around them creak with strain.

Coral acted on instinct and covered her head with her arms as she hit the ground, the reverberations of the blast pulsing under and around her. A large form landed on top of her. Trevor.

"We're good, babe." His words, his voice in her ear was all she needed. Trevor was okay.

"We can't stay here any longer." Trevor watched the fire engines put out the raging fire from the safety of the side drive next to the safe house. They stood in a cluster with Colt, Claudia and Josh.

"No." Coral's reply was little more than a whisper. She'd been unusually quiet over the past hour as they ascertained that all of the classified material and equipment in the operations room would be destroyed by the blast, eliminating the need for anyone to go back in and ensure total destruction.

Then they'd called in the fire department, but they'd arranged to have SVFD instead of a more local unit, as there were a couple of trusted TH employees who also happened to be Silver Valley firefighters.

"Where do you want to go? Hershey Lodge?" He tried to lighten the mood. Anything to get her to smile, break out of the place she'd mentally retreated to.

"That's hilarious. I was hoping to stay closer to home, as I have that event in less than two days."

Her wedding gig tomorrow afternoon. He'd forgotten.

"We'll make sure you're there to get the event going and keep it safe, don't worry."

She gave him a knowing smile. "Don't patronize me. There's no way to guarantee the security of my guests. I'm going to have to either move it or cancel last minute."

"I can help with that," Claudia interrupted. "Sorry, I couldn't not overhear you. I have a place, a cabin on a lot of acreage, in the mountains. It'd be only ten minutes' difference for most of your guests, I'm sure. You and Trevor can stay there tonight, see if it works for you." Claudia waved at the safe house. "This place will be back up and running soon enough, but it's too exposed right now."

"I couldn't impose…" Coral began to protest, but Trevor saw her eyes spark again. The tight ball of concern in his chest loosened a fraction. Coral's well-being meant more to him than anything. And being with her seemed to be the only way to manage it. He'd had to face facts as the clock ticked down on the bomb. Only a month ago he'd have pushed it to the utmost limit, risked losing it all, even his own life, to outwit the device.

Instead he'd figured out a way to get the plastic bag from under the bomb and left himself enough time to get out of the house. He'd known that he could live with the destruction, to the tune of millions of dollars, of the TH edifice.

There was no living without Coral or the hope of a future with her.

As he watched her, cold realization dawned. They were never going to have a future as long as Markova and ROC had their targets on each of them. He was tired, bone weary of running from lethal threats.

Trevor wanted to be able to go home at night and be with the woman he loved.

But she'd already watched him leave her. She'd never trust him again.

He didn't know how, but he had to regain her trust.

* * *

Coral stood with Trevor, Josh, Claudia and Colt and knew the catering event would work out if it was meant to. She was too emotionally exhausted to worry about it at the moment. Her mind couldn't let go of the fact that another explosion, clearly the work of Markova, had taken place on her property.

Wasn't losing her barn the first time enough?

"You've been quiet, Coral." Claudia had convinced her to accept the generous gift of her cabin, where Trevor said they were headed as soon as the fire department cleared the building.

"I'm trying to figure out why Anna Markova sent in thugs to blow a hole in the dirt. There's nothing left in the barn, and the foundation has been cleaned up, right down to the original eighteenth-century stones."

"The key is, what was there before January? Before the gala?" Josh had been at the gala with Annie, his fiancée.

A sense of missing something plagued Coral. "I can't put my finger on it, but there's something obvious here." She pictured the driveway, the barn's entrance the night of the gala. The welcome sign that was set on boulders had been blown down, as had all of the entryway decor, from oversize terra-cotta urns that she kept perennials in and had used for several of the ice sculptures that night, to the paver pathway her grandparents had laid down in the 1950s. All destroyed by Markova's vengeful act. "Josh, do you have the photos SVPD sent you?"

"Sure." Josh pressed on his screen and then handed it to her. She blew up the photos, one by one, and settled on the one that showed where the corner of the foundation lay.

"There's nothing left there. She wouldn't have dug under the driveway or path to the main entrance. It'd have been too obvious." Colt shoved his hands in his pockets. They all watched the fire team move methodically around the safe house. The initial fire had been put out, and now all that remained was for them to determine how far-reaching the blast had been. So far it looked like the living area of the safe house remained untouched, just as the kitchen and main bathroom in Coral's farmhouse had been left standing while the rest was totaled—nothing more than a pile of toothpicks.

"No, you're right. She wouldn't have left it there." Coral's gaze hitched on the image of the front face of the foundation. It missed one stone, the stone she'd taken out after the gala to be resurfaced. The stone that she'd decided to have professionally polished for the future unveiling of the new barn. The stone that represented not only her ancestors and their legacy, but hope for her future at the barn. The stone with "1763" chiseled into it. Excitement teased her stomach, and she grabbed Trevor's arm.

"Trevor, the keystone."

"Yeah, what about it?" He was still a bit of a mess from running out of the building before the explosion could have killed him. But even with dust in his hair and his face heavily lined, his eyes sparked with interest.

"It was exactly where the bomb went off. I mean, Markova must have told her men to excavate the place where the keystone was. She doesn't know it's not there, that it was taken out."

"By 'taken out,' do you mean unearthed and put in the pile of rubble that you and Trevor found the lockbox in?" Claudia took Josh's phone from Coral's shaking hands and shared the image with Colt and Josh.

"No, that's just it. The day after the gala, weeks before the construction crews came and did the final demolition, I saw that the keystone was still there and relatively intact. I wanted to keep it that way, but better. It hadn't been polished or revitalized since it'd been laid for the original, smaller barn back in the 1700s."

"So it's not under the ground anymore." Trevor appeared to be putting it all together, just as she had.

"No. I had one of my event crew's brothers, who happens to be an architect, come out and give me suggestions. At the end of the day, we had the help of three guys to dig it up and hoist it onto a flatbed pickup."

"Where did you take it?" Trevor's interest had ignited into the same urgency that was making her tremble with excitement. She'd figured out where the third set of data might be hidden.

"To the headstone manufacturer on the outskirts of town. Henley's."

"Wait—you took it to a cemetery-marker maker?" Josh's confusion made her laugh.

"Of course. They're the experts when it comes to big chunks of granite. And this isn't that big—remember, it had to be manageable to use for a foundation almost three hundred years ago."

"You think Markova hid something under the keystone. That means her thugs probably found it or destroyed it when they blew up that makeshift bomb earlier." Colt didn't mince words.

"No, that's just it. The keystone has always been a family heirloom. It has two spaces carved out inside it to store things. It looks like it's just a layer of mortar to the average eye. But there's no row of continuing bricks to correspond to it—it's faux bricklaying at its best." Coral allowed the laughter to bubble out as she watched the team around her comprehend what she was telling them. "Back in the day, they'd store money, jewelry, wills in the spaces."

"But how would Markova know about these hiding places?" Claudia wasn't sold. "And didn't you notice anything different about the keystone when you moved it?"

"I have the story of the keystone printed on my business brochures, to entice potential clients with the historical significance. It's a family rumor that drafts of the original Declaration of Independence were stored there. I've never confirmed it, though. It's part of the draw of my barn for wedding couples—they love to find a place that's been here as long as Pennsylvania has. As a way of symbolizing that their love will survive the years." A blush rose in her cheeks, and she knew she had to look like a beet as she spoke about everlasting love while her own marriage to Trevor had failed.

But that had been before she really understood all he did, why he was so passionate about his work. Now that she'd experienced the other side of his life, she knew she'd be able to handle him being gone on missions. More significantly, she wanted to be the one at his side.

"The gala detonation didn't take the mortar off?" Colt stood next to Claudia, more readily accepting Coral's story.

"No. I don't know—I wasn't worried about that at the time. There was a lot of dirt frozen to it, and all I wanted was to get it out for cleaning and rehab." She bit her bottom lip. "It was all I had left of the original barn, save for the remaining foundation stones. They're rebuilding all of those, of course, and the keystone's due to go in by the end of next week. That's why no framework has been built over the western portion of the property yet."

She allowed the silence to descend over their Trail Hiker huddle. Coral knew her place; she was but a volunteer in this mess that Markova made. While she was doing her part to the best of her abilities, the next moves weren't up to her.

"What time do they open tomorrow   the grave stone business?" Trevor was the first to break through their resistance.

"Ten." It was now midnight. "I was supposed to stop by this past week to check on the keystone and approve the work they've done, but…it's been a little busy. Could we go there now, open it out of a sense of urgency?"

"Not without a search warrant, and I need time to assemble a SWAT team for backup. Tomorrow morning will have to be soon enough, and it's clear Markova doesn't know you've moved the stone or where it is. Call the owner now," Claudia said. "Tell him not to touch it, to stay away from it. We don't know how it's rigged if she did anything to it. Once we have our team ready, we'll get to the place before they open. Report back to me." Claudia turned to Colt. "I'd say it's time to call it a night."

Colt nodded. "Josh, I'll see you at SVPD tomorrow."

"Coral and I will head to Claudia's for a few hours' sleep." Trevor walked toward their car.

"Hang on, you'll need the key." Claudia handed him their housekey as she and Colt followed him. Josh put his hand on Coral's arm.

"Coral, wait. I want to let you know that Annie and I are amazed at what you've taken on and how you've handled it."

"Thanks. But how much does Annie know?"

"As the SVPD psychologist, enough."

Curiosity piqued, Coral smiled. "She's involved with TH, too, isn't she? No, stop—I don't have a need to know, unless we're going to be working together. And I'm just in this for the short run. It's not like I'm an agent or anything." She laughed, trying to make light of the whole thing. The gravity of their situation needed some levity, and she longed for the days before the gala explosion, before her life and job had imploded.

Josh allowed a small smile but didn't share in her hilarity. "It's not my place to say anything about you and Trevor, or whether you'd be a good agent. I do want to tell you that sometimes the toughest among us are the ones who need an understanding partner."

"You mean, a law enforcement partner." She'd just told him she wasn't an agent. What did Josh not understand about her temporary work with TH and SVPD?

"Whatever it needs to be, Coral. You and Trevor have a shared history, and that's rare nowadays. Annie and I almost blew it when we got our second chance last year. I'd hate to see either you or Trevor lose out on what could be your second chance." He removed his hat and scratched his head. "Heck, I'm sorry, Coral. It's none of my business."

"It's okay. You've known me forever, as has Annie. I trust your judgment. It's a fact, however, that Trevor and I got divorced for a good reason."

But did that reason—his constant absence and her refusal to accept he'd want to do a job like undercover work—hold any longer?

As she followed the rest of the group to the front of the house and got into the car with Trevor, she didn't have an answer. But she knew she wanted to find out.

Would Trevor be willing to try again if he knew she wanted to?

Chapter 15

"What did Josh want to talk to you about?" Trevor drove along the main route to where Claudia's cabin was nestled in the Appalachian Mountains, just south of Silver Valley.

"Uh, he wanted to tell me that he and Annie thought I was doing a good job. You know, handling the barn and my business since the night of the gala." She worried her bottom lip with her pearly teeth, and his tongue burned to do the same.

Stop. He thought that Josh had said something more to her but didn't want to push too far and make Coral shut down. He'd done enough of that when they were married.

"He's right. You've done a remarkable job. I remember how your property was when Aunt Brenda owned it and never imagined anyone would be able to breathe life back into it. You did that, plus so much more." Too tired to ignore the weight of his emotions, he relented. "I'm sorry you had to come back to Silver Valley and rebuild your life on your own, Coral. It's a regret I know I can't change, but I do want you to know that I've thought of you a lot these past three years. About us."

"Do you think you're the only one who's had regrets, Trevor?" She sniffed, and in the darkness he wasn't sure if it was from disgust or the same sadness he was swimming in. Three years of life they couldn't get back, time that could have been used to rebuild their partnership. He wiped his hand over his head.

"No, I know you've done your share of suffering." And it'd all been on him. He could have prevented her heart from breaking if he'd not been so dang selfish. If the ghosts of his past could turn back the clock, he'd go for it. This had to be the explosion talking—the close brush with death.

Or maybe it's time to face the truth that you still love her.

"*Suffering* is a hard word, Trevor. I was miserable, sure, but if I was wallowing in self-pity, that was on me. I was so young, so selfish when we got together. I had no way of understanding what you were dealing with on a daily basis. At least when you were in the Marines, I had the other spouses and command support to rely upon."

"And when I got out, you thought I'd be home more. That we'd have a normal life like all our friends from high school and college."

"Well, yes. When you put it that way." She let out a short laugh. "I was the epitome of naive, wasn't I?"

"We both were."

"You were a lot of things but never ignorant, Trevor. You were the one who had the job with the heavy lifting."

"Hold on there. Just because you weren't in the military or doing the same kind of work I was doesn't make your life and job and less valid."

"But now I know what you do, at least a lot better than I did. Trevor, I was such a jerk! I used to whine and complain about you missing dinner, and you were out facing the worst possible criminals, in terrible situations."

He didn't answer at first, because she was right. "I should have filled you in more. My intent to protect you only ended up hurting both of us."

They were on the winding drive up to the cabin, and he had the headlights on high beam.

"Look at the doe and fawn!" Her voice was infused with pure delight, and he couldn't help but join her as he stopped the car to allow the deer to pass.

"There's bear up here, too. Claudia and Colt tell us stories about how they can't leave anything out on the kitchen counter or they'll have attempted break-ins. One time Colt came downstairs and found two cubs chowing down on a bowl of strawberries."

"Where was the mama bear?"

"On the deck, emptying the bird feeder." They laughed together, and he almost began to cry. He'd missed the sound of their shared laughter more than sex. Well, almost more than the sex.

Lovemaking is more like it.

The drive opened into a large pullout area, the cabin a modest-appearing A-frame.

"That wasn't a long drive." Coral yawned. "Good thing, as I'm beat."

He looked at his watch. They'd been driving for over an hour, but he agreed with Coral. It'd felt more like ten minutes. Time had a way of being so fleeting when it was spent with your favorite person.

"Let's go in."

Within a few minutes, they'd toured the entire cabin, making sure it was free of wildlife as well as any other more unwelcome intruders—like Markova.

"I don't see a security system here." Coral peered around the kitchen.

He laughed. "No, it's not going to be like the safe house. But we weren't followed here, and only TH knows about this cabin. It's where Claudia used to come to regroup before she married Colt."

"They haven't been married that long, then?" Coral's face was a study in noncommittal detachment. He knew her better, though. Underneath her feigned casualness, he sensed she was tossing the same questions around.

Had they made a mistake in divorcing? Could they make a go of it again after this case resolved?

Or was it all an illusion, feelings churned up by the intensity of the last week?

"A few years, tops. They may have been involved longer, but I was working West Coast ops when I first joined TH and only saw Claudia when she came out to California or when I had to check in to headquarters back here."

She stilled. "Have you been back to Silver Valley other than for this op?"

Crap. "Yes. Twice before." And he'd stayed clear of her. Avoided the entire three-mile radius around her property. He'd even stayed an hour away in Lancaster, in an old Amish B&B. "I used my trips back here as retreats, downtime from the undercover work. Until this time, when I came back for you."

"What?"

Ah, hell.

"Yes, it's true, Coral. When I read the reports and found out that Markova was using your property as a hiding place for her goods, I couldn't keep my hands off the op."

"Why didn't you tell me this before, or at least last week?"

"I couldn't. I didn't want to." He blew out a breath, frustrated. "I don't know. What I am sure of is that we're both tired and we've got a big day tomorrow. It's best we get some sleep."

His body longed to take her to the place where he knew she was completely free of any worries, totally involved in his lovemaking.

But not tonight. He had to stay alert to any possible intruders, and she needed rest.

Anna Markova couldn't remember a time she'd been more angry. This was the second pair of ROC castoffs who'd disappointed her. By blowing up the ground next to the barn to enable their digging, all they'd done was alert SVPD and FBI and the entire law enforcement world that she was still desperate to find the data she'd buried before the gala last winter.

They'd found nothing for her, either, and had begged her over their burner phones to help them hide from the local police. If they'd been face-to-face, she would have finished them on the spot. As it was, she'd told them to get out of the state and to never contact her again.

She was leaving ROC, and all she needed was the last set of data from Ivanov's stolen files. Ivanov and his top men were after her now, squeezing her. She didn't think he knew she'd copied his most important information, but the fact that she'd not reported to him since she'd broken out of jail said enough. He had to know she was avoiding him and no doubt suspected her treason. Since she'd gotten out of prison, she'd taken on several different disguises—nothing new to her, but she wanted her freedom from all of this. As soon as she had the money from Ivanov, she'd use one of the dozen or so passports she possessed to go to an overseas plastic surgery clinic and permanently change her looks. There would be no more running, no more scratchy wigs.

First, she had to get the information. She knew that the one place she'd hidden it no longer existed on the property, but there was only one person who knew that area well enough to find it.

Coral Staufer, the event planner that Misha had been watching. Anna had almost panicked when she found out about the most recent bust at the farm property. Until her GPS signal from box two of the safe boxes lit up like New Year's fireworks in Red Square. She'd only put a GPS marker in one box, and the signal had led her to a hole of a house about an hour north of Silver Valley, where she'd found Coral huddled with people she assumed were police and FBI. The box exploded as she'd wired it to, but not before she was able to put eyes on the event planner and the man who'd shadowed her every move since the first time Anna sent men in to find her treasure.

Her data had been destroyed, but she still had a backup option.

The most important part of the data was in the hiding place that had been moved, a large stone she'd discovered when she'd cased the barn before the gala last winter. She hadn't had to drill a hole in it, as she'd found a tiny compartment already built into the rock. Americans had a history of innovation, and the hiding spot made her smile at the time. Her people had been devising clever ways to protect information since the first Tatars crossed the steppe. The keystone's mini safe was rudimentary at best, but it was good enough for her purposes. She'd used industrial-strength adhesive to seal it. The precaution ended up being fortuitous, since she hadn't been able to get the box before the bomb blast she'd triggered during the gala evening.

All she needed now was to get the event planner bitch to lead her to the stone.

A rustling drew her eyes to the back porch of the cabin the couple had spent the night in. The black bear had come out on command, thanks to the fresh birdseed she'd found in the sealed box on the deck and spilled for him. She'd run into the bear last night as she'd camped on the property. Far enough into the woods so that the couple couldn't see her but close enough to know when they came and went. When the bear had rumbled by a few hours ago, she'd regretted not being able to shoot him as her father had taught her at their dacha in Russia. Until she realized she could use the bear to draw the couple out sooner, in case they decided to linger in their sex den.

A smile felt foreign on her face, but she couldn't help it. How fitting that a bear might help her undo her American quarry.

Coral tossed and turned for at least the first hour that she spent between Claudia's guest room sheets. She should have been asleep immediately, but Trevor's words haunted her.

He wrestled with the same thoughts she did. The same possibilities.

But none of it mattered if they didn't get Markova in custody, if the data wasn't in the keystone. That was the only thing that allowed her to drift into sleep. She had to do her part to help save Silver Valley and her business.

If there was any hope for her and Trevor, she had to table it until after the case was closed.

Trevor had assigned them to separate rooms and she didn't argue. They needed to figure out their future after they survived this case.

Loud footfalls woke her from her semislumber, and she wondered who was in her camper. It took her another heartbeat to remember she wasn't at home but in Claudia's cabin. Claudia and Colt. *Trevor.*

A pounding on the other side of her wall woke her

fully and she sat up, listening in the pale dawn light. She got out of bed, in her underwear and T-shirt, and peeked through the bedroom window's curtains. Shock ran over her as she saw a huge shadow moving across the deck, replaced by relief when she recognized a bear. The animal pawed around the deck chairs, its snout poking into every corner. Her heart still pounded, as she'd never been this close to a bear, but she'd take it over Markova or an ROC thug any day.

"Trevor!" She shouted toward the bedroom door in an effort to not startle the animal. The cabin was sturdy, but couldn't bears go through doors and windows?

"I see him." Trevor's shout sounded from outside her room, and she left the window, quickly donning shorts. At least this time they were working together to prevent something fairly normal from happening, instead of fighting off thugs.

She joined him in the kitchen, where he stood by the back door, which opened onto the deck.

"Is there a shotgun in here?" She looked around the cozy but plain kitchen. It boasted the most up-to-date appliances while still maintaining an air of retreat from the everyday.

"We don't need a shotgun unless this bear decides we look good enough to taste." Trevor's amusement laced his voice, and she inwardly balked.

"You're making fun of me."

His gaze never left the bear as his lip curled up, making his dimple appear. She'd almost forgotten about his dimples, how she used to wonder, if they'd had kids, would they have dimples, too?

"Not really—well, okay, yeah, I'm poking a little fun at you." A flash of white as he smiled and offered her a quick glance. "Black bears are cuddle bugs compared to grizzlies. They won't bother you unless they're really hungry, with no other option, or you get between them and their cubs."

"You sound like you've encountered a lot of bears." She walked up next to him and couldn't help but put her hand on his back, and then her arm around his waist. It seemed so natural to stand here next to him and share the moment. His muscles tensed under her fingers, but then he relaxed into the gesture and matched it with his own.

She loved the sense of security that his strength gave her as his arm wrapped around her shoulders, the warmth making a robe or sweatshirt superfluous.

"I've run into a grizzly a time or two." The rumble of his laugh reached the bottom of his rib cage where her hand rested. "Both times weren't a lot of fun. It's impossible to outrun them, so I had to wait and see if they were interested in me or not."

"Were they?"

"No, thank goodness. The first time I was near a stream in Alaska, and the bear was with two cubs, fishing for salmon. Once she had her cubs situated with their lunch, she ignored me and caught her own fish."

"What were you doing in Alaska?" She knew he must have had vacations and fun since the divorce, but it didn't take away the sting of envy that he'd shared a similar moment with anyone else.

"Business stuff, believe it or not."

"I picture Alaska as a huge nature preserve, not a place to track ROC."

He grunted. "I wish it were. Let's just say it's a good place to practice Russian."

The bear was taking its time finishing up the bird-seed, licking any extras from between its claws.

"I can't believe we're this close and it's not both-ered by us." And she couldn't get over how standing like this with Trevor was so fulfilling and soul baring.

As they watched, the bear pivoted and looked straight at them as they stood behind the screen and main doors.

"Don't move." Trevor breathed the words, and she didn't have to hear them to do just that. It was hard not to imprint her emotions onto the bear's face, so expres-sive and full of intelligence as it made eye contact with each of them, sniffed the air as if to smell them through the wall and then ambled down the steps toward the woods. Within seconds it disappeared, swallowed by the trees and ground-level bushes.

"That—that was incredible." Coral wanted to hold on to this forever. The closeness of such primal strength while feeling safe inside with Trevor. She looked up at him only after she was certain they'd seen the last of the bear and was startled to find he'd already been looking at her, watching her reaction.

"You're incredible, Coral." He gently turned her in his arms and embraced her. "This is what matters." His lips came down on hers, and she didn't waste time responding, needing to show him she agreed. What-ever they decided next, in this moment, this kiss, she was all in.

"What time is it?" She asked the question against his lips, half-afraid of the answer.

"It's…" He looked at his watch and then lifted his head. "Dang. We have to be at the granite works in twenty minutes. Claudia texted and thinks we need to go in now, before the owner shows up for business hours." He looked at her. "I wanted to talk to you before we do this again, anyway, Coral."

"Wait—don't. I know what you're going to say."

"No, I don't think you do." His enigmatic expression made swirls of anticipation leap in her belly while her mind tried valiantly to shut the hope down. She couldn't handle losing Trevor again.

Maybe you never lost him.

"I'm afraid, Trevor." There. She'd said it.

"Babe, you're not alone. I'm scared, too."

"You are?"

"Dang straight." He traced her cheek with his finger. "We were so young before, and we never gave ourselves a chance to work things out. This last week, and the months before when I knew I was heading back here, to be near you, have made me see what I hope the truth for us is."

"Me, too."

"But we can't take the time we need to hash this out right now."

She nodded. "I know. We have the case to solve."

"It's solved as far as I'm concerned. We need to get the remaining data, yes, and get Markova and any of her thugs locked up. But we've done most of the heavy lifting."

"I thought you said a case isn't closed until the last

criminal is incarcerated." Or dead, but she didn't want to say that aloud.

"The last criminal in this case is Dima Ivanov, the head of the East Coast ROC. There's a bigger net casting out for him, and our job is to get the rest of Markova's stolen data so that TH and FBI can cinch the closure. Let's go."

They grabbed bananas and poured coffee into to-go cups they found next to the single-serving machine. Claudia and Colt had quite the setup, and with a hard pang, Coral realized she wanted this, too. A partnership with the man she loved, in all ways. Not that she thought of herself as an agent, but she liked the challenge of solving the case, knowing that she was in step with Trevor.

"What are we going to do if the owner isn't there?" She balanced a bag of frozen muffins she'd found in the freezer and her coffee cup as they walked down the gravel driveway to the car. The warm morning would thaw the muffins in a few minutes. The air was heavy with summer humidity, but for once she didn't mind the overbearing heat. She was with Trevor, and the glimmer of possibility that this could be the new normal for her—being beside him each day—made her steps light, her load not as overwhelming.

"We have means to access your keystone without anyone there. The team will already have the door open for us." He looked at her over the car's top as he set his cup on it and unlocked the doors.

"I'm not sure—" Her concerns about breaking and entering were halted as the sound of gunfire followed by the ping of bullets against the car had her reacting as trained. Without thought and on pure instinct she was on her belly, peering under the car toward Trevor.

"Get around the car, now!" She didn't need his shouts to move across the ground, wincing as bullets flew, ricocheting off the metal body and sending up dust clouds from the ground where they hit.

Please, please, please. She heard her mind scream the mantra but had to detach from it, had to let her body do what she'd learned and what Trevor told her to do.

Their lives depended on it.

Chapter 16

Coral ran around the vehicle and came up into a crouch behind a wheel, mimicking what Trevor was doing.

"Here." He slapped a .45 into her hand, and she held it pointed up, away from him but ready to fire at the shooter. "Cover me while I get the rifles out of the trunk."

Without waiting for her reply, he quickly moved to the back of the vehicle and used the key fob to pop the trunk. As soon as the lid sounded, a flurry of gunshots hit the lid, the side of the car, narrowly missing Trevor as he ducked.

"I said cover me!"

"Okay, okay!" She looked to where the shots were coming from and saw the end of a rifle around the back of the cabin. The shooter had been waiting for them to leave. Cold dread poured over her, but she had to fight it, had to protect Trevor. Carefully aiming, she fired off a shot, hitting the corner of the cabin and forcing the rifle snout out of sight.

Take that.

Trevor retrieved their two rifles and tossed her one before they both knelt behind the car again. Unlike Aunt Brenda's rustic hunting rifle, there was nothing vintage about these state-of-the-art weapons.

The bullets stopped, and Coral looked at Trevor for guidance. "Do you think they saw you get these rifles out of the trunk?"

"Maybe." Trevor kept his weapon aimed at the woods as he spoke, his eye in the scope. "We'll give it a few more minutes."

"They have to know they're no match for us." Coral didn't mean the words in an arrogant matter. It was simple math—two shooters to one.

"If it's Markova out there, superior firepower means nothing. She's an expert sniper."

Coral allowed his words to sink in and mentally crossed her fingers that if it was Markova, she'd opted to leave the scene.

After five minutes of complete silence and no sign of the shooter, Trevor's hand grasped her shoulder. "Let's get in the car and go. You drive."

She complied, sliding into the front seat while keeping her head down after Trevor did the same in the back seat. Only after she turned the key and had to step on the gas did she raise her head.

Two shots rang out, and she instinctively ducked but kept driving. She had to get them out of here.

The car shook violently and leaned to the right, in the direction of the shots fired.

"Dang it, she's hit the tires." Trevor issued answering shots from the back seat, through the half-lowered rear passenger window, but it didn't matter.

They weren't going anywhere.

Panic fluttered along the edges of Coral's awareness. "What are we going to do?" She felt in her pockets, looked around the car interior. "I don't have my phone—I left it inside."

"Damn it. I dropped mine." Trevor's clipped reply told her everything. They were sitting ducks.

"We have to get out of this car and make a run for it, Trevor."

"I have a better idea." He spoke from the back seat, and she remained slumped down in the driver's seat. "We're going to get out and run back toward the house. Zigzag the entire way until you hit the building. We can't go back in—the chance of being trapped is too great. We'll use the cabin as our shield until we can make a break for the warehouse we passed on the way in. It's less than one hundred yards through the woods on the east side of the property. There's a clear path."

"A warehouse? What, so that Markova or whoever's out there can follow us and shoot us in the back?"

"She probably doesn't know about the other building. I'm sure she followed us here."

"You said you weren't followed!"

"I'm not perfect, and we were spent last night. I might have missed something."

Was this her ex, the man who never admitted wrongdoing?

"I don't want to bleed out in the middle of the woods from ROC bullets, Trevor."

"We're both going to die in this vehicle if we don't move." The urgency in his voice convinced her to trust him.

Trevor considered their options—with two blown tires and Markova coming for them and probably bringing in reinforcements, there was only one.

The warehouse was a makeshift airplane hangar, and the back of it opened onto an airstrip the perfect size for the Cessna 150 that Claudia kept there. She and Colt used it for quick overnights to the shore, and Claudia had taught Colt to fly.

It was also a backup escape that the couple kept, knowing that their business sometimes attracted unsavory types.

"What's in the warehouse that's going to help us, Trevor? Shouldn't we head down the drive toward the main road?"

"There's an airplane there. We have a better chance of getting out of here alive if we make it to the warehouse than back in the cabin. I know her methods—she's already made our vehicle useless." The flat tires made that obvious. Two more shots hit the car, and he opened the door behind hers for extra shielding. "Let's move, now."

They didn't exchange any further words, and he had to trust that Coral would work alongside him without hesitation. It was their only chance to get out alive.

The gravel was too noisy under his feet, and he hated the several steps they were both completely ex-

posed to the shooter. He knew it had to be Markova—
she was the only one capable of following him without
his knowledge. The expert shots at the tires validated
his suspicion.

As they both zigzagged across the short open space,
he was impressed with how Coral not only kept up with
him but edged ahead, reaching the safety of the cabin
wall right before he did.

She flattened herself against the wall, rifle across
her shoulder, aiming at the back of the house, ready
to fire as needed.

"Now where do we go?"

"To the other edge of the house, then through about
ten yards of trees. It's meant to look like we're surrounded by forest, but there's a clearing. Wait for me to
give the signal, then run." He left her then and headed
for the opposite end of the cabin to clear the area they
had to get through.

He carefully crept around the building, muzzle
first, staying steady and making every move delib-
erate. Sweat poured from his temples as the morning
sun heated the hazy air to sweltering, and he blinked
perspiration from his eyes.

A round of rapid fire burst from the trees, and he
jumped back just as several chips of wood flew from
the building's corner.

As soon as the barrage stopped, he quickly retraced
his steps and shot up the entire forest in front of him,
spraying bullets across the trees. Whoever the sniper
was, they were lying flat to avoid his assault. Which
put them at a visual disadvantage.

He signaled Coral, and as soon as she was even with

the clearing, he began to fire into the woods, laying down cover for her to run. Only after she disappeared did he take off and follow her, his weapon ready to fire again.

At least he'd gotten Coral through the worst of it. All he had to do was join her, and they'd have a shot at getting out of here alive.

Coral ran through the thick forest layer, and just when she began to think that Trevor was wrong and had led them deeper into the woodland darkness, away from hope, the path opened into an area where she located the warehouse.

It was barely the size of a garage but otherwise appeared like any other storage building. Corrugated steel walls and a flat rooftop were what she noticed but didn't dwell on. They had to make it to the building in order to call for help.

She ran through several inches of dried pine needles to the storage facility, then turned the corner farthest from where the shots had come from and ran up to the other side.

Where she stopped midstride at the site of a short runway.

A runway.

She turned back to the building and saw the garage doors across the front, the small side entryway. Wasting no time, she tugged open the metal door and entered a tiny office area, which led to the main space.

A Cessna was parked in the middle of the room. It was the same model she'd learned to fly with, and she wanted to shout with relief. She could get them out of here with little trouble.

As long as there was fuel and they could get the garage door open.

She turned back to the office to find the phone just as Trevor burst through the door. The receiver in her hands, her fingers trembled over the numbers. "Do I call 9-1-1 or TH?"

"She's right behind us. Come on." Trevor grabbed her upper arm, and as they ran back into the storage bay, she saw him reach up to a hook over the threshold.

The keys.

Quickly she yanked the chocks from under the wheels.

"I haven't flown in months." Her declaration was punctuated by her gasps. Climbing into the cockpit seemed natural, though, as did taking the keys from Trevor once he was in the passenger side.

"You're still better than me."

She knew this to be true. Trevor hadn't had a pilot's license when she'd been with him, had never shown an interest in anything but serving the Marines as intelligence.

"Where's the door opener? It has to be in here." She groped around in the dim interior.

"Start the engine. I have the remote for the door. We'll go—"

"Stop!"

Horror froze Coral in place as she heard the yell, then recognized Anna Markova running through the office doorway. It was the same woman from the parking garage. Coral had read her file while at TH and memorized the woman's features. They appeared more stark, far more frightening in person than they had on the dossier.

"Start the engine!"

Coral saw Markova through the office door window that Markova was trying to open the door into the warehouse that Trevor had locked behind them. But she didn't fire. Yet.

It took a shaky few seconds, but the propeller began to spin, and the fuselage shook.

"When I get the door open, you have to get us out of here as quickly as possible."

"Got it." She jammed on the headset and adjusted her seat belt. "Let's go."

Trevor aimed the remote, and the door spooled open, gliding to the left as it let in the daylight an inch at a time. Coral's awareness flipped into slow motion as she willed the hangar door to open faster.

The roar of the small engine drowned out any other noise, but she saw Markova take a chair to the office door's window, saw huge shards of glass fall onto the cement floor.

Please, please, please.

Finally the space was wide enough, and she pushed the stick, moving the plane forward with an initial jerk. With no further thought, she acted on pure instinct and shoved the stick as far as she dared, taking them to maximum velocity before the wings caught the air and they had liftoff.

"You're doing it! Way to go." Trevor shifted in his seat and looked out his passenger-side window. All Coral saw was his back, as she couldn't look any farther to her right—she had to steer the plane free of the treetops.

"We lost her! Now she's trying to shoot at us again."

He looked at her. "Did you talk about evasive maneuvers during the Trail Hiker training?"

"We did." Before he questioned her further, she'd already begun to change direction, make her profile as tiny as possible and therefore impossible for Markova to shoot her down.

"Good job." He leaned back in his seat and looked at her with wonder. "You did it."

"No, Trevor, we did it." She made out a familiar aviation radio tower. "Where to? I haven't filed a flight plan." She grinned at him, her fear wiped away by the jubilation of not only evading a huntress like Markova but because she was thrilled to be in the air again.

"You don't need to. I'll radio in to TH if you'll get us to the community landing strip." He referred to Silver Valley Municipal Airport.

"On our way."

As she went through the checklists she'd memorized during flight training years earlier, she was struck again by how natural this felt. They'd just been attacked and tracked down by one of the most lethal women on the planet. And yet they'd survived. Together.

"We could have made it out on two flat tires if we had to." She knew they were safer up in the air, but she wanted to know Trevor's decision process.

"Markova's got her own vehicle, if not right around here then close enough to get to it and catch up to a severely impaired car. We really didn't have a choice, not if we wanted to get out of there alive and not have her able to follow us."

"It bothers you that she followed you last night, doesn't it?"

He shook his head. "Dang right. I'm falling down on my job lately."

"Because I'm a distraction."

"No, don't put this on you. It's my problem. The fact is I've been working undercover for a long time with few breaks. Too long."

"Sounds like you need one—a break."

He didn't answer, and she let it go. Her very limited insight into the kinds of operations he did was enough to know that no human being could be expected to go full throttle for an indeterminate time. Trevor was going to have to take some time off, in her opinion.

"It's hard for you to not tell me your thoughts, isn't it?" His teasing tone reassured her that no one knew her as well as he did.

"Sometimes." Trevor wasn't the only one who could keep his private musings close to his vest.

She knew they needed to finish their conversation from earlier, but whether because of her fear that their time together wouldn't end as happily as she envisioned, or from her concerns that they were doing so well right now only because they were in Markova's crosshairs and had no other choice, she didn't know.

This was the hardest place to live. Knowing that all she'd only just discovered with Trevor could be gone with one well-aimed bullet.

Trevor was in awe of Coral's abilities as she flew them back into Silver Valley and landed the plane on the town's airport runway. It was much larger than the tiny strip at Claudia and Colt's cabin, and she had little problem making the touchdown smooth.

"You'd think you were the one with the military training." Trevor's admiration warmed her, but she fought it, not wanting to get used to his constant praise and approval.

"You can teach anyone to fly, really." She taxied up to a row of similarly sized aircraft and shut the prop down. "I've been wanting to get back in the air but had no idea when the opportunity would pop. This is quite the surprise."

"You're full of surprises, Coral Bell."

She took off her headset and turned to him. "Trevor, about that—you were going to say something earlier, in the kitchen."

"You mean before we were shot at and then had our tires blown out and, oh yeah, before we were followed out to the hangar and almost hijacked by Markova?"

"Trevor, stop it. You know what I mean."

"I do." He unbuckled his seat belt. "I don't think this is where we need to have the conversation, either. Claudia and Colt are going to be pulling up in front of the office here within two minutes."

"They're going with us to the granite expert's?"

He shook his head. "Doubtful. They've got half a dozen other ROC-related ops simmering. More like they're checking in on us, making sure we're okay. They'll have an extra car for us to use."

As they deplaned they were met planeside by Colt. It should have surprised or frightened her how closely TH followed them once they were in contact from the plane, but at this point Coral found it comforting.

"Claudia and I have a vehicle out front for you. Go to the granite facility as we planned and report in as soon as you have the stone. We were ready to do this ourselves, but Claudia thinks you'll have a better chance of knowing what to look for." He spoke to both Coral and Trevor, as if he met couples escaping from a sniper every day. "We're canvassing the land around the cabin. We'll have Markova in custody in no time."

"You sound confident." Trevor didn't look convinced.

"She's running out of options." Colt's mouth was a grim line as he handed Trevor the car keys.

"Thanks." Trevor looked at Coral and nodded. "Next stop."

Coral followed him out through the hangar and to where two SUVs were parked side by side. Claudia was in the driver's seat of one and rolled down her window. Colt walked around and got into the passenger seat.

"You two okay?" Claudia looked as strong as always, and Coral wondered if the woman had slept at all. Running an organization as critical and far-reaching as Trail Hikers had to be a strain, and yet the former Marine never exuded anything less than total confidence in her people and their mission.

"I'm good," Coral answered.

"How are you, Trevor?"

"Fine. Thanking our stars that Coral knew how to fly your plane."

"Wait—I didn't even refuel it or do a postflight." Coral knew they were in a hurry, but she'd flown Claudia's plane without a second thought during the heat of the moment. "Thank you so much for having it ready to go."

"It's how we always keep things—force of habit."

Claudia's quick smile let Coral know that she needn't worry about leaving the plane as it was. The mission came first. "Glad you enjoyed your flight. Do you think this vehicle can handle the weight of your keystone?" Claudia motioned at the car Trevor and she were going to use.

"No, definitely not. The keystone needed a commercial pickup and a lift. But that's not important—I can open up the hidden compartment with a chisel and hammer. We won't have to move the stone."

"All right, then. Let us know as soon as you have any more information. SWAT is standing by." Claudia rolled up her window and was backing out of her space before Coral had a chance to blink.

"Claudia's a mission-oriented person." Trevor had his hand on her shoulder. "C'mon, let's get this over with. Then we'll talk."

Coral put her rifle in the back seat before she got into the passenger seat. As Trevor settled into the driver's side, she reached over and grasped his hand. "Trevor, what if we don't get a chance to talk?"

He stilled and his gaze met hers. "We're going to have all the time we need, babe. As soon as we finish up this job." He leaned over and gave her a firm kiss that made her lips tingle. The extra sizzle wasn't from the sexual heat they shared, but from the promise of what might come.

As Trevor drove them to the granite shop, she licked her lips and let the sensation settle over her. Trevor's kiss had tasted of hope.

Chapter 17

Trevor's gut warred with his mind the entire drive to the headstone shop. Claudia was rarely wrong, nor was Colt. If they thought Markova was going to be caught again, he believed them. But he also knew that a former FSB agent was a formidable foe. One who wouldn't go down without a brutal fight.

He reconciled his concern to being so close to working things out with Coral. Finally he'd seen the sliver of light that might be the chance he had to tell her what a fool he'd been for leaving their marriage. He could have backed off on his undercover work or let her in on more of what he did. It wasn't his job to protect her, not from who he was as a person. He'd failed her by not sharing his thoughts and how rough his work was with her. OPSEC aside, as his spouse and partner, she'd deserved more than he'd given her.

"It's there, on the left." Coral spoke for the first time in the ten-minute drive. He figured she'd been sorting through her emotions, too. Did she think he was going to leave her again, let what they'd found again with one another go so easily?

There was no time to contemplate their future after he parked the car. They entered the shop and looked around.

"Back there is the actual storage facility." Coral pointed to a rear door.

Trevor followed Coral through the back to a long room—another building, really—that he hadn't noticed from the road.

"Good thing I've got you here, to make it so easy to find."

"TH helped us by unlocking the shop and making sure the owner isn't here. And I know you'll keep me safe." She smiled.

He loved this, the way they fit together so perfectly, and for once he wasn't thinking about the physical way they connected. Their sexual bond was as incredible as it was because of this—the way they were attuned to one another's intuition. He physically felt more alive around Coral.

He never wanted to live without her again. But he had to save his proclamations and newfound enlightenment for after this op.

Soon.

He followed her into a dusty space that appeared stuffed to the gills with tombstones. As they meandered through the rows of granite blocks, he noted a few tall monuments in the back and a fountain or two.

"What am I looking for?" He wanted to help her. The sooner they found the keystone, the quicker they'd be able to wrap this up. His gut was firing again, and he didn't like the close confines of the workshop.

"It's about two feet tall and as wide. Nothing like these polished markers." She walked down one aisle and he the other.

Trevor wasn't surprised that they couldn't find it right away. The place was filled with stone objects of all shapes and sizes. The first row or two were neat and had the finished items, while the items were less organized and closer together as they walked farther back. The building seemed much longer and narrower than it appeared from the front. Its narrowness explained why he hadn't noticed it from the road.

"There it is." Coral sprang forward to a lump of what looked like concrete but had to be limestone if it was the original keystone from 1763. He opened his mouth to tell her to be careful—Markova may have rigged the keystone as readily as she had the second safe box. But a blinding pain seared through his head, and his world went dark.

Coral's relief at finding the stone intact rushed through her, spurring her on.

"Let me check it out." She spoke to Trevor but her focus was completely on the marker. She ran her fingers over the surface, around to the side opposite of where "1763" was chiseled. The rough edges gave way to a smoother, more contemporary-feeling substance.

Bingo.

"It's sealed where the compartment is." Trevor had

been correct—Markova must have put something in the stone and then, knowing she was going to blow up the barn, covered it with a resilient caulking or adhesive of some kind.

Expecting Trevor to tell her to be careful, she let out a chuckle. "Don't worry, I'm not going to move it. There's always the possibility of explosives. We don't want to bring this building down, too." But as she spoke, she heard a loud *thud*, and her cautious jubilation swirled into cold, hard dread.

"Trevor?" She turned, intending to meet his gaze, to see his eyes with the warmth she believed was solely for her. Instead she met the cold arctic-blue glare of Markova, her short pixie-style hair dark as night, holding an AR-15 rifle pointed directly where Trevor lay in a heap, his head under the barrel of the deadly weapon.

"Trevor's skull is going to explode into a bloody mess if you make one move that I don't order you to." The woman's voice was almost congenial, and if Coral wasn't looking at the lifeless form of the love of her life on the concrete floor, she'd not believe the horror the woman had set in motion.

"What did you do to him? Trevor!" She couldn't stop the scream from erupting, and the only thing holding her feet in place was the threat of the shot by the evil woman. Coral knew it was Anna Markova—she was dressed like a fast food server and a blond wig was at her feet. No longer needed the disguise—did that mean she was going to kill both of them?

Coral knew she had to stall. Her hands itched for the weapons in the back of the SUV. Weapons they never should have left there, but it wasn't normal to walk into a local Silver Valley business with rifles in hand.

Why was her mind racing like this?

There's no telling how the stress will hit you.

Trevor's words stilled her, centered her. She was only a wannabe TH agent, but she was all Trevor had right now.

Coral had to save them both.

"You're coming with me." Markova spoke with icy calm. Coral knew the woman could have already killed her if she wanted to. Trevor's chest was moving, so despite the deathly pallor of his skin, she clung to the fact that he was still alive.

"Why? You have what you want. Take the stone and go." Coral wasn't running anymore. She belonged next to Trevor no matter the consequences.

"Sit down next to your lover and keep your mouth shut or I'll put a bullet through each of your skulls. I'll kill him first, to give you the extra pain before you leave the world." Markova motioned her pistol to the spot between Trevor and a huge tombstone. Coral sat, the cold floor echoing the chilling fear that pumped through her. She should have ignored Trevor and told him how she felt in the plane. Or when they were being shot at, in the car. Any time would have been good. Now he might never wake up, or they could both be dead before she had a chance to ever tell him what he deserved to hear.

He was her everything.

Markova paid no more attention to her or Trevor as she knelt by the stone and pulled a long chisel out of the black duffel Coral hadn't noticed. The woman was deft as she pounded and chipped away at what Coral now realized was a ridge of newer material, not the centuries-old mortar she'd mistaken it for when she'd had the keystone moved here for repair.

Would it have made any difference if she'd questioned the vein that ran through the rock back in March? No one had known Markova had hidden Ivanov's most valuable information yet.

With Markova's gaze averted toward the other side of the stone, Coral took the risk to look at Trevor. His breathing appeared normal, and his eyelids were twitching. If he wasn't already conscious, he would be soon.

Could she help them both get out of here, away from Markova? Markova was only keeping them alive until she had her data in hand.

She slowly moved her hand to cover his and squeezed. And almost jumped when he responded with his own squeeze. Careful to make sure Markova didn't notice, she looked at Trevor's eyes, which were open. She pressed her finger to her lips, the universal sign for "be quiet."

"Don't even think about moving from where you are." Markova's warning made Coral fake a cough into her hand to cover for the sign language she'd aimed at Trevor.

"Let us go. You don't need us."

"I decide what I need or not." Markova grunted as she used more force to pry the adhesive from the rock's crevice. Her gloved hands moved with purpose, and even though her weapon was on the floor, Coral knew

Markova's reflexes were lethal. She had to come up with something other than turning the murderer's gun on her.

"What's in the rock that you want so badly?"

"Like you don't know." Markova paused and looked at her. Coral had never seen such soulless eyes before. The woman had to be some kind of sociopath to kill as many as she reportedly had. For the former FSB agent all that mattered was the mission and saving her own hide.

"I don't."

"You're the fool for getting wrapped up in this again, after your little party blew up last winter." Markova's lip was lifted on one side in a sneer that rivaled any cartoon villain's. "That would be enough warning for a normal person to stay away from their property."

"Why shouldn't I rebuild?" She had to keep Markova talking long enough to figure out how to get her and Trevor out of here, or at least save Trevor's life.

"Please. You can't help yourself. All of you Americans suffer from a disease of not letting go."

"Some call that resilience." Coral tried to make out what Markova was withdrawing from the small opening she'd scratched into the limestone. Markova ignored her as she lifted her hand and peered at the small object between her slim fingers. She expected another USB stick. To her surprise what Markova withdrew was much larger, about the size of a deck of cards.

It was a portable disk drive. She recognized the logo on the side as the same type she used for her business. Markova's smile of triumph made Coral want to throw up. Now that the woman had her objective, there was little time to try to outwit her.

Something primal came to life in Coral. She might not stand a chance against the former FSB agent who'd been trained by retired KGB operatives, but she wasn't going to die without a fight, either. With a last quick squeeze of Trevor's hand, she gave him a wink and moved onto her knees.

"What do you think you're doing, Anna?" The rich, heavily accented baritone came from behind Markova. Markova's eyes widened fractionally before she licked her lips and turned to face the man.

"Dima. What are you doing here?" Markova's use of the Russian first name was like a slap of cold air. Dima Ivanov had come here, personally, to track down Markova?

It only meant one thing. He was going to kill Markova. Maybe he hadn't seen Coral or Trevor yet, but they were toast the minute he was aware of them or had finished off Markova.

A long, low laugh that was anything but humorous rolled across the workshop, bouncing off the stone sculptures. Coral swore she heard death in the man's voice. "Oh, Anna, it's a delight to see you struggle so valiantly."

Coral looked at Trevor, who was moving into a sitting position very slowly, now that Markova's back was to them. Blood dripped down the side of his face, and she gave him a quick shake of her head. Mouthing the words *don't move!* did nothing. Trevor's grace was remarkable considering his head injury.

"Dima, listen, I've had a few hiccups as they say

here, but I just had two things to take care of, and then I was coming to report to you." Coral noticed that Markova had her hands behind her back, one with the handgun and the other holding the portable hard drive. If she could have told Markova to keep the man busy in conversation, she would have. The longer they spoke and Markova's back was to her and Trevor, the better.

"First you get yourself locked up in the county jail. Then you miraculously escape, when I specifically told you to wait for my lawyers to do the job for you. You draw too much attention to my operations, Anna. My people are supposed to make my job easier. You've done anything but."

"I had to get out sooner, Dima. There's important information that I safeguarded for you."

Ivanov's evil laugh sounded strained. "Your task had nothing to do with information, Anna. You're supposed to be keeping my heroin flowing through the Cumberland and Susquehanna Valleys. Instead you get locked up and then draw more attention to us by breaking out."

Coral moved to crouch behind the tombstone in between her and Markova, and hopefully Ivanov's out of line of fire. There was no doubt Ivanov had come prepared to kill.

The click of a gun safety sounded, and Markova's hand twitched on her weapon.

Coral sized up the tall monument to Markova's right, just behind the woman. It was a long shot, but if she hit it at the right angle, there was a chance she'd topple it onto Markova. It might not kill the woman, but it would stop her and give Coral the time she needed to get her and Trevor out of harm's way. But her timing had to be perfect, because Ivanov would either take off or kill all three of them and risk being caught.

"Dima, come on, you know me. I'm your most trusted employee." Markova still sounded like the hardened agent she was, and she was thoroughly distracted by Ivanov. Coral knew in that moment that it was go time.

She turned back to make eye contact with Trevor, to try to communicate what she planned to do, but where he'd sat seconds before was empty. Coral was alone with only a few hunks of granite between her and the ROC's most lethal persons.

A movement in her peripheral vision revealed that Trevor was at the other end of the building, circling around from where Ivanov's voice sounded. A flash of one of her TH classes reminded her of this very scenario. While she couldn't read Trevor's mind, she trusted that he was going with the best protocol for this situation. She had no choice but to trust that he'd take care of Ivanov.

Eliminating the threat from Markova was up to her.

"Don't make this harder on yourself, Anna. Give me the little treasure you just took out of that rock or I'll put one of my golden bullets through your skull."

Coral had read about the golden bullets in the TH intel reports. Ivanov wanted everyone, including LEA, to know he'd killed Markova if he was going to leave the signature piece in her head. She had no desire to have that kind of gold in her body, though. Or Trevor's.

When Markova's arm moved to use her weapon, Coral took it as her signal to proceed. She leaped up and ran as fast as she could toward the tall monument, on the diagonal.

Markova's face turned toward her, but not before Coral tackled the column with her right shoulder, pretending it was one of the larger agents she'd practiced with. Fortunately for her, the monument hadn't been completely fused together, so the large square base was separate from the obelisk, which was separate from the smallish ball atop it. The ball crashed to the ground first, cracking into several pieces.

Shots rang out, and she expected to feel a hit as she watched the obelisk topple onto Markova, who moved to evade the stone but was stopped by a shot. Blood spurted from Markova's shoulder, and she fell to the ground a split second before the column of granite crashed onto her. The weight of the stone held Markova in place, arms splayed and both hands empty. Coral ignored the threat of being shot by Ivanov and ran the few steps to retrieve the hard drive and handgun.

As Coral shoved the drive in her back pocket, she didn't allow herself to look at Markova's face, to worry if she was still alive or not. Getting to Trevor was her focus.

From the sounds of scuffling in the back of the room, Trevor had engaged Ivanov. Fear sprang anew, the cold dread pushing against her exultation that she'd neutralized Markova.

A gunshot rang out, followed by a guttural grunt of pain. The voice was Trevor's.

Trevor.

The next seconds turned into a blur of gunfire, footsteps, sirens and crashing glass. Coral ran forward and aimed Markova's pistol at the heart of a man who stood over Trevor, pointing his weapon at Trevor's head. Trevor was prone on the ground, blood seeping out of the back of his skull. Coral couldn't determine if it was from his head injury or if Ivanov had shot him in the head. With a cold determination she'd never experienced before, she raised the weapon and fired.

Ivanov anticipated her and was already behind a large headstone as he returned fire. Coral dived behind a monument, firing at the assassin as she hit the ground. Bullets ricocheted off all of the stone surfaces until there was a pause in Ivanov's shots. Her ears strained for the next sound he'd make—would he come up to her here, try to shoot her point-blank?

Soft footsteps followed by the sound of shattering glass was the last she heard of Ivanov. He'd jumped out of a large back window, and when she ran after him, he disappeared behind into a storage facility that abutted the monument shop's property. Confident that SVPD could track him down in the enclosed lot with row after row of storage garages, she ran over to Trevor.

"Trevor!" She put her head on the floor next to his, praying he was still here. Because if Trevor had died, her world, her life was over.

His eyes were tightly closed, but his lips moved. "Help me turn over."

"Thank goodness, oh my gosh—" She kissed his cheek, felt along his back and sides for obvious injuries. "Where did he shoot you?"

"He didn't. He just missed my foot, but I pretended he'd hit me." Trevor had his arms under his chest and was pushing himself up. "It's just hard to move with this pounding headache." As he righted into a sitting position, she saw the blood on the back of his head came from the same temple injury he'd sustained earlier.

"Trevor, I need you to do something for me." She had to get them both out of here—there was no telling if Markova had left another surprise explosive for them in the keystone.

"Anything." He groaned the word out, and she knew he was in excruciating pain. But he was conscious and mobile, two things that she desperately needed.

"Keep your eyes on me. Don't hold your head. I've got this."

He looked at her, and she saw the comprehension dawn. "I'm bleeding all over the place, aren't I?"

"Shh, don't go there. Follow me." She grasped his hands and helped him to his feet as she got to hers.

"Markova—what did you do to her?" His gaze was locked on hers, and she sidestepped them down the row of stones toward the closest exit. There was no way they'd be able to climb out of the window Ivanov had so adeptly bounded from. Time felt like gelatin as her feet didn't move fast enough in response to her mind's screams to get the heck out of the building *now*.

"She's going to face consequences like never before. I don't think we have to worry about her going anywhere, if she's still alive." Imagining the woman being lost to the impending explosion, she cast a quick look at the toppled monument. Where Markova had lain only moments earlier.

The spot was empty, and footprints in the dusty mess led to the window Ivanov had smashed through.

It wasn't the outcome she'd wanted, but Coral was focused on saving Trevor at this point.

Without telling Trevor what she knew, she kept their momentum toward the door. Wailing sirens and the sound of a helicopter's blades gave her hope that help was at hand—all she had to do was get them out of here.

Chapter 18

"They both got out through the back window, the large one. I saw Ivanov run into the storage center." Trevor watched Coral report to Claudia, surrounded by Colt, Josh and several other SVPD officers. The county EOD team had swarmed the building as soon as he and Coral emerged, and so far there hadn't been an explosion. Trevor was on a gurney positioned outside the estimated blast radius, being triaged by EMTs. Coral held his hand tight.

"Both Markova and Ivanov were in the workshop with you?" Claudia's tense tone told Trevor all he needed to know. The two nemeses had escaped.

Coral nodded, biting her lower lip. He wished he wasn't such a dang weakling when it came to the sight of his blood. If he hadn't listened to her and followed her out of the building, eyes on her, he'd have risked both of them being blown up.

"But I have what matters, I think." She reached behind her and pulled the disc drive from her back pocket. "Now we have all three parts of the puzzle, right?"

Colt's vigorous nod and the way he grasped Coral's shoulder was as effusive as Trevor had ever seen the man. "Good job. Excellent."

"I'll take that." Claudia smiled and handed the object to Josh, who gave Trevor a quick nod before disappearing.

"So I didn't totally screw up by not getting Markova? I really thought I'd killed her with that small obelisk." Trevor immediately looked at her shoulder, where he'd watched her make contact with the rock.

"That had to weigh at least a couple hundred pounds. You're a tough one, Coral Bell." As the endearment left his lips, he saw Claudia's brow raise, heard Colt's soft chuckle. They probably thought all was well now, that he and Coral would patch things up and reunite.

No such luck. He'd failed to keep her safe from near disaster each step of the way. While Coral had added skills she'd learned from TH, it was as if he'd forgotten all of his.

"You two make a great team. That was incredibly quick thinking on your part to fly out of our cabin property." Claudia nodded at Colt. "We wouldn't have done it any differently."

"You wouldn't have allowed Markova to follow you there in the first place." Trevor felt like a man giving his last confession. "And you wouldn't have allowed

Ivanov or Markova to get off any shots in the workshop."

"That's absolutely not true, Trevor. We've each had ops together and individually where it was impossible to decide which action was best." Colt was having none of Trevor's self-deprecation.

"I'm the one who messed up. If I'd been able to stop Markova at the hospital, or moved on her sooner, we'd have both of them in custody." Coral turned to Claudia. "Are Trevor and I both still targets, then? Do I have to stay off my property?"

"No, I'd have to say we've seen the last of them for the time being. Markova will either convince him she's on his side or he'll kill her. Ivanov is probably already out of the state, if he follows his usual pattern, and she's with him. Ivanov can't do much with his assets frozen by the US government, which will happen in about an hour if not sooner." Claudia looked at Trevor. "All you need to do is heal that egg on your head and take a break." He saw the meaning behind her words. Like him, Claudia had been an agent and a US Marine. She had to know that what he was planning to do, and this was her way of telling him not to make any rash decisions.

"Yes, ma'am." He was too tired and disgusted with himself to argue. He'd already made his choice.

"We've got to get him to the hospital for an MRI." The EMT was at his other side, across from Coral.

"I'm going with you." Coral's voice remained as steady as her grip on his hand.

"No, wait. Can you give us a minute?" He dismissed

the EMT and surrounding colleagues. It was just him and Coral and a beautiful summer day.

"Trevor, what's wrong?" Lines etched on her forehead, indicating her concern.

"Look, let's not make this harder than it has to be." He hated how gruff and emotional he sounded. He cleared his throat.

"What are you talking about? I know I messed up, but did you hear what Colt and Claudia said? We did some great teamwork together! And I know you have to go back undercover if you can, or at least work overtime with TH to eventually capture Markova and Ivanov, but we got their information! We've stopped Markova from the escape she'd planned, and Ivanov doesn't have the resources to keep bringing heroin into the States. Win-win." Her bright smile cut through him as if she'd stabbed him with a steel blade. Coral had every right to be jubilant—she'd acted the part of a hero today, and every day since he'd arrived on her property in the guise of Grisha.

"Don't turn the last week into more than it was. We needed the time to figure out where we went wrong when we were married. Now we can both move on."

"Trevor, you took a hard hit to your head. We aren't going to have this conversation here and now." Anger hid the hurt he knew he was inflicting, but he had no choice.

"No, this is the deal. I'm going to the hospital on my own, then being transferred to another mission as soon as I'm back on my feet. You're going back to the farm, to your house and barn. We're moving on because we can now." He didn't deserve her. He had to let her go.

Tears glistened in her eyes, and he hated that he'd put them there, but the knowledge that she was safe from Markova now that the data wasn't on her property allowed him to continue with his intention. Coral deserved a man who didn't screw up when the heat got to be too much. He'd let her down in their marriage once—he wasn't going to risk it again.

"We're done, Coral Bell." He looked for the EMT and motioned him over. "I'm riding to the hospital solo, pal. Let's go."

For the first time since she'd helped him off the workshop floor, he didn't keep his gaze firmly on her. If he saw his blood and passed out, it would be preferable to the anguish he feared seeing reflected in her eyes.

Coral watched the EMTs lift Trevor into the ambulance and fought against the urge to run to him, to scream at him to stop being such a stubborn ass. It was futile, as he wore the same stony expression he'd had the night they'd agreed to divorce. The years melted away, and she was the same hurt woman who'd not even begun to mourn her marriage.

No.

This time was different, because Trevor had left her with something she hadn't had before—a sense of her power as a woman, the knowledge that she was able to have compassion and understanding of what Trevor did in service to his country. The long days and nights apart didn't seem such an unfair trade now that she'd experienced a slice of what he lived and worked with each day.

She turned away, determined to give him what he wanted. Wasn't that what true love was really about, anyway? Letting someone go who didn't want to be with you.

"You okay?" Claudia had walked up next to her, her face unreadable.

"I'm good." She wiped her eyes with the back of her hand. No sense hiding her emotions—she had nothing to be ashamed of. "It's hard to believe I can go back to my property and not worry about being stalked or thugs showing up to dig around anymore."

"Believe it. You have an event scheduled soon, if I recall?"

"Yes, it's tomorrow, actually."

"Are you sure you didn't get hurt in there?"

"Positive. I know I have to give a debrief."

"You do, and you can do that with Josh at SVPD. It'll be the quickest for now. One more thing, Coral." Coral remained silent as the CEO of TH, retired US Marine two-star general and wife of SVPD chief of police Colt Todd regarded her. "Love's not a straight line."

"I'm not sure what you're getting at, but thank you." She really didn't want to disrespect Claudia, but she wasn't about to share her deepest feelings with her. Not yet, not when her heart felt like a raw mess of sorrow.

"It might not be today, or tomorrow, or next year, but if you and Trevor are supposed to make a go of it, you will. The only thing I can tell you is that it's important that you take the opportunity when it shows up."

Coral nodded. Maybe Claudia knew more than she realized. "Thanks."

"Enjoy getting back to your normal life. You have

a job at TH if you ever want to change careers." Claudia's smile conveyed her sincerity. Coral watched her as she walked off toward Colt and tried hard to soak up the praise she'd just received.

But even adulation from a woman who was a national treasure wasn't enough to lift her sinking thoughts. So Coral did what she'd always found best during those early days after the first time Trevor broke her heart. She refocused on her life, her career, and moved forward. No matter how many sad days she knew awaited her.

Chapter 19

"It's spectacular." Annie Fiero, Josh's fiancée, stood next to Coral under the big-top tent, the summer breeze perfect as the sun's late-afternoon rays began to slant across the fields. Annie had been invited to the wedding reception of a mutual high school classmate of theirs and had offered to show up early to help Coral with last-minute details.

"Thanks. I appreciate your help, but really, I'm fine."

"Fine, my butt. You went through an awful lot yesterday, and to be back here throwing such a large party is quite the feat. And in case you don't know it, Trevor is okay. They released him this morning after observation last night. He has a mild concussion and several stitches."

"No, I didn't know that. Thanks for telling me." She was grateful to know how he was, no matter how much it stung that Trevor's well-being—or lack thereof—was no longer any of her business. Again. "Are you sure you're not here to keep an eye on my state of mind?" Coral teased Annie, a police psychologist.

Annie grinned. "Nope, sorry. I'm off duty at the moment. And it would only matter if you wanted to join TH."

Coral looked at her. She figured that Annie knew about TH, as Josh was both SVPD and TH, but she had never asked. "Stop looking so serious. I know you had three days of training this past week, thank goodness. I do contract work for Claudia when the occasion calls for it."

"Do you ever miss the NYPD?"

"No. I miss the people I worked with, but I'm back where I've always felt most myself. And with Josh here, too, it's a no-brainer. I'm a lifer as far as Silver Valley goes."

They laughed, and Coral nodded at the huge floral bouquets anchored around the tent's perimeter. "This family spent more on flowers than the food, if you can believe it. And they never told me—they were just delivered twenty minutes ago." Coral had accepted the delivery and opted not to be annoyed at the surprise. Event hosting involved surprises, and if flowers were the big one for this reception, she'd take it.

"I don't doubt they cost a pretty penny— they're beautiful."

"I can't wait to host your wedding here, Annie."

"Neither can we! Do you think the barn will be finished in time?"

"I do. Now that I don't have ROC distracting me, I'm

going to put full pressure on the construction crew." It was more like she didn't have Trevor here, or her wonderings about their future, anymore. Trevor had made his decision, and while it had only been yesterday, it felt years behind her.

Except for her heart. That still ached.

"We're happy to have a tent if we have to. This is lovely."

Coral looked at her watch. "I've got to get back to the kitchen and make sure they're all doing okay. Since you're here, I'd love it if you'd hang out and make sure the flowers don't tip over. The band should be arriving within twenty minutes."

"I told you I'm happy to do it. I only wish you could catch a catnap before the guests arrive."

"I know I look like heck, but I'm good, trust me. It's wonderful to be hosting an event on my property again."

Coral left Annie and made the walk to her farmhouse, not expecting to find any issues but mentally preparing herself for anything unplanned. It was the secret to success as an event planner—always have backup and don't be surprised when things didn't run smoothly.

She was still dressed in a plain white T-shirt, khaki shorts and a simple black apron. Her evening wear was laid out in her camper, to be donned minutes before the first guests arrived. A longing to have the barn finished hit her. It made for much smoother operations.

Trevor's last words and, more importantly, the words he hadn't spoken yesterday—or the entire time they'd shared together—continued to haunt her. No matter how much she focused on the event or tried to distract herself, she couldn't shake the fact that it was the hardest thing she'd ever done to let him go as he'd asked. Not going to the hospital today to check on him had been equally difficult, and she was glad to know he'd not needed to stay.

As she turned the corner to the back of the house where the kitchen entrance stood, confusion hit her. Where were all the cars from the staff? Two had arrived earlier in the day, and then more had trickled in as the event's start grew closer. But the only vehicle on the mowed field next to the house was Chef Mike's.

Coral hurried up the back steps, concerned that Chef Mike had needed to send the workers out for last-minute supplies. She'd double-checked her list to prevent just such an incident. It was never good to have the staff unavailable this close to when the first guests arrived.

When she entered the kitchen, she found cookie sheets of frozen savory pastries out to thaw, but no staff and no Chef Mike. Anxiety roared as she concluded her chef had been hurt.

Feeling for her phone to tell Annie what was going on, she realized she hadn't brought it with her when she'd left the farmhouse almost an hour ago. The counters were cluttered with the pastries. She lifted tray after tray, looking for the device, wondering where the heck Chef Mike was. Worry trickled in, because without him to help tonight, it'd be her and her staff. Except her staff was nowhere to be found.

"Looking for this?" Chef Mike's voice sounded very close—too close as she whirled and found him directly in front of her, holding her phone up with one hand. In the other hand he held his chef's knife, the eight-inch blade in the air between them.

"Chef Mike! Yes, thank you. Where's everyone else?" Before she could put the cookie tray back on the counter, he stepped forward and held the knife at her throat.

"Wha—" She dropped the tray, and it clattered to the linoleum floor.

"The staff left when I told them the event is canceled." He let it sink in before he told her what his motive was, why he was acting so unbalanced. "You made a big mistake when you killed Markova." His breath stank of alcohol, and she saw pure hate in his dark eyes.

"I didn't kill her—what do you know about Markova?" She fought for every second, for the time to clear her head of event lists and focus on saving her life. Again.

"I know everything about Anna Markova. And I told her all that I knew about you." He sneered. "You're the fool who believed I was a real chef. You didn't even check my references!"

His anger frightened her more than the knife. A blade was predictable—it would cut and she could choose to use her hands to save her throat, her face. But his ire was uncontrollable and equally unpredictable.

Calm amid the high pressure of being murdered is your best weapon.

The TH trainer's voice sounded in her mind and grounded her. But it wasn't going to be able to stop Chef

Mike, a man much larger than her and at present hulking over her with a deadly weapon, from killing her.

Why hadn't she stopped Trevor from leaving her yesterday?

Trevor spent all Saturday morning preparing for his confrontation with Coral. He told himself it wasn't adversarial, that she'd be willing to hear him out. His deepest fears disagreed.

He loaded the custom bouquet of cream roses into his car, careful not to crush the delicate blooms, and got into the driver's seat. Time to roll.

He'd screwed up royally yesterday. Only after the hospital had quieted down for the night and he'd been left awake with his thoughts did he realized he'd been kidding himself. He chalked it up to the head injury. He'd not been thinking straight.

He needed Coral with every molecule of his being. There was no other woman for him. And contrary to what he'd let her believe, what he'd told himself yesterday, there were plenty of other job options for him that didn't involve putting the woman he loved in jeopardy.

Swallowing his pride, he'd called Josh and asked if Annie was available to help him make it up to Coral. He'd need all the support he could get. It turned out Annie had already volunteered to help Coral with the wedding reception, a break he appreciated. He asked Annie to make sure Coral was at the farmhouse about an hour before the guests were to arrive. He wanted time to talk to her and also hoped that if she agreed with his thoughts, she'd be able to enjoy hosting this first event back on her property with complete ease.

Without the hurt he'd caused her yesterday.

Anticipation rolled in his gut as he turned in to her drive, and when he passed the tent, he saw the flowers surrounding it. Good. At least that part had happened. He parked by the barn site, hoping to be waiting for her at the tent with the bouquet when she came back, dressed to meet the guests. Annie's recent text told him that so far, his timing was perfect.

It made him nervous when things went too smoothly. He slicked back his hair one last time and straightened the bow tie in the car's rearview mirror. He hadn't worn a tux in eons, usually wearing his Marine uniform when the occasion warranted. It had taken more time than he'd wanted to, but he was glad he'd found one that fit this morning.

He got out of the car and walked toward the tent. Still no sign of Coral, but it wouldn't be more than a few minutes. She'd never been one to take too long getting ready. She didn't need to, and while she laughed off his compliments that she didn't need makeup, it was the truth.

"Annie." He waved from the edge of the tent.

"Hey, Trevor!" She walked quickly to him. Her smile was radiant. "I'm so excited for you. Josh filled me in on some of the happenings over the past few days. Don't worry, Coral's not going to be able to resist your charm."

"Uh-huh." It was like being in middle school again, but with his very adult heart on the line.

"How's your head?" She winced as she looked at the bandage that covered most of the bruise and all of the stitches on his scalp.

"Sore but manageable." And the least of his problems. "When did you say Coral went to the house?"

"About twenty minutes ago. She should be coming back any time now."

The first warning bell clanged in his mind. "And when do the first guests show up?" He pulled up the security app on his phone.

Annie frowned. "In fifteen minutes." Her lips puckered in puzzlement. "She is cutting it close, isn't she?"

A second sense of imminent danger made the hairs on his nape stand up. When the app opened and the security camera revealed an empty kitchen, he didn't need a third red flag. Trevor took off for the farmhouse.

"You stay here—call SVPD," he shouted to Annie over his shoulder as he ran, each step jarring to his sore body and tender head.

"Trevor, wait, you might need backup!" One thing about Annie being a police psychologist was that she was always the first one to encourage someone to trust his gut. She didn't try to prevent him from going after Coral.

"No time." He kept going, trusting Annie to make the needed call.

When he rounded the back of the house, his stomach flipped with fear. There was only one car where there should have been at least eight. Where was her staff?

He bounded the last steps to the back porch and called to her as he opened the screen door.

"Coral!"

Walking into the kitchen, all he saw was a bunch of food on baking pans, but no Coral. He called again, hating the emptiness in the battered house. Some of the walls had been repaired, but it was far from being reconstructed.

A scuffle of footsteps, a low voice from the back hallway that had remained intact after the explosion. He still clutched the bouquet, the blooms crushed by his herculean effort to get here as fast as he could.

Coral stepped into the hallway, her figure backlit by the sunlight pouring in from the far window. Her hair was a mess, and she still was in work clothes. This wasn't how Coral acted when she was running an event. It may have been over three years since he'd witnessed her event planning, but she'd always dressed the part of her clientele.

"Trevor." She jutted her chin out, her bottom lip trembling. "What are you doing here? I'm in the middle of an event."

He knew she was, but it wasn't the wedding reception. With Markova and Ivanov verified to be out of the state by TH as of an hour ago, who was in the house with her?

More importantly, what did they want?

He fought against his rage and used the energy to focus and ascertain all he could before he took out whoever was making the love of his life this upset.

They'd come too far to lose one another now.

Coral's knees shook, but with Chef Mike to her side, pointing the knife at her, she mustered the courage to stay calm and do whatever it took to get Trevor out of here.

"Why are you here, Trevor?" He still hadn't answered her, just stood there in a tuxedo, looking more attractive than she could remember. She wanted to weep with the injustice of it. The man she loved stood here with a beautiful bouquet of roses—cream, her favorite, he'd remembered—and at least one of them was about to be killed. Mostly likely her.

Chef Mike had made it clear that if he saw her clue Trevor in on what was going on, he'd stab him first, then kill her.

"I wanted to make up for what I said yesterday. It was the hit to my head talking."

"I see you've got quite the wound there. I'm sorry, but I can't discuss this right now. I have two hundred people showing up within minutes." Maybe if Chef Mike realized that not only was Trevor here, but dozens of guests were on the way, he'd relent.

She saw him wave the knife and thrust at the air with it in her peripheral vision. Nope, he wasn't going to give it up.

"Coral, come here. We can work this out."

She shook her head. "That's not possible right now." As she spoke, she saw his gaze go from her to the bedroom door, back to her. He mouthed the word *someone* and pointed.

Unable to nod, she decided to do what she'd done in the warehouse when she'd trusted Trevor to take out Ivanov. She locked gazes with him and tried to convey how much she loved him, and that, yes, there was a very bad man in her bedroom.

"You know I'm not going to ever let you go again, babe." Trevor spoke the sweet words she'd wanted to hear yesterday. The words that would have kept her with him and maybe somehow prevented this situation with Chef Mike. Trevor always saw trouble coming before she did.

"You don't have to. We'll work this out after my event." More gestures from Chef Mike stretched her nerves taut. Without a weapon or any other way to protect Trevor, she had no choice but to urge him to go. "You have to go now, Trevor. Wait for me at the tent."

"At least let me give you these flowers." He held out the bouquet with squashed petals, and only then did she see the weapon in his hand. A Sig Sauer. She bit back a smile, knowing what she had to do. What they had to do. Together.

"Thank you." She reached for the flowers and felt the tips of his fingers before he hissed the action word.

"Duck!"

Coral sprang into action, tossing the flowers at Chef Mike, who tried to slice them with his knife. On her knees so that Trevor could jump over her in the narrow corridor, she looked back to see him square off at the doorway and hold his pistol forward.

"Drop the knife. On your knees."

Only when she heard the clatter of the metal hitting Aunt Brenda's worn wooden floor did she stand back up and walk over to Trevor.

"Trevor, meet Chef Mike. Apparently he's a close acquaintance of Anna Markova's."

SVPD and TH arrived on scene only seconds after Trevor apprehended Chef Mike. He'd told Coral to go and get dressed for her event, with an SVPD officer next to her until Chef Mike was taken to jail.

Coral was able to call back her staff, who were

working like demons in the farmhouse kitchen, somehow putting a meal together and keeping the guests fed.

"Is that it, boss?" He looked at Claudia, eager to be at the tent with Coral. He didn't have the flowers any longer, as Chef Mike had crushed them, but he had a lifetime to buy her flowers. If she'd have him.

"Good job. Now go ahead and enjoy the rest of the evening. And I mean it when I say you need to take at least a month off."

"You'll get no argument from me on that."

He wasted no time heading toward the big tent. The sun had set, and the air was cool compared to the blazing sun of the day. Twinkling lights edged the massive canvas structure, and the candle flames seemed to float in the air. The band was playing a fast number, something about rock and roll never dying. He had no idea about rock and roll, but he knew that his love for Coral would never die. All he had to do was convince her.

A tall woman broke away from the crowd and approached him. Annie clasped her hands in front of her.

"You're good to go. The bride and groom are one-hundred-percent behind you. This is so exciting!" Annie's grin lit up her face.

Trevor didn't have time to get excited. Not until Coral agreed to his plan for her future. "Where's Coral?" He scoured the crowd for her with no joy.

"She's over there, in the corner. I'll tell Josh to do his thing." Annie paused, then put her hand on his shoulder. "Good luck, Trevor. Now, go get her!"

He didn't need any prodding as he walked slowly to the dance floor. The fast music faded, and the deejay—Josh—asked the crowd to clear the floor for a special number. Trevor walked into the middle of the floor, under the ridiculous disco ball that somehow seemed full of magic in this moment. He saw Annie next to Coral and reveled in how her expression went from annoyance at being interrupted in the middle of an event to confusion, to surprise and then, when her eyes met his, to something else entirely.

He held out his hand in an unquestionable offer. She allowed Annie to slip the electronic tablet from her hands and took her first steps toward him.

Trevor heard nothing after that, only the pounding of a heart that had spent too many nights away from its mate. There were scores of people in the tent, surrounding the parquet dance floor, but all he saw was Coral, her hair floating around her sexy shoulders, her every curve illuminated by her sparkling black gown. The dress was tasteful enough for a professional working a wedding reception, but over-the-top sensuous for Trevor, who knew what she looked like under the fancy fabric.

When he looked back up at her face, he caught her happy smile, saw that she knew he'd been checking her out as if they were both naked and alone.

It was only a few seconds but felt like forever until she finally reached him and placed her hand in his.

"Can I have this dance, Coral?" He knew he looked ridiculous with the huge bandage on his noggin and wearing his now rumpled tux. The bow tie had taken a hit during the takedown, and he'd shoved it in his pocket, leaving his collar open. But Coral looked at him like he was the most handsome man she'd ever seen.

"I was hoping you were going to ask for more than a

dance." Her words sank in as Josh said something inane that Trevor made a note to give him hell for later. The soft strains of a popular ballad began, and they moved together perfectly, as they always had.

"You were?"

She looked up at him, her body pressed to his as they shared the intimate moment in front of two hundred strangers. "Why did you come back, Trevor? You were so sure yesterday."

"I was a fool. I want you to have the man you deserve, and it's not going to happen."

"Why not?"

"Because I have to have you, Coral. You deserve someone who would never put you in the situations I have, someone who's not working such a dangerous job. Someone who can be home every night."

"But?"

"No buts. I'm changing my job. I'll have a desk job from now on, for the most part. And I can't change our past, but I sure as heck can make a difference going forward. We make the best team. I didn't see that before, had no idea that we'd work so well together. I'm not saying we should work together in law enforcement, but if we wanted to, we could. You accept me as I am—you don't care if I'm afraid of the sight of my own blood. You get me." He sucked in a deep breath. "No one knows you or loves you like I do, Coral. I'm as crazy about you as I ever was, and I want to spend the rest of my days with you. Will you have me?" He stopped moving his feet and got down on his knee.

Coral's laugh and then gasp when he winced at having to bend his head back to look at her made him laugh. They really were a pair.

"Please say yes, Coral."

"Yes, Trevor. Please get up before you give yourself a migraine." When he stood she wrapped her arms around his neck and gently tugged.

He lowered his lips to hers and let the pent-up need from the last few days—heck, the last three years—go. Her lips were soft and tasted of pure love.

A roaring sound filled his ears, and only after several seconds did he recognize applause. He lifted his mouth from hers and saw the tears streaming down her cheeks. But she wasn't sad.

Coral's gaze reflected nothing but love.

"I love you, Coral Bell."

"I love you, too, Trevor."

* * * * *

Don't miss the other thrilling romances in
Geri Krotow's Silver Valley PD miniseries:

Snowbound with the Secret Agent
Reunion Under Fire
The Fugitive's Secret Child
Secret Agent Under Fire
Her Secret Christmas Agent
Wedding Takedown
Her Christmas Protector

All available now
from Harlequin Romantic Suspense.

#2103 COLTON 911: DETECTIVE ON CALL

Colton 911: Grand Rapids • by Regan Black

Attorney Pippa Colton is determined to overturn a wrongful conviction but must find a way to get the truth out of the star witness: Emmanuel Iglesias. The sexy detective is sure the case was by the book. When Pippa starts receiving threats, her theory begins to look much more convincing, if they can unearth evidence before the true killer stops them in their tracks.

#2104 COLTON'S SECRET HISTORY

The Coltons of Kansas • by Jennifer D. Bokal

When Bridgette Colton's job with the Kansas State Department of Health sends her to her hometown to investigate a cluster of cancer cases, she uncovers long-hidden family secrets that lead her back to her first love, Luke Walker.

#2105 CAVANAUGH IN PLAIN SIGHT

Cavanaugh Justice • by Marie Ferrarella

A feisty reporter has always believed in following her moral compass, but this time that same compass just might make her a target—unless Morgan Cavanaugh can protect her. Her work gets her in trouble and anyone could want to silence her—permanently.

#2106 HER P.I. PROTECTOR

Cold Case Detectives • by Jennifer Morey

Detective Julien LaCroix meets Skylar Chelsey, the daughter of a wealthy rancher, just when she needs him the most: after she stumbles upon a murder scene. Now they fight instant attraction and a relentless killer, who will stop at nothing to silence the only living witness.

YOU CAN FIND MORE INFORMATION ON UPCOMING HARLEQUIN TITLES,
FREE EXCERPTS AND MORE AT HARLEQUIN.COM.

HRSCNM0820

Great. She'd get to endure another visit with the dubious
sheriff. Except now he'd be hard-pressed to doubt her
claims. Clearly she must have seen something to make
the hole digger feel he needed to close loose ends.

Julien ended the call. "While we wait for the sheriff,
why don't you go get dressed and pack some things? You
should stay with me until we find out who tried to kill
you."

He had a good point, but the notion of staying with
him gave her a burst of heat. Conscious of wearing only
a robe, she tightened the belt.

"I can stay with my parents," she said. "They can
make sure I'm safe." Her father would probably install a
robust security system complete with guards.

"You might put others in danger if you do that."

Her parents, Corbin and countless staff members might be in the line of fire if the gunman returned for another attempt.

"Then I'll beef up security here. I can't stay away from the ranch for long."

"All right, then let me help you."

"Okay." She could agree to that.

"Don't worry, I don't mix my work with pleasure," he said with a grin, giving her body a sweeping look.

"Good, then I don't have to worry about trading one danger for another." She smiled back and left him standing there, uncertainty flattening his mouth.

Don't miss
Her P.I. Protector *by Jennifer Morey,*
available September 2020 wherever
Harlequin Romantic Suspense
books and ebooks are sold.

Harlequin.com

Get 4 FREE REWARDS!

We'll send you 2 FREE Books plus 2 FREE Mystery Gifts.

Harlequin Romantic Suspense books are heart-racing page-turners with unexpected plot twists and irresistible chemistry that will keep you guessing to the very end.

FREE Value Over $20

YES! Please send me 2 FREE Harlequin Romantic Suspense novels and my 2 FREE gifts (gifts are worth about $10 retail). After receiving them, if I don't wish to receive any more books, I can return the shipping statement marked "cancel." If I don't cancel, I will receive 4 brand-new novels every month and be billed just $4.99 per book in the U.S. or $5.74 per book in Canada. That's a savings of at least 13% off the cover price! It's quite a bargain! Shipping and handling is just 50¢ per book in the U.S. and $1.25 per book in Canada.* I understand that accepting the 2 free books and gifts places me under no obligation to buy anything. I can always return a shipment and cancel at any time. The free books and gifts are mine to keep no matter what I decide.

240/340 HDN GNMZ

Name (please print)

Address   Apt. #

City   State/Province   Zip/Postal Code

Email: Please check this box ☐ if you would like to receive newsletters and promotional emails from Harlequin Enterprises ULC and its affiliates. You can unsubscribe anytime.

> ### Mail to the **Reader Service:**
> **IN U.S.A.:** P.O. Box 1341, Buffalo, NY 14240-8531
> **IN CANADA:** P.O. Box 603, Fort Erie, Ontario L2A 5X3

Want to try 2 free books from another series! Call 1-800-873-8635 or visit www.ReaderService.com.

---

*Terms and prices subject to change without notice. Prices do not include sales taxes, which will be charged (if applicable) based on your state or country of residence. Canadian residents will be charged applicable taxes. Offer not valid in Quebec. This offer is limited to one order per household. Books received may not be as shown. Not valid for current subscribers to Harlequin Romantic Suspense books. All orders subject to approval. Credit or debit balances in a customer's account(s) may be offset by any other outstanding balance owed by or to the customer. Please allow 4 to 6 weeks for delivery. Offer available while quantities last.

Your Privacy—Your information is being collected by Harlequin Enterprises ULC, operating as Reader Service. For a complete summary of the information we collect, how we use this information and to whom it is disclosed, please visit our privacy notice located at corporate.harlequin.com/privacy-notice. From time to time we may also exchange your personal information with reputable third parties. If you wish to opt out of this sharing of your personal information, please visit readerservice.com/consumerschoice or call 1-800-873-8635. **Notice to California Residents**—Under California law, you have specific rights to control and access your data. For more information on these rights and how to exercise them, visit corporate.harlequin.com/california-privacy.

HRS20R2

**IF YOU ENJOYED THIS BOOK
WE THINK YOU WILL ALSO LOVE**

INTRIGUE

Seek thrills. Solve crimes. Justice served.

Dive into action-packed stories that will keep you
on the edge of your seat. Solve the crime
and deliver justice at all costs.

6 NEW BOOKS AVAILABLE EVERY MONTH!

Love Harlequin romance?

DISCOVER.

Be the first to find out about promotions, news and exclusive content!

Facebook.com/HarlequinBooks

Twitter.com/HarlequinBooks

Instagram.com/HarlequinBooks

Pinterest.com/HarlequinBooks

ReaderService.com

EXPLORE.

Sign up for the Harlequin e-newsletter and download a free book from any series at **TryHarlequin.com**

CONNECT.

Join our Harlequin community to share your thoughts and connect with other romance readers!
Facebook.com/groups/HarlequinConnection

HARLEQUIN

Heartfelt or suspenseful, inspiring or passionate, Harlequin has your happily-ever-after.

With new books published
every month, you are sure to find the
satisfying escape you know you deserve.

HNEWS2020